WITHDRAWN

VOICES
THAT
COUNT

A COMICS ANTHOLOGY BY WOMEN

W9-AOZ-366

Facebook: **facebook.com/idwpublishing**
Twitter: **@idwpublishing**
YouTube: **youtube.com/idwpublishing**
Instagram: **@idwpublishing**

ISBN: 978-1-68405-917-1   25 24 23 22   1 2 3 4

Cover Art by
Esther Gili

Letters by
Nathan Widick

Edits by
Megan Brown

Special Thanks to
**David Hernando for his
invaluable assistance.**

VOICES THAT COUNT. FIRST PRINTING. JUNE 2022. © texts and illustrations of each story belong to each author. "Por una falda de plátanos": © Almudena Grandes, 2010. Published through an arrangement with Tusquets Editores, S.A., Barcelona. "Soledad": © Amaral, 2019. Included in the song album "Salto al color" (Antártida/Sony Music). "Morder la manzana": © Leticia Dolera, 2018. Published by Editorial Planeta, S.A., Barcelona. First published by Editorial Planeta, SA. Diagonal, 662-664, 08034 Barcelona. Copyright © 2021 Editorial Planeta, SA for the Spanish edition. All Rights Reserved. The IDW logo is registered in the U.S. Patent and Trademark Office. IDW Publishing, a division of Idea and Design Works, LLC. Editorial offices: 2765 Truxtun Road, San Diego, CA 92106. Any similarities to persons living or dead are purely coincidental. With the exception of artwork used for review purposes, none of the contents of this publication may be reprinted without the permission of Idea and Design Works, LLC. Printed in Korea.

IDW Publishing does not read or accept unsolicited submissions of ideas, stories, or artwork.

Nachie Marsham, Publisher
Blake Kobashigawa, SVP, Sales, Marketing & Strategy
Tara McCrillis, VP, Publishing Operations
Anna Morrow, VP, Marketing & Publicity
Alexandra Hargett, VP, Sales
Mark Doyle, Editorial Director, Originals
Lauren LePera, Managing Editor
Joe Hughes, Director, Talent Relations
Keith Davidsen, Director, Marketing & PR
Topher Alford, Sr. Digital Marketing Manager
Patrick O'Connell, Sr. Manager, Direct Market Sales
Shauna Monteforte, Sr. Director of Manufacturing Operations
Greg Foreman, Director DTC Sales & Operations
Nathan Widick, Sr. Art Director, Head of Design
Neil Uyetake, Sr. Art Director, Design & Production
Shawn Lee, Art Director, Design & Production
Jack Rivera, Art Director, Marketing

Ted Adams and Robbie Robbins, IDW Founders

WITHDRAWN

Cover illustration by Esther Gili

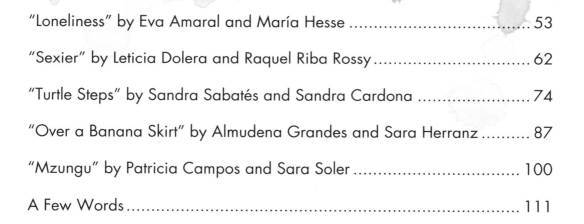

Translated by Diego Jourdan Pereira

VOICES THAT COUNT—AN INTRODUCTION

"I have nothing interesting to tell."

As we began to assemble this anthology, that was the phrase I heard the most and yet the one I never expected to run into. When I contacted the authors finally gathered for this volume, each of a self-evident social and cultural relevance and importance, I never thought their first reaction would always be the belief that they didn't have anything interesting to bring to the table or know what story to tell. Just by looking at their names, one realizes that's impossible. Be it in the professional or the personal field, all of them have hundreds of exciting stories, tales that would help other women see themselves reflected or represented. That very reaction made me realize this project was even more necessary than originally thought at first glance.

An anthology of the present volume's characteristics was long overdue from an editorial standpoint. It wasn't until I got their first replies that I gathered how meaningful this collection could be and how pertinent it was to bring it to fruition, because in those moments, I recognized the "I have nothing interesting to tell" sentence would never have come up had this been an anthology by male authors—there wouldn't have been enough pages to tell everything *they* would have thought relevant to tell.

The voices gathered in this volume not only count, they matter. They are a model for personal stories dealing with overcoming adversity, realizing true callings at particular moments in life, and becoming who one is today—slice-of-life tales that many will surely see reflected in their own daily lives that would otherwise be left silenced. "I have nothing interesting to tell" proved quite the opposite, and it was clear that this collection needed to see the light of day.

Thanks to the work of all these authors, the anthology expresses different realities and situations that appeal to a wide range of readers, regardless of their gender—because these tales not only target women, but also men. From my perspective as an editor, working with the authors, discussing different story options, and seeing them visually applied in preliminary character designs, layout sketches, and final illustrations has made me see many things I previously hadn't been aware of.

At the end of the day, that is essentially what a publisher hopes from what it publishes: pursuing reflection around universal themes through its authors, its pages, its stories. They collect different types of storytelling, ranging from the influences of mothers, fathers, grandmothers, and great-grandmothers, to career paths found along the way.

This is possibly the most heartfelt, intimate, and personal foreword I have written so far, but the occasion deserves it. It is truthfully satisfying having taken part in this book, and all that's left is to thank these writers and illustrators for their time, their talent, their know-how, and their help throughout the entire creative process that has led us to *Voices That Count*. It has been one of the most gratifying creative moments of my career, and it's been thanks to Almudena Grandes, Eva Amaral, Diana López Varela, Estefanía Molina, Leticia Dolera, Lola García, Julia Otero, Patricia Campos, Sandra Sabatés, Ada Diez, Agustina Guerrero, Akira Pantsu, Ana Oncina, María Hesse, Raquel Riba Rossy, Sandra Cardona, Sara Herranz, and Sara Soler. Thank you. And here's to many more stories left to tell!

DAVID HERNANDO
Editorial Director at Planeta Cómic

JULIO

WRITTEN BY JULIA OTERO

DRAWN BY ADA DIEZ

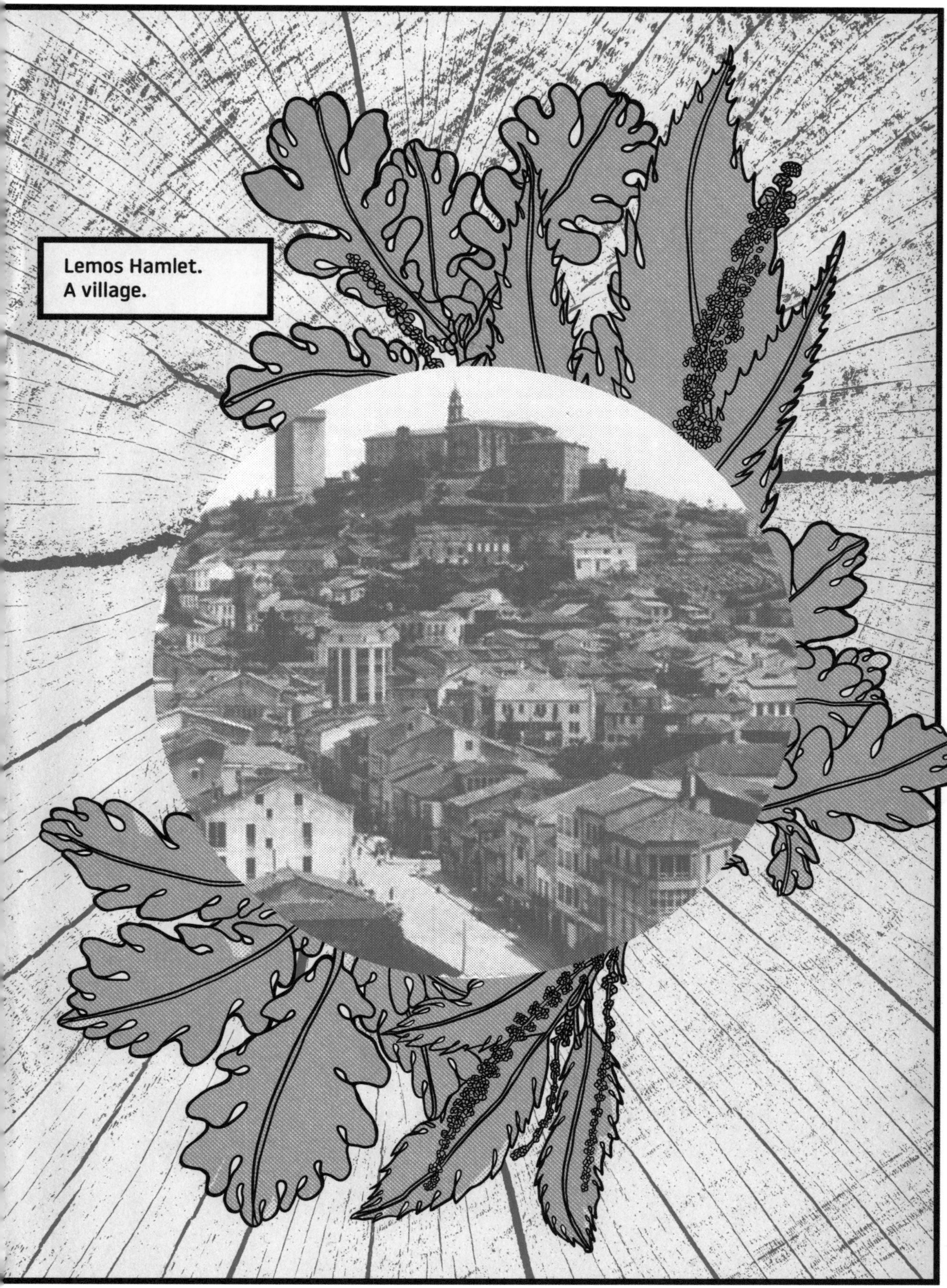
Lemos Hamlet.
A village.

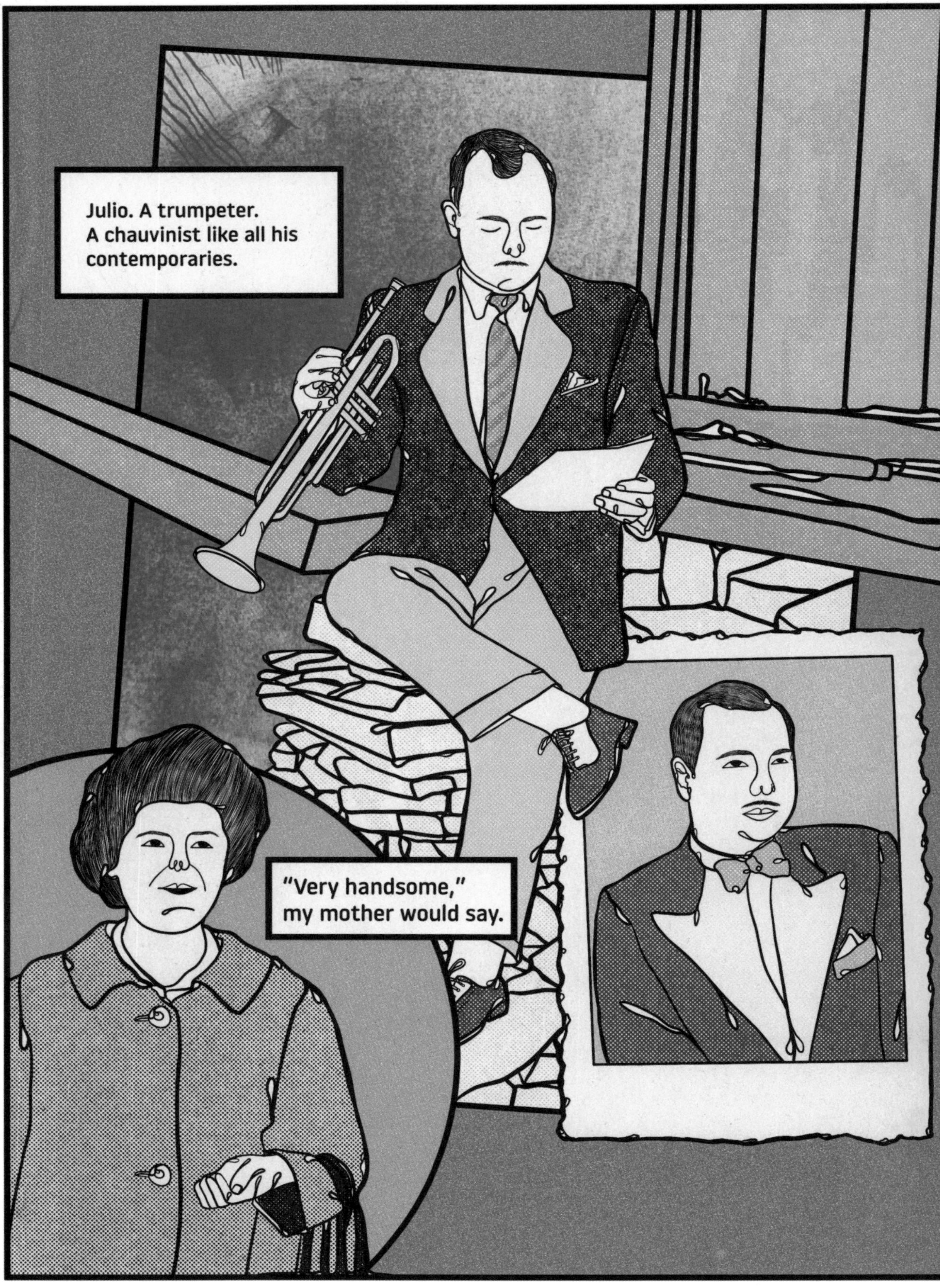
Julio. A trumpeter.
A chauvinist like all his
contemporaries.
"Very handsome,"
my mother would say.

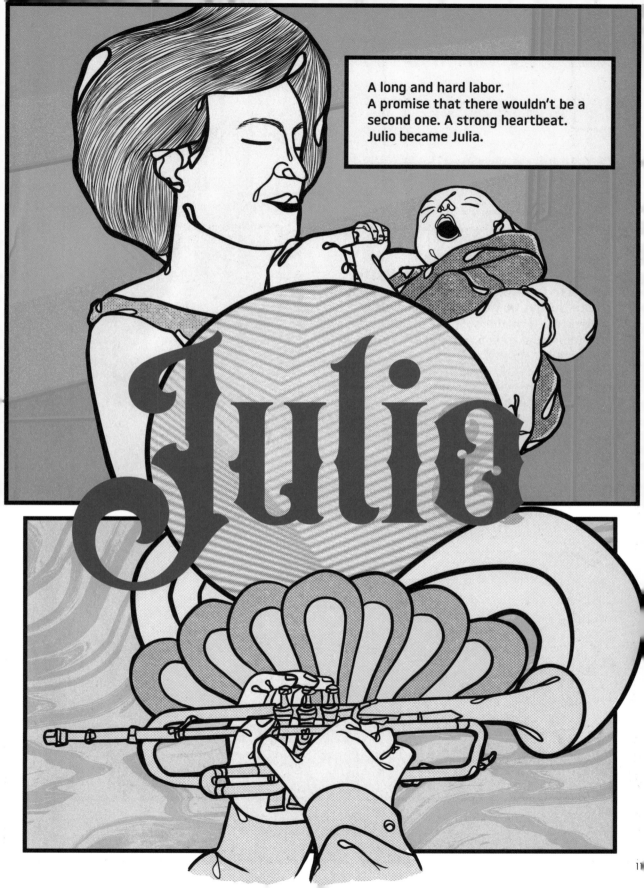

A long and hard labor.
A promise that there wouldn't be a
second one. A strong heartbeat.
Julio became Julia.

Julio

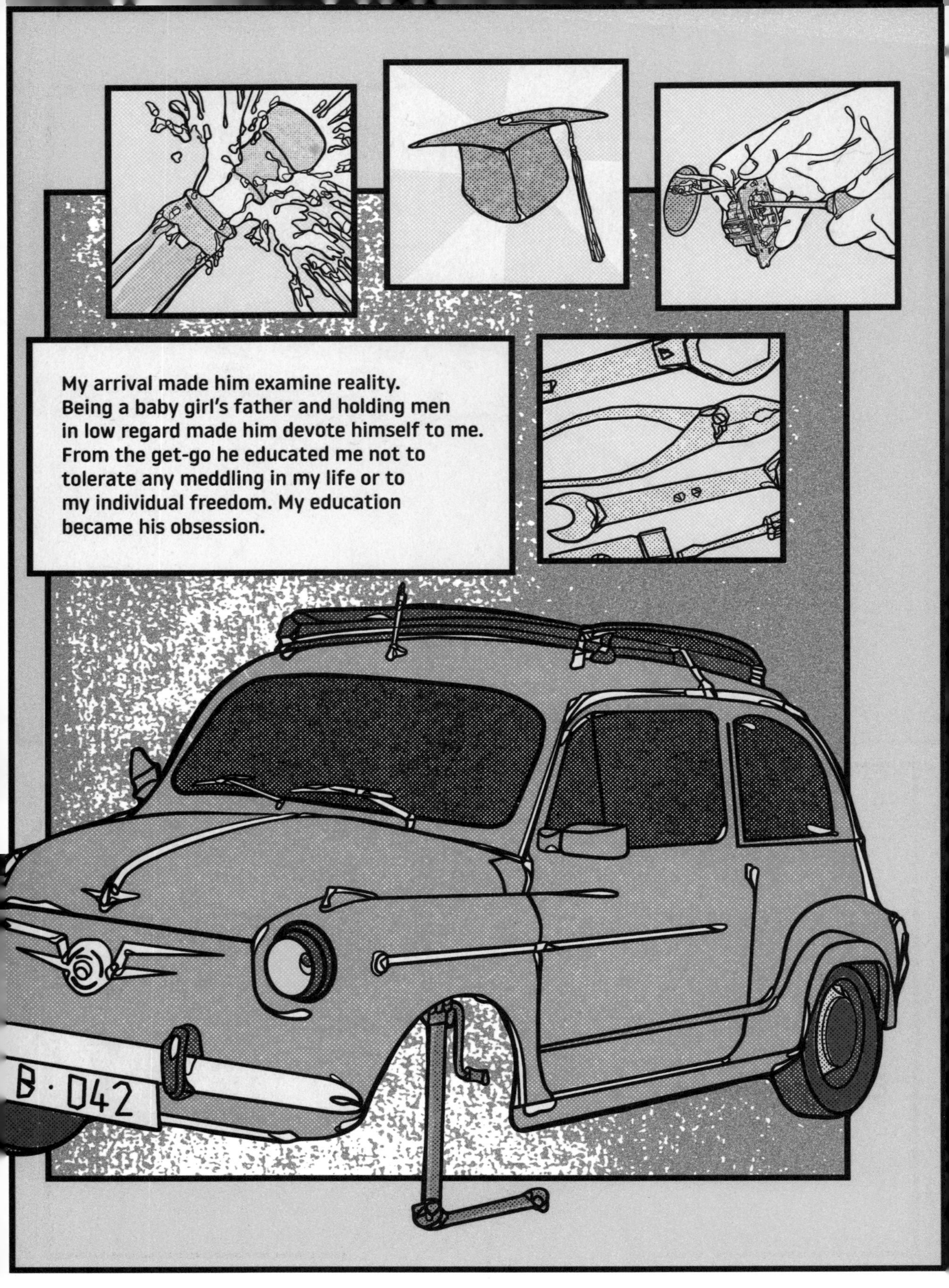
My arrival made him examine reality. Being a baby girl's father and holding men in low regard made him devote himself to me. From the get-go he educated me not to tolerate any meddling in my life or to my individual freedom. My education became his obsession.
B · 042

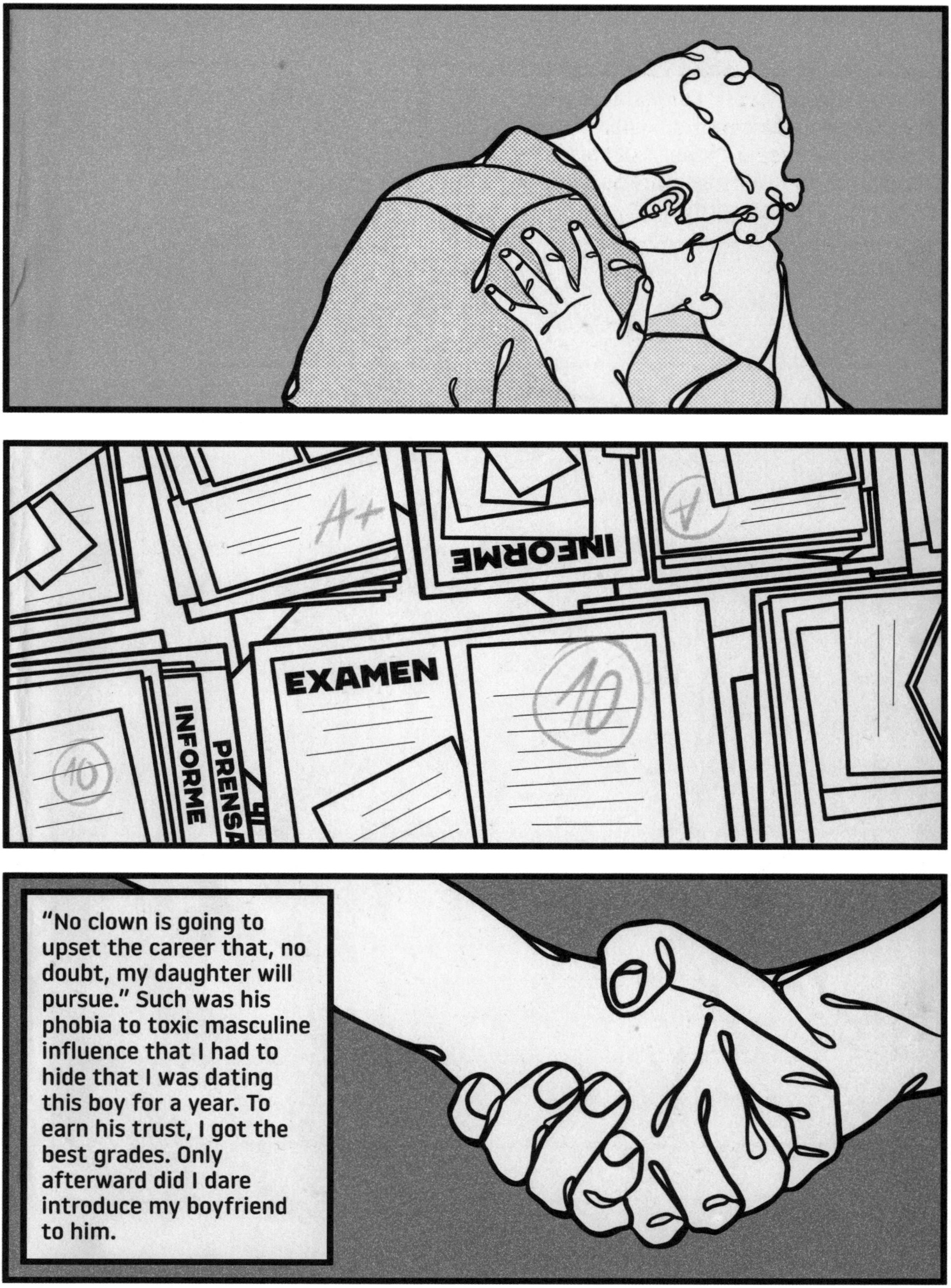
A+
INFORME
EXAMEN
PRENSA
INFORME
"No clown is going to upset the career that, no doubt, my daughter will pursue." Such was his phobia to toxic masculine influence that I had to hide that I was dating this boy for a year. To earn his trust, I got the best grades. Only afterward did I dare introduce my boyfriend to him.

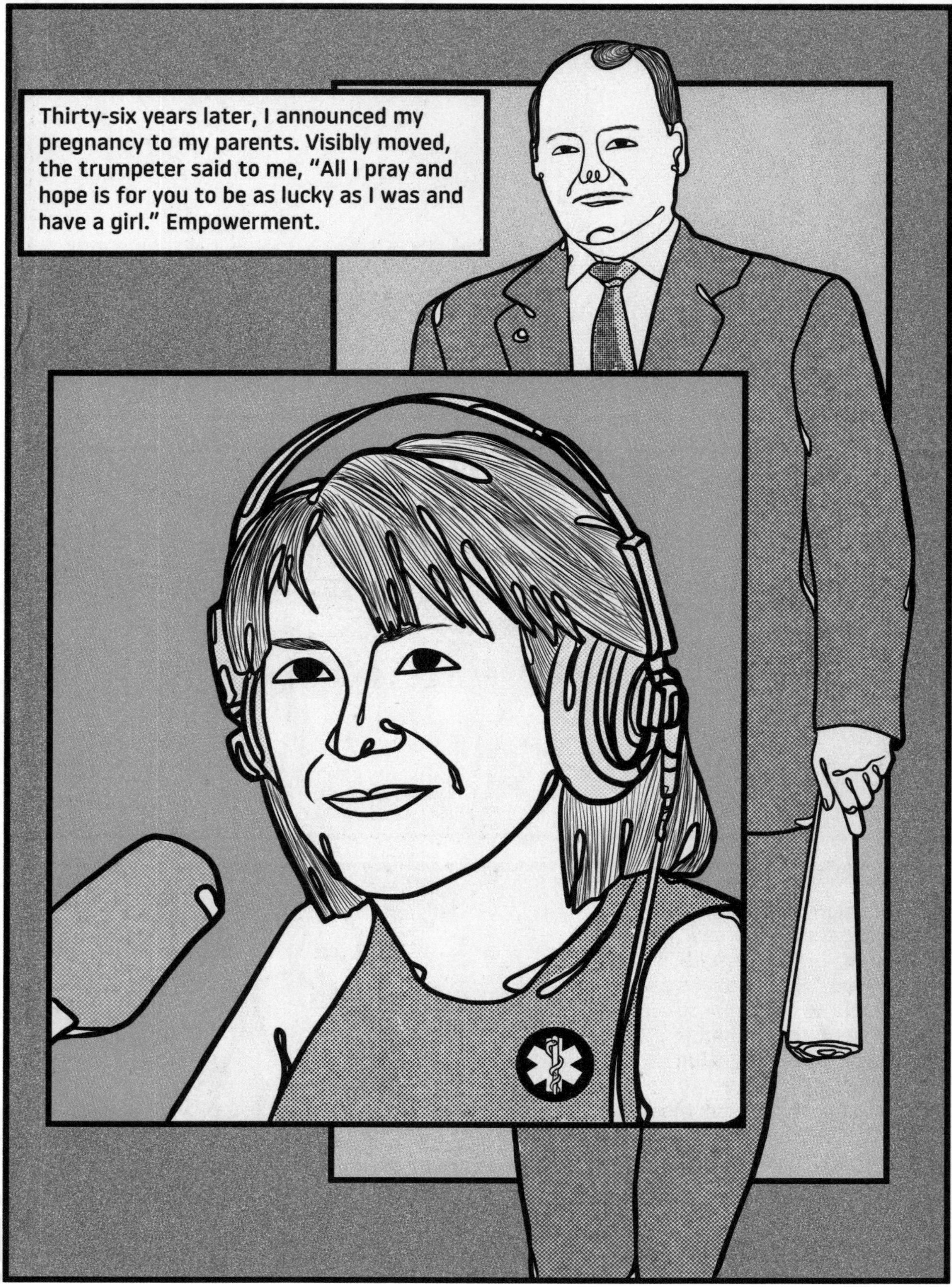
Thirty-six years later, I announced my pregnancy to my parents. Visibly moved, the trumpeter said to me, "All I pray and hope is for you to be as lucky as I was and have a girl." Empowerment.

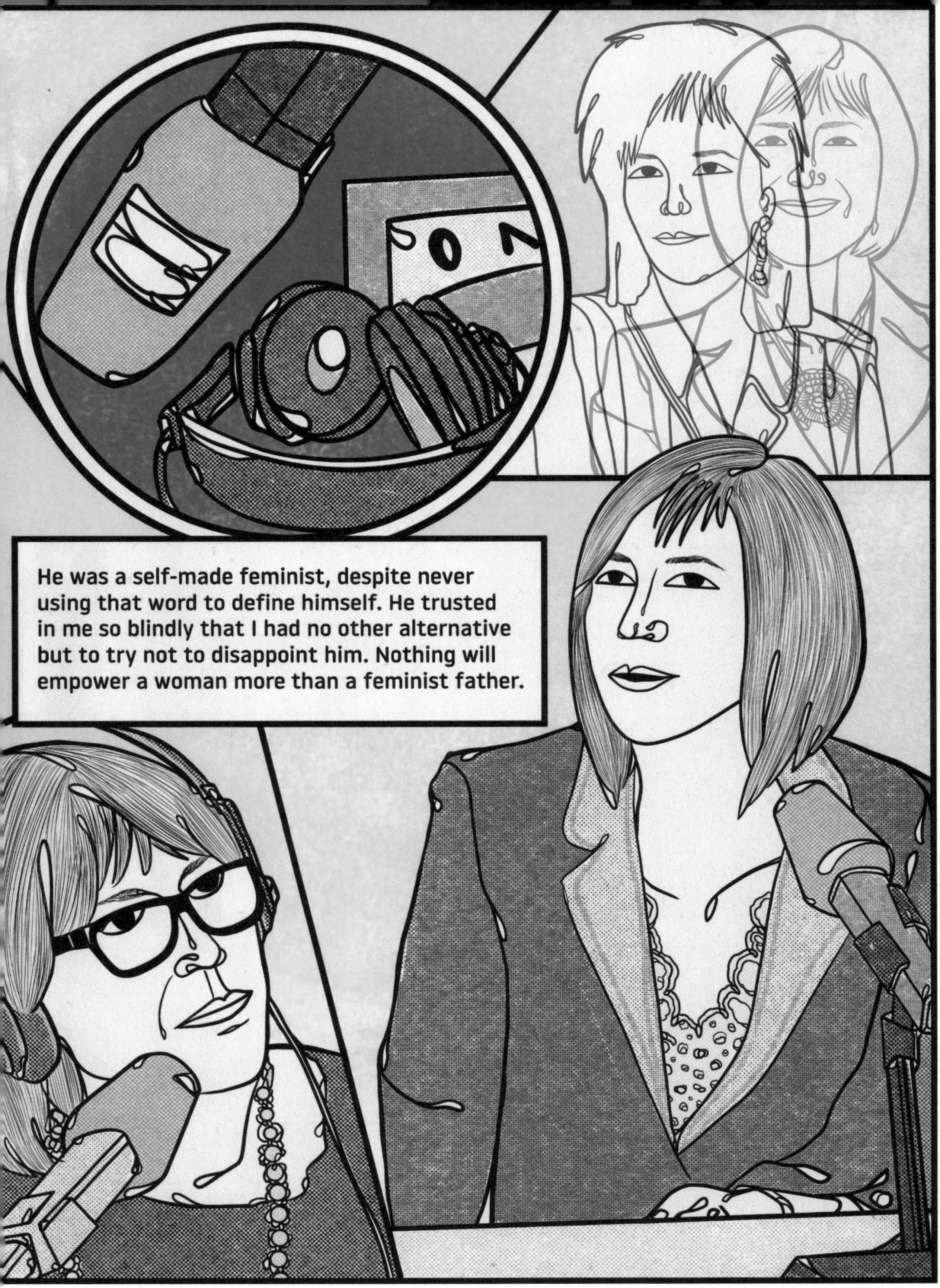
He was a self-made feminist, despite never using that word to define himself. He trusted in me so blindly that I had no other alternative but to try not to disappoint him. Nothing will empower a woman more than a feminist father.

24 HOURS

WRITTEN BY LOLA GARCÍA

DRAWN BY AGUSTINA GUERRERO

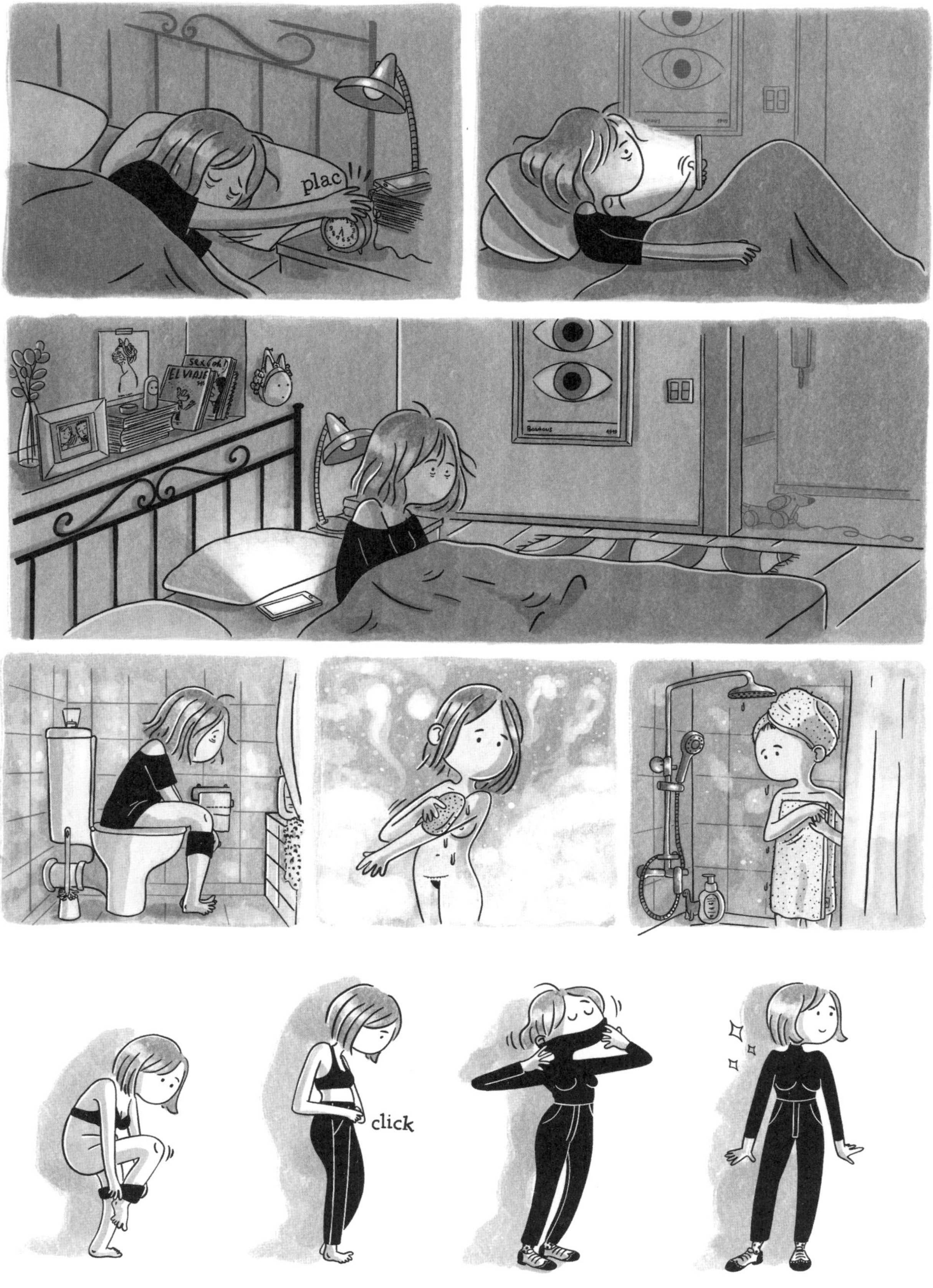
plac
EL VIAJE
click

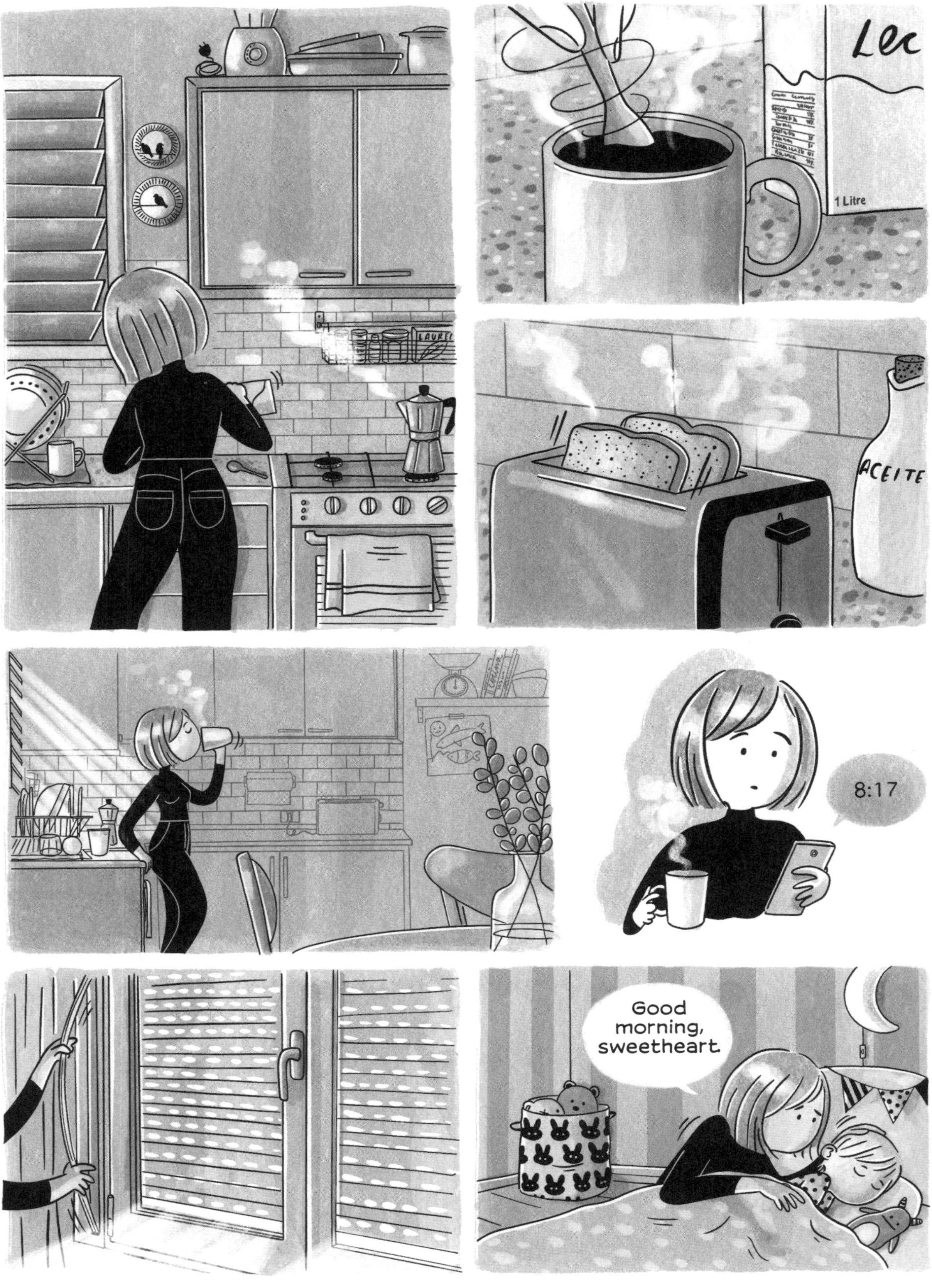
Lec
1 Litre
ACEITE
8:17
Good morning, sweetheart.

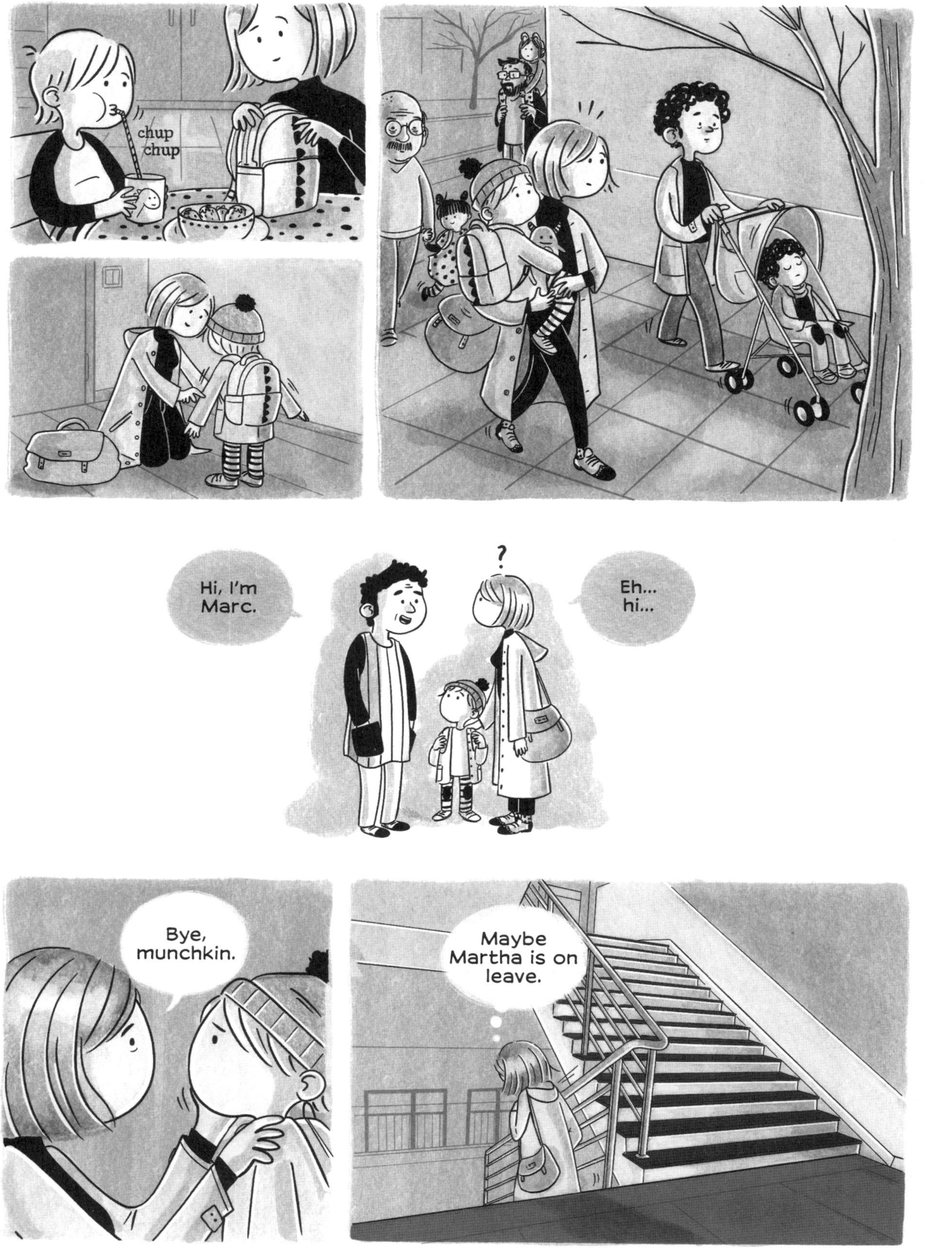

chup
chup
Hi, I'm Marc.
?
Eh... hi...
Bye, munchkin.
Maybe Martha is on leave.

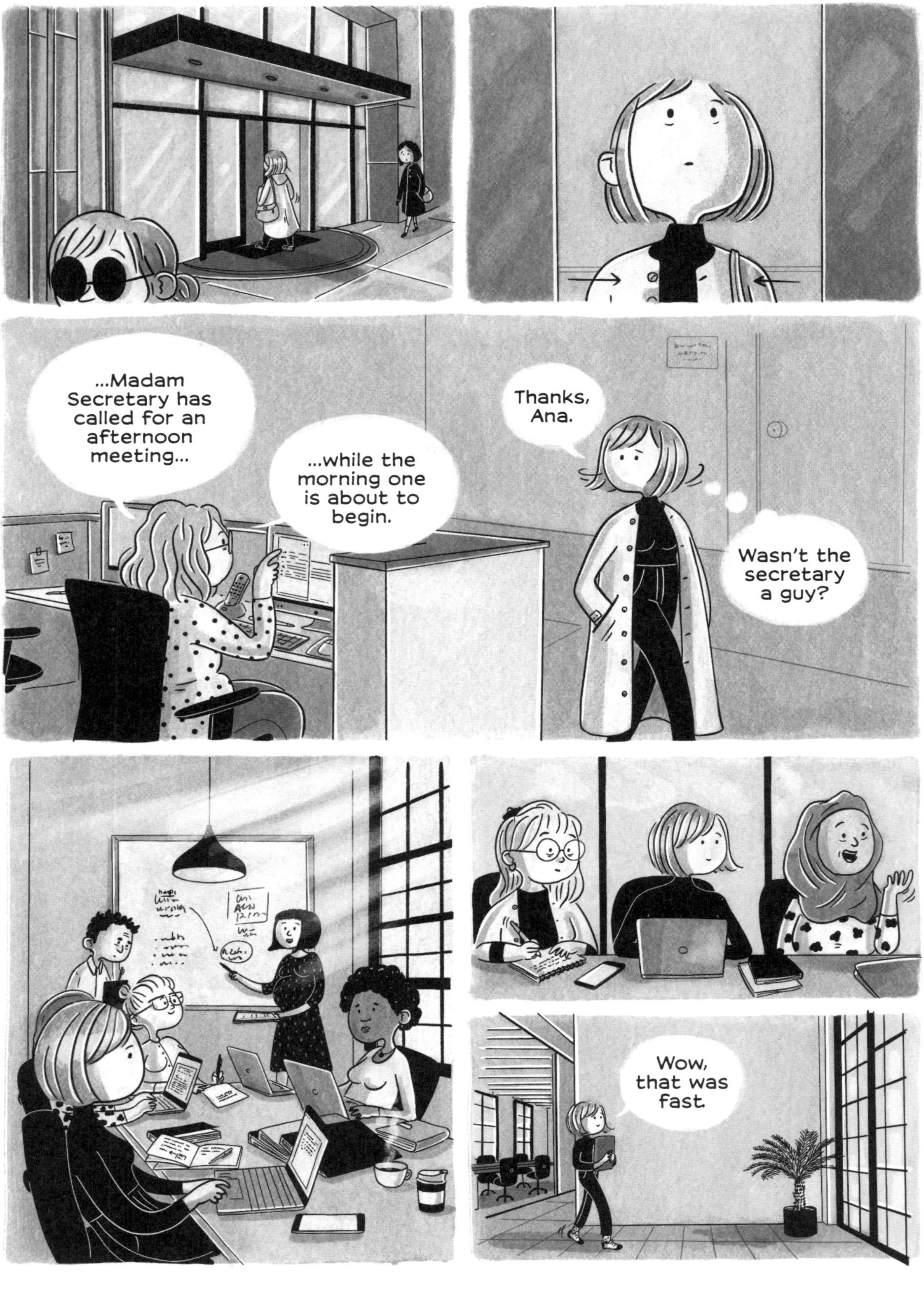
...Madam Secretary has called for an afternoon meeting...
...while the morning one is about to begin.
Thanks, Ana.
Wasn't the secretary a guy?
Wow, that was fast.

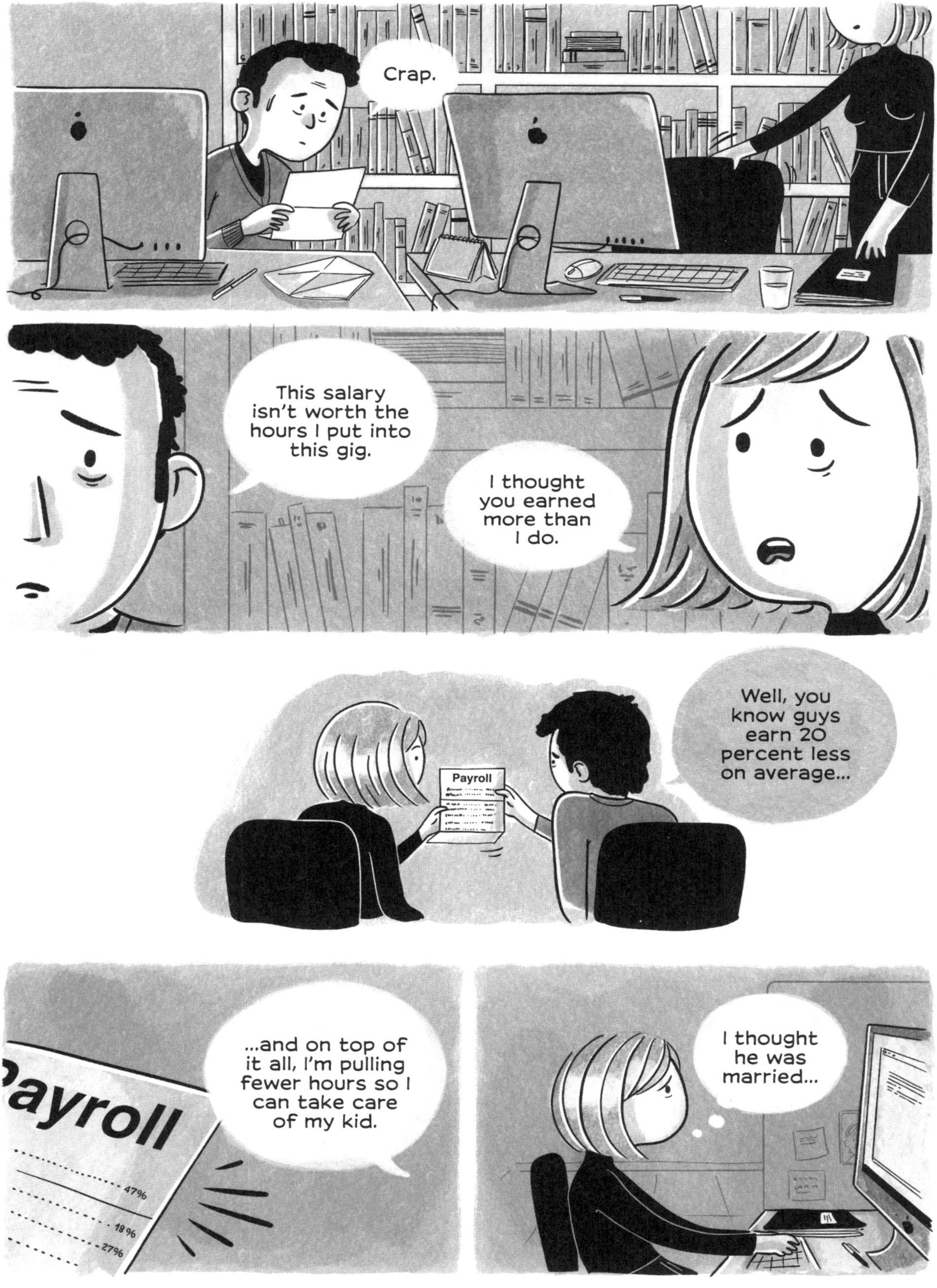
Crap.
This salary isn't worth the hours I put into this gig.
I thought you earned more than I do.
Payroll
Well, you know guys earn 20 percent less on average...
Payroll
47%
18%
27%
...and on top of it all, I'm pulling fewer hours so I can take care of my kid.
I thought he was married...

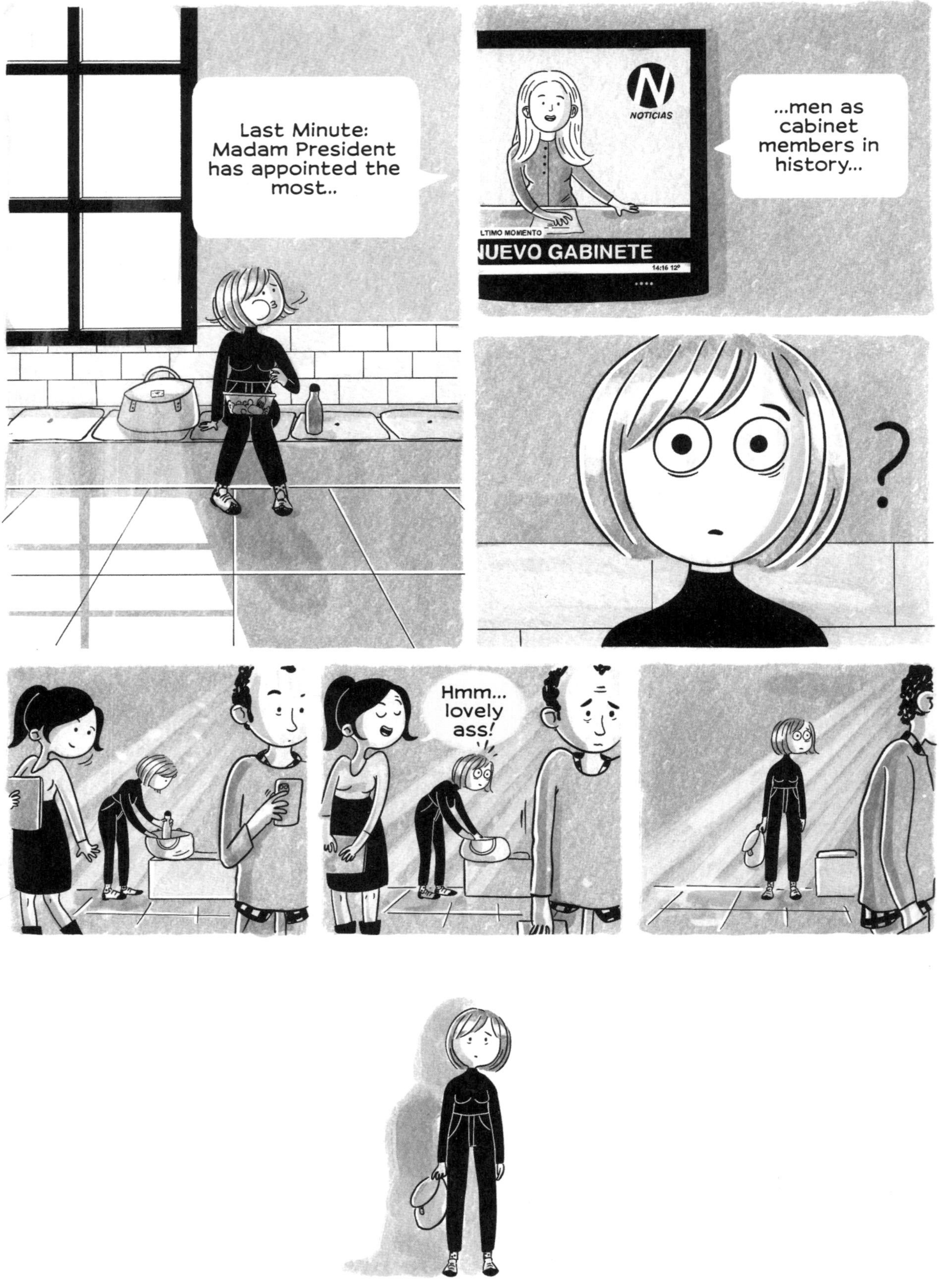
Last Minute: Madam President has appointed the most..
NOTICIAS
LTIMO MOMENTO
NUEVO GABINETE
14:16 12º
...men as cabinet members in history...
?
Hmm... lovely ass!

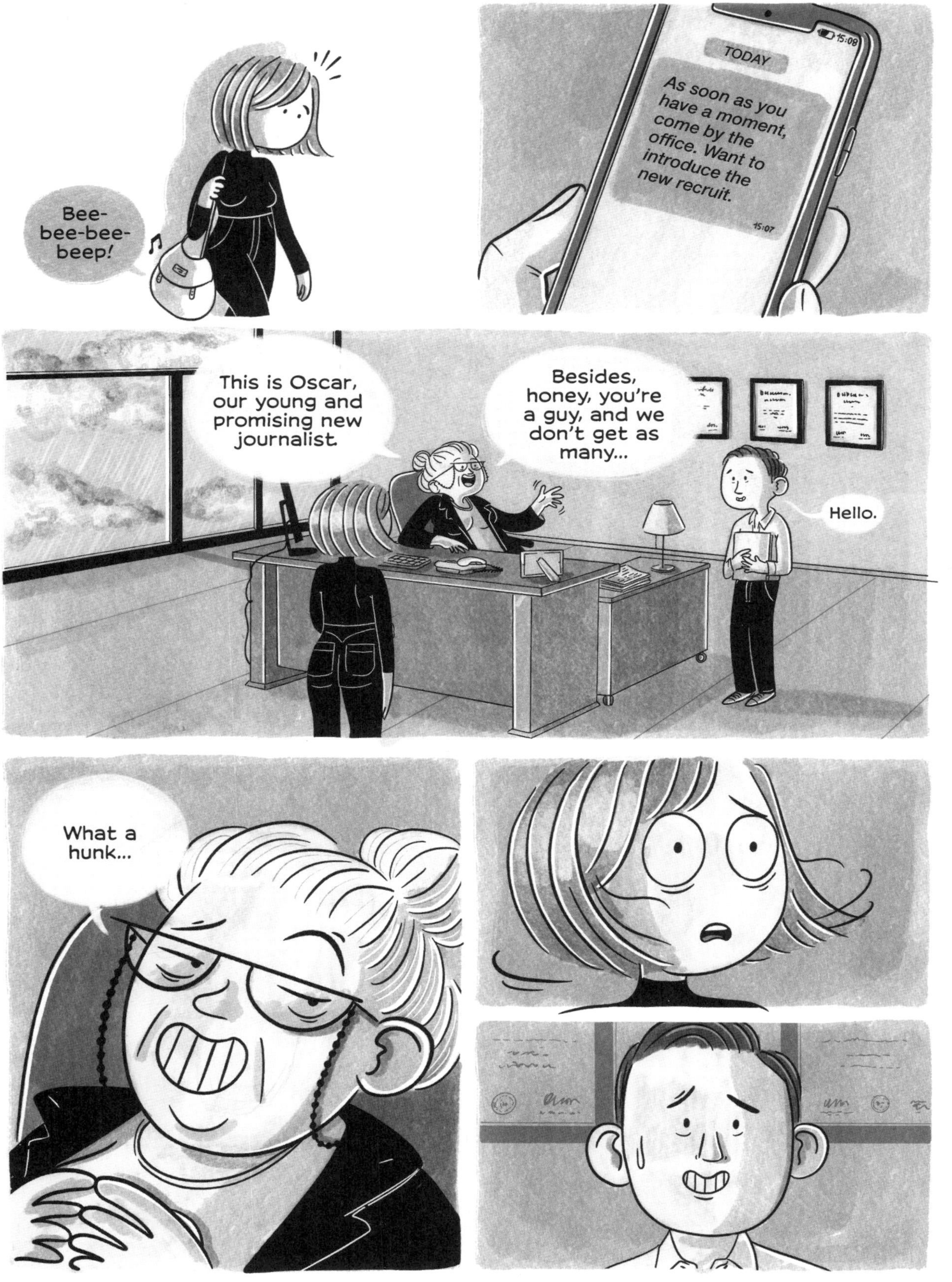

Bee-bee-bee-beep!
TODAY
As soon as you have a moment, come by the office. Want to introduce the new recruit.
15:07
This is Oscar, our young and promising new journalist.
Besides, honey, you're a guy, and we don't get as many...
Hello.
What a hunk...

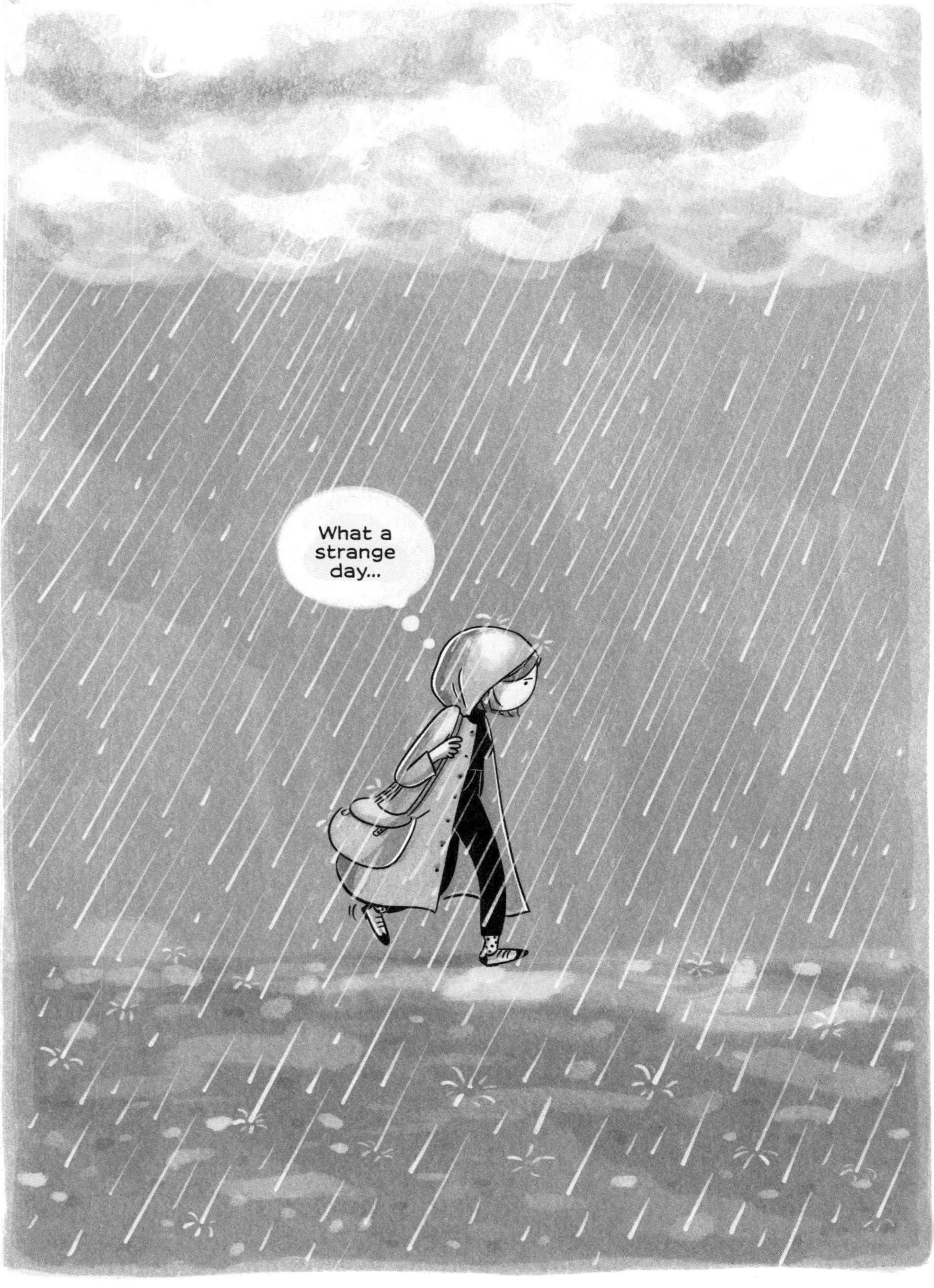
What a strange day...

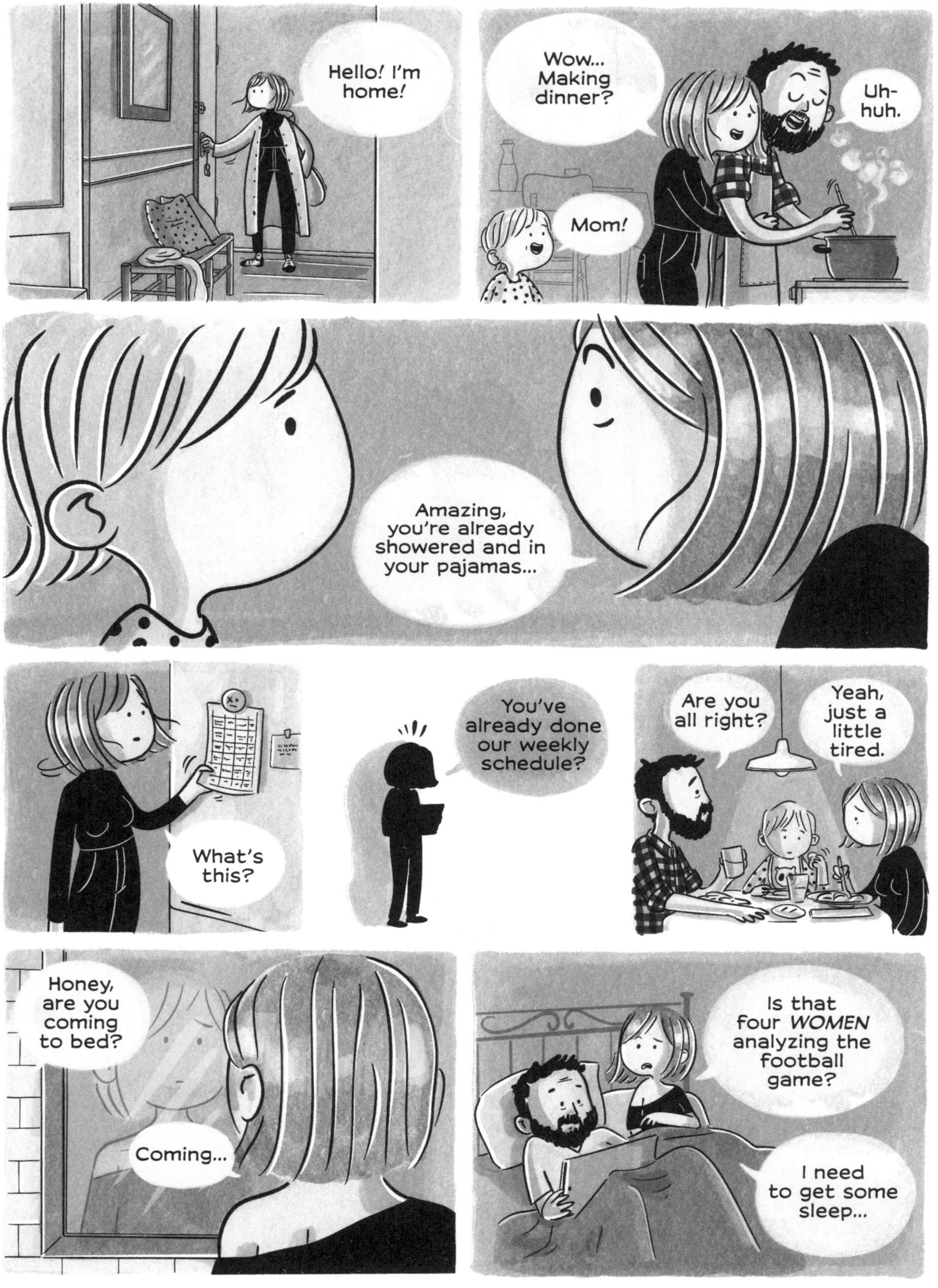

Hello! I'm home!
Wow... Making dinner?
Uh-huh.
Mom!
Amazing, you're already showered and in your pajamas...
What's this?
You've already done our weekly schedule?
Are you all right?
Yeah, just a little tired.
Honey, are you coming to bed?
Coming...
Is that four *WOMEN* analyzing the football game?
I need to get some sleep...

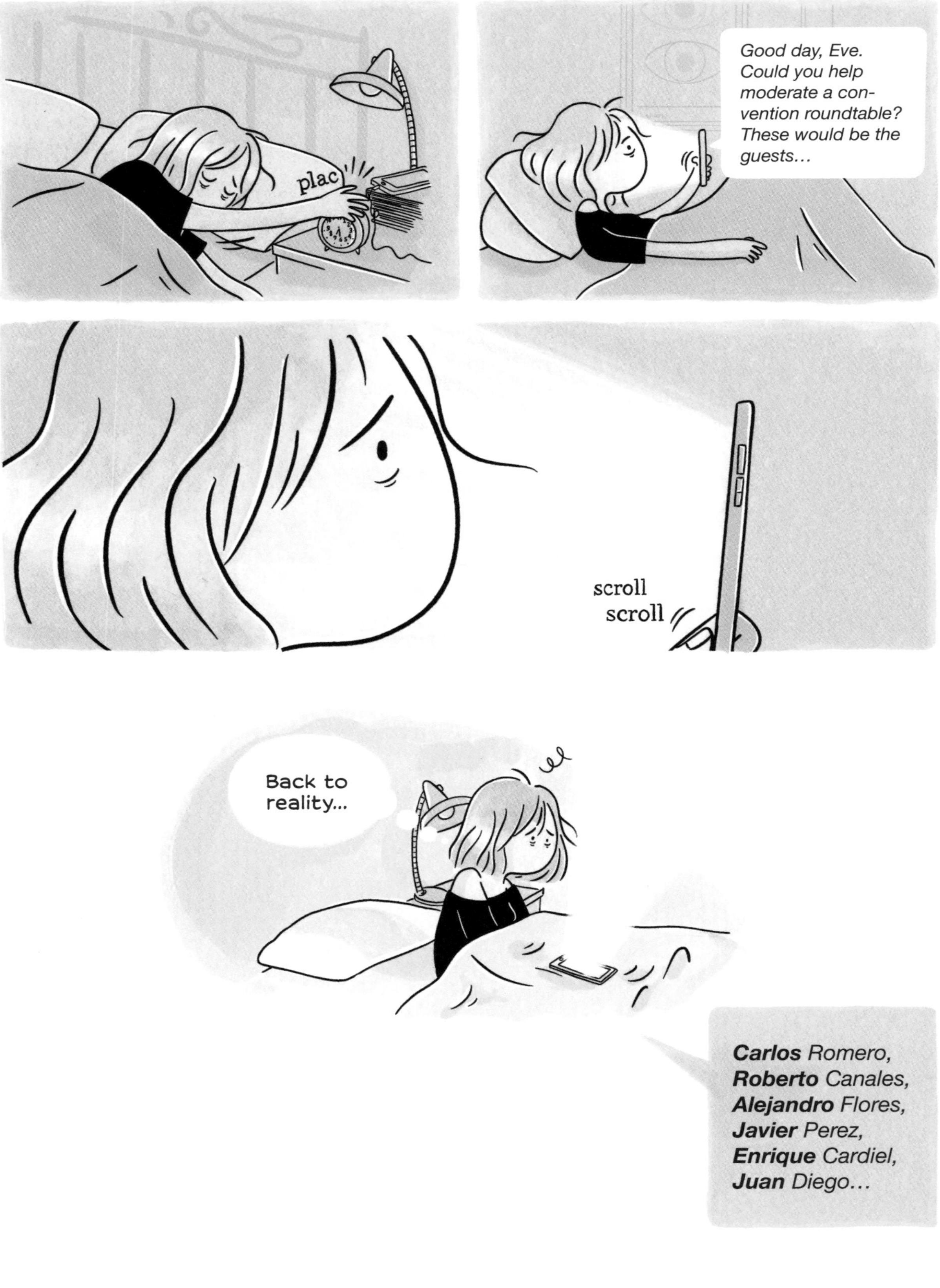
plac
Good day, Eve. Could you help moderate a convention roundtable? These would be the guests...
scroll scroll
Back to reality...
Carlos Romero, **Roberto** Canales, **Alejandro** Flores, **Javier** Perez, **Enrique** Cardiel, **Juan** Diego...

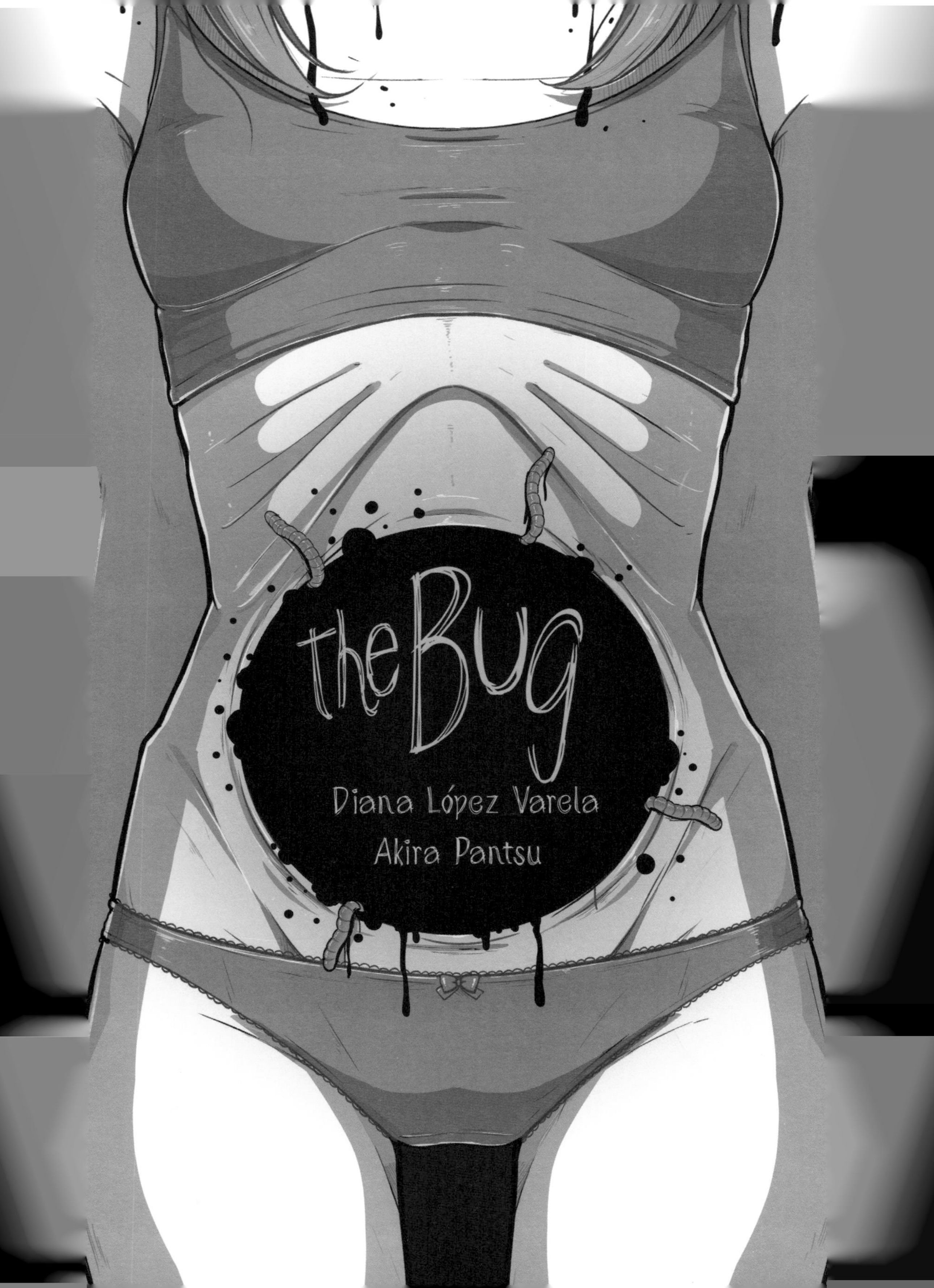
theBug
Diana López Varela
Akira Pantsu

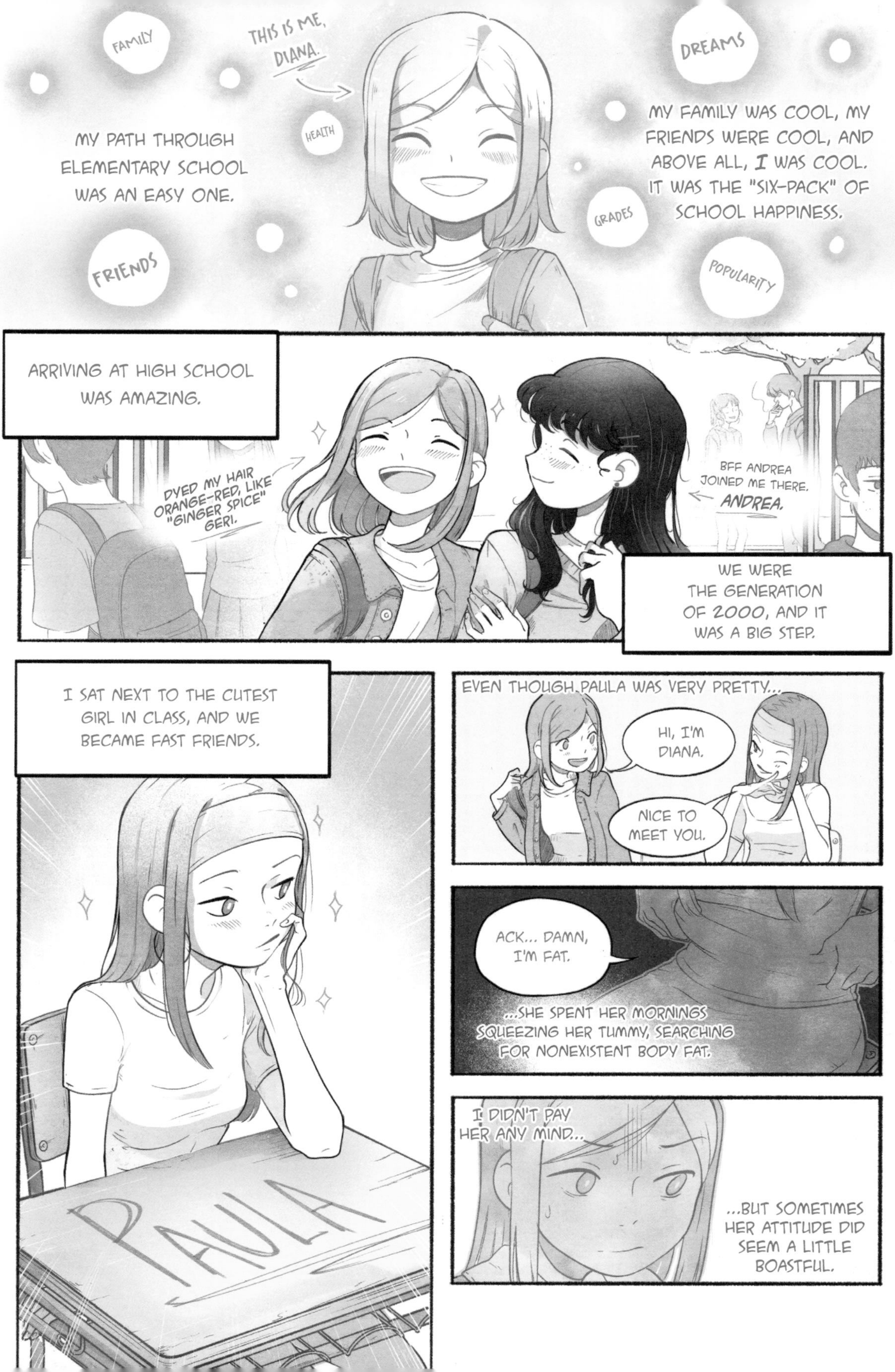

THIS IS ME, DIANA.
FAMILY
HEALTH
FRIENDS
DREAMS
GRADES
POPULARITY
MY PATH THROUGH ELEMENTARY SCHOOL WAS AN EASY ONE.
MY FAMILY WAS COOL, MY FRIENDS WERE COOL, AND ABOVE ALL, I WAS COOL. IT WAS THE "SIX-PACK" OF SCHOOL HAPPINESS.
ARRIVING AT HIGH SCHOOL WAS AMAZING.
DYED MY HAIR ORANGE-RED, LIKE "GINGER SPICE" GERI.
BFF ANDREA JOINED ME THERE.
ANDREA.
WE WERE THE GENERATION OF 2000, AND IT WAS A BIG STEP.
I SAT NEXT TO THE CUTEST GIRL IN CLASS, AND WE BECAME FAST FRIENDS.
PAULA
EVEN THOUGH PAULA WAS VERY PRETTY...
HI, I'M DIANA.
NICE TO MEET YOU.
ACK... DAMN, I'M FAT.
...SHE SPENT HER MORNINGS SQUEEZING HER TUMMY, SEARCHING FOR NONEXISTENT BODY FAT.
I DIDN'T PAY HER ANY MIND...
...BUT SOMETIMES HER ATTITUDE DID SEEM A LITTLE BOASTFUL.

I WAS MAINLY CONCERNED WITH GRADES AND BOYS.

FIRST KISS

Dear Diana,
I'm thrilled to be in high school.
Do you think it will be tough?
How should we dress?
Are there gonna be cute boys?
Will we... fall in love?
Ack! Already getting nervous!

Andrea

DWARF!

DO-GOODER!

WIENER DOG!

SOME HAD ALREADY BEGUN TO MESS WITH ME.

BUT ANDREA SUFFERED THE BRUNT OF IT.

GOT GUM IN HER HAIR...

SPIT ON HER TABLE...

TRASH DIE
ANDREA IS UGLY

THEY WERE FAR CRUELER TO HER...

SHE CRIED HER EYES OUT EVERY DAY.

PAULA, AS CUTE AS SHE WAS, WAS HARASSED, TOO.

SLUT!

SKANK!

QUICKLY I LEARNED THAT LAUGHING LIKE PAULA WAS A FAR BETTER STRATEGY THAN CRYING LIKE ANDREA.

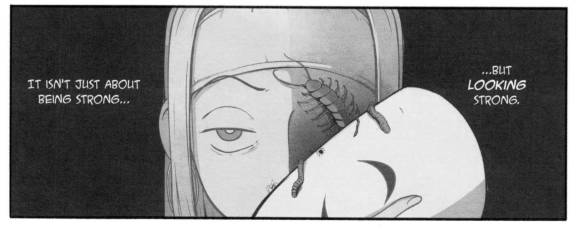

IT ISN'T JUST ABOUT BEING STRONG...

...BUT *LOOKING* STRONG.

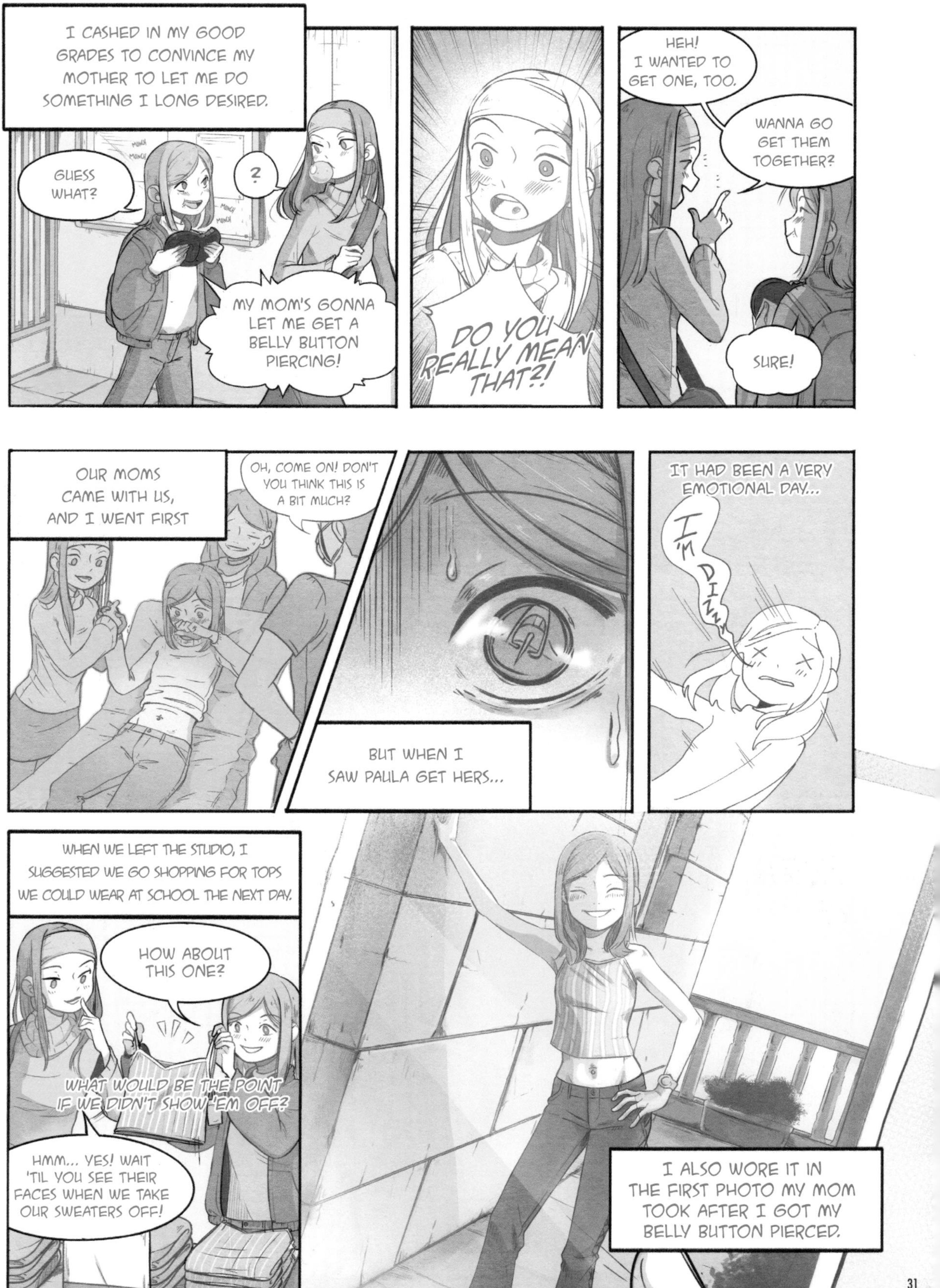
I CASHED IN MY GOOD GRADES TO CONVINCE MY MOTHER TO LET ME DO SOMETHING I LONG DESIRED.
GUESS WHAT?
?
MY MOM'S GONNA LET ME GET A BELLY BUTTON PIERCING!
DO YOU REALLY MEAN THAT?!
HEH! I WANTED TO GET ONE, TOO.
WANNA GO GET THEM TOGETHER?
SURE!
OUR MOMS CAME WITH US, AND I WENT FIRST
OH, COME ON! DON'T YOU THINK THIS IS A BIT MUCH?
BUT WHEN I SAW PAULA GET HERS...
IT HAD BEEN A VERY EMOTIONAL DAY...
I'M DIZZY
WHEN WE LEFT THE STUDIO, I SUGGESTED WE GO SHOPPING FOR TOPS WE COULD WEAR AT SCHOOL THE NEXT DAY.
HOW ABOUT THIS ONE?
WHAT WOULD BE THE POINT IF WE DIDN'T SHOW 'EM OFF?
HMM... YES! WAIT 'TIL YOU SEE THEIR FACES WHEN WE TAKE OUR SWEATERS OFF!
I ALSO WORE IT IN THE FIRST PHOTO MY MOM TOOK AFTER I GOT MY BELLY BUTTON PIERCED.

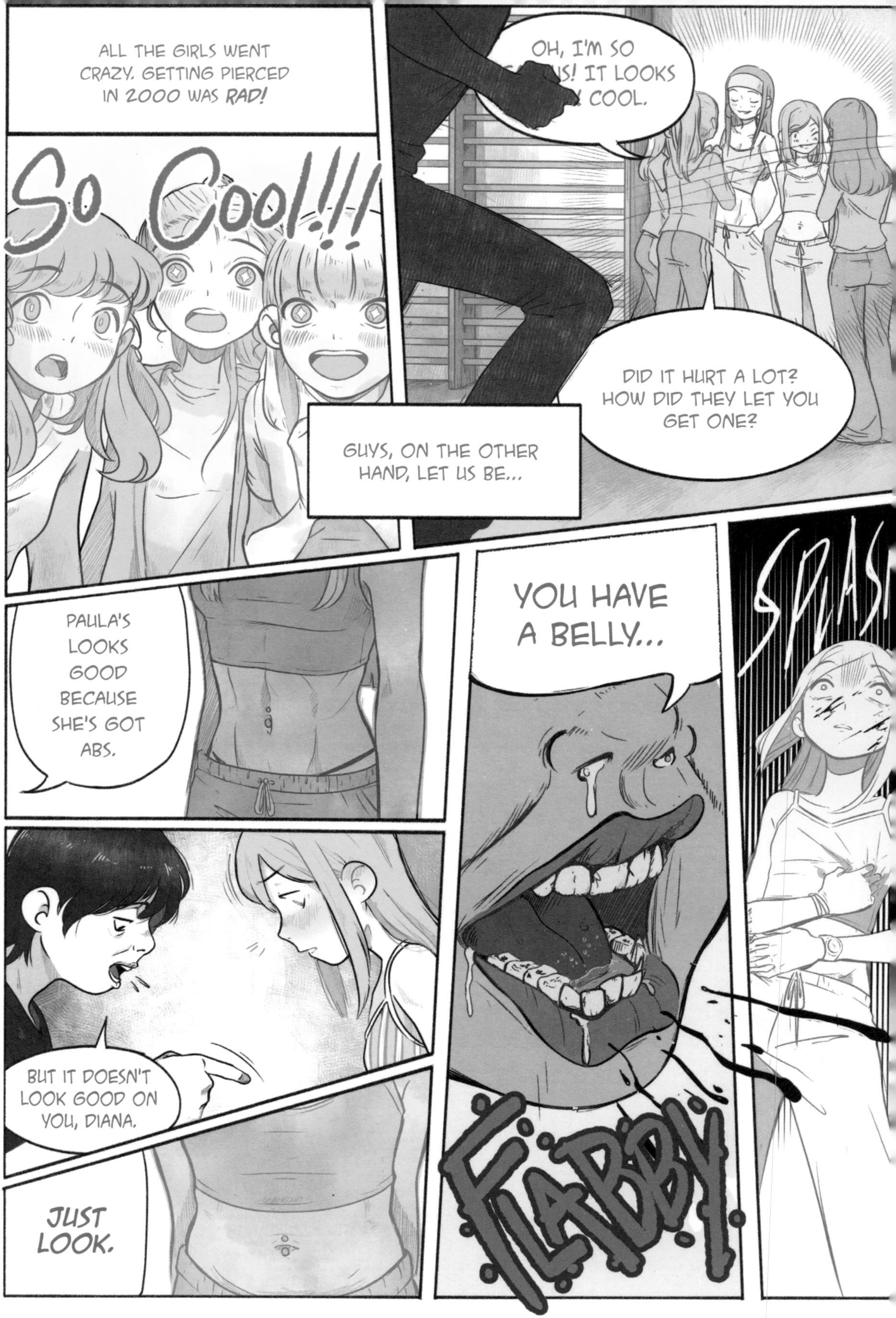
ALL THE GIRLS WENT CRAZY. GETTING PIERCED IN 2000 WAS *RAD!*
So Cool!!!
OH, I'M SO ...US! IT LOOKS ... COOL.
DID IT HURT A LOT? HOW DID THEY LET YOU GET ONE?
GUYS, ON THE OTHER HAND, LET US BE...
PAULA'S LOOKS GOOD BECAUSE SHE'S GOT ABS.
BUT IT DOESN'T LOOK GOOD ON YOU, DIANA.
JUST LOOK.
YOU HAVE A BELLY...
FLABBY.
SPLAS

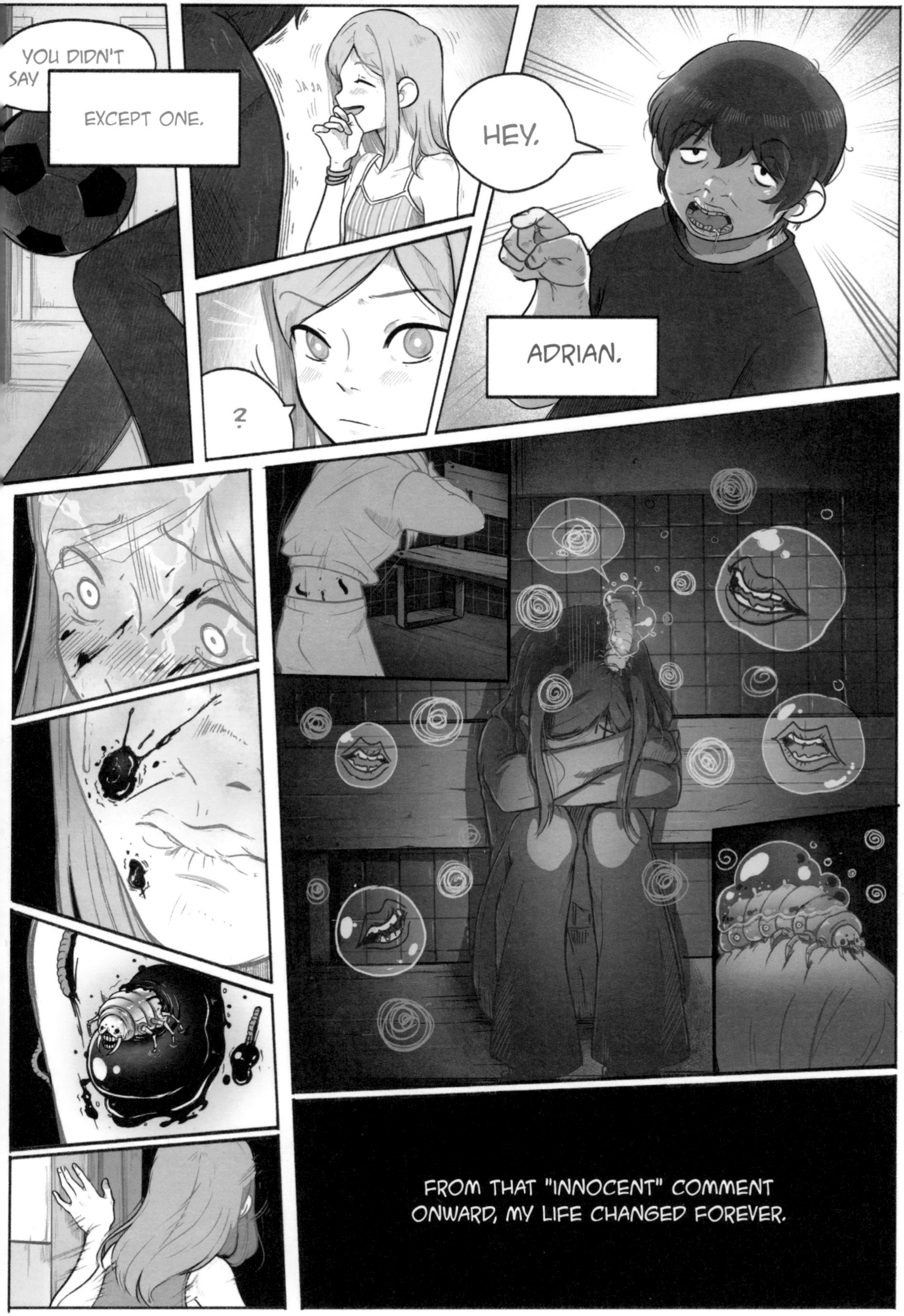

YOU DIDN'T SAY
EXCEPT ONE.
JAJA
HEY.
ADRIAN.
?
FROM THAT "INNOCENT" COMMENT ONWARD, MY LIFE CHANGED FOREVER.

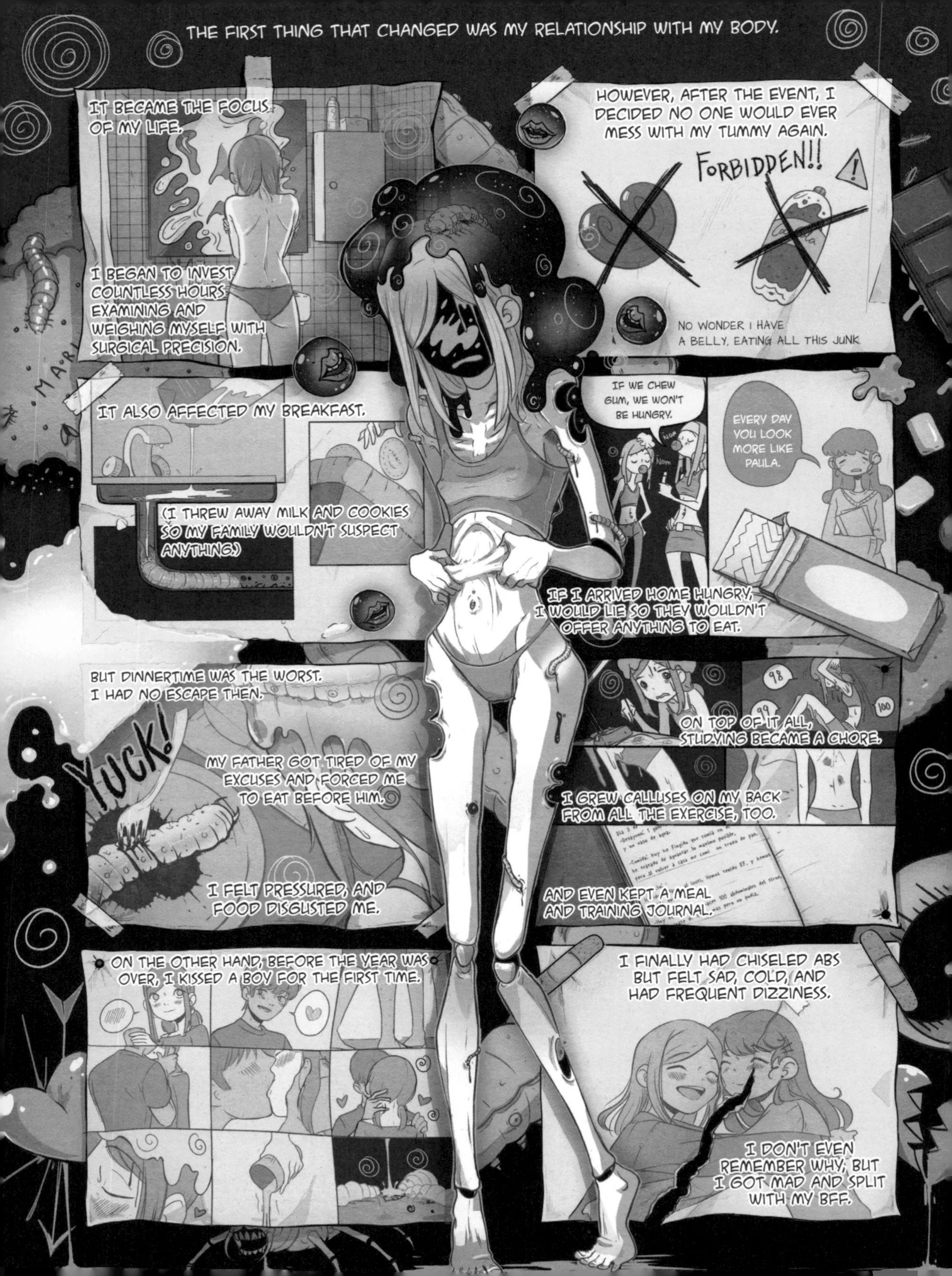

THE FIRST THING THAT CHANGED WAS MY RELATIONSHIP WITH MY BODY.
IT BECAME THE FOCUS OF MY LIFE.
I BEGAN TO INVEST COUNTLESS HOURS EXAMINING AND WEIGHING MYSELF WITH SURGICAL PRECISION.
HOWEVER, AFTER THE EVENT, I DECIDED NO ONE WOULD EVER MESS WITH MY TUMMY AGAIN.
FORBIDDEN!!
NO WONDER I HAVE A BELLY, EATING ALL THIS JUNK.
IT ALSO AFFECTED MY BREAKFAST.
(I THREW AWAY MILK AND COOKIES SO MY FAMILY WOULDN'T SUSPECT ANYTHING.)
IF WE CHEW GUM, WE WON'T BE HUNGRY.
EVERY DAY YOU LOOK MORE LIKE PAULA.
IF I ARRIVED HOME HUNGRY, I WOULD LIE SO THEY WOULDN'T OFFER ANYTHING TO EAT.
BUT DINNERTIME WAS THE WORST. I HAD NO ESCAPE THEN.
YUCK!
MY FATHER GOT TIRED OF MY EXCUSES AND FORCED ME TO EAT BEFORE HIM.
I FELT PRESSURED, AND FOOD DISGUSTED ME.
98
99
100
ON TOP OF IT ALL, STUDYING BECAME A CHORE.
I GREW CALLUSES ON MY BACK FROM ALL THE EXERCISE, TOO.
AND EVEN KEPT A MEAL AND TRAINING JOURNAL.
ON THE OTHER HAND, BEFORE THE YEAR WAS OVER, I KISSED A BOY FOR THE FIRST TIME.
I FINALLY HAD CHISELED ABS BUT FELT SAD, COLD, AND HAD FREQUENT DIZZINESS.
I DON'T EVEN REMEMBER WHY, BUT I GOT MAD AND SPLIT WITH MY BFF.

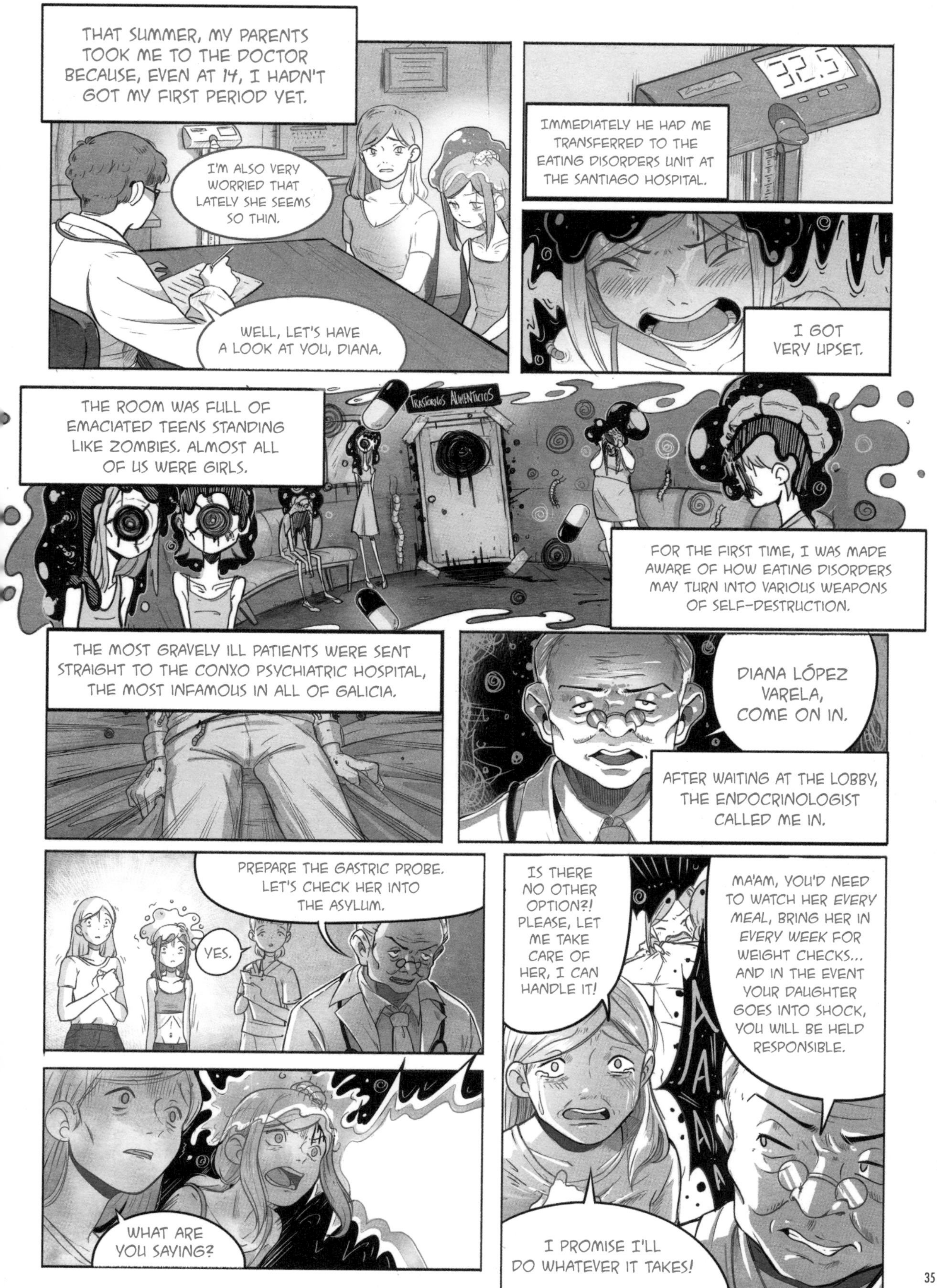

THAT SUMMER, MY PARENTS TOOK ME TO THE DOCTOR BECAUSE, EVEN AT 14, I HADN'T GOT MY FIRST PERIOD YET.
I'M ALSO VERY WORRIED THAT LATELY SHE SEEMS SO THIN.
WELL, LET'S HAVE A LOOK AT YOU, DIANA.
32.5
IMMEDIATELY HE HAD ME TRANSFERRED TO THE EATING DISORDERS UNIT AT THE SANTIAGO HOSPITAL.
I GOT VERY UPSET.
THE ROOM WAS FULL OF EMACIATED TEENS STANDING LIKE ZOMBIES. ALMOST ALL OF US WERE GIRLS.
TRASTORNOS ALIMENTICIOS
FOR THE FIRST TIME, I WAS MADE AWARE OF HOW EATING DISORDERS MAY TURN INTO VARIOUS WEAPONS OF SELF-DESTRUCTION.
THE MOST GRAVELY ILL PATIENTS WERE SENT STRAIGHT TO THE CONXO PSYCHIATRIC HOSPITAL, THE MOST INFAMOUS IN ALL OF GALICIA.
DIANA LÓPEZ VARELA, COME ON IN.
AFTER WAITING AT THE LOBBY, THE ENDOCRINOLOGIST CALLED ME IN.
PREPARE THE GASTRIC PROBE. LET'S CHECK HER INTO THE ASYLUM.
YES.
WHAT ARE YOU SAYING?
IS THERE NO OTHER OPTION?! PLEASE, LET ME TAKE CARE OF HER, I CAN HANDLE IT!
MA'AM, YOU'D NEED TO WATCH HER EVERY MEAL, BRING HER IN EVERY WEEK FOR WEIGHT CHECKS... AND IN THE EVENT YOUR DAUGHTER GOES INTO SHOCK, YOU WILL BE HELD RESPONSIBLE.
AAAAA
I PROMISE I'LL DO WHATEVER IT TAKES!

I WAS SO SICK, THEY HAD TO FEED ME HYPER-CALORIC SHAKES TO COMPENSATE MY MALNOURISHMENT.
"IT'S FINE, BUT YOU NEED TO KNOW YOU'RE BRINGING A TICKING TIME BOMB HOME. SHE COULD DIE AT ANY MINUTE."
MOM
DAD
TENSION
I HAD TO DRINK MY FIRST SHAKE UNDER MY PARENTS' WATCHFUL GAZE THAT NIGHT.
IT WAS A DISGUSTING, THICK, DOG-FOOD-TASTING CONCOCTION.
NO PUEDO
NO PUEDO
OF COURSE, I TRIED PUKING IT ALL OUT, BUT FORTUNATELY NEVER MANAGED TO DO SO.
TO THIS DAY, I GET NAUSEATED JUST THINKING ABOUT THOSE SHAKES.
GULP
FIGHTS AT HOME, ESPECIALLY DURING MEAL TIME, BECAME MORE FREQUENT. MY PARENTS' OWN RELATIONSHIP TOOK A DOWNTURN DUE TO MY ANOREXIA.
I KNEW I WAS RESPONSIBLE AND FELT CONSTANT SHAME.
EACH WEEK I FACED THE SCALES, SO IT DIDN'T TAKE ME SO LONG TO START GAINING WEIGHT AGAIN. IF I LOST AS LITTLE AS THREE OUNCES, I'D BE CHECKED INTO THE CONXO.
345.
369.
I CHEATED, TOO. BEFORE EACH CHECKUP, I'D LOCK MYSELF IN THE TOILET AND GORGE MYSELF WITH WATER.

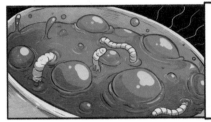

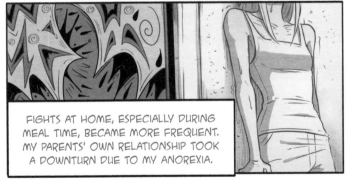

THE NEXT YEAR OF HIGH SCHOOL WAS NO DOUBT THE WORST.

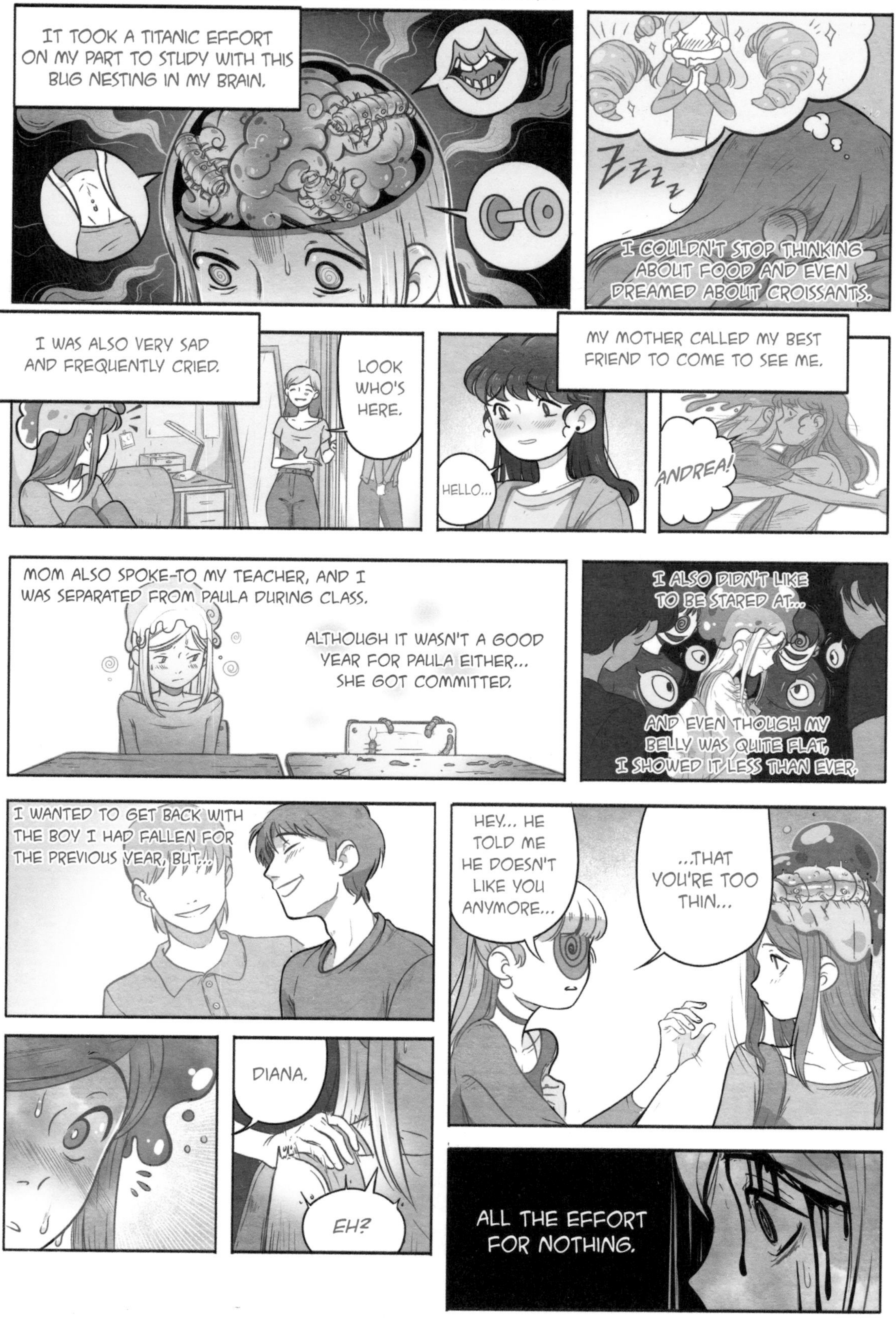
IT TOOK A TITANIC EFFORT ON MY PART TO STUDY WITH THIS BUG NESTING IN MY BRAIN.
ZZZZ
I COULDN'T STOP THINKING ABOUT FOOD AND EVEN DREAMED ABOUT CROISSANTS.
I WAS ALSO VERY SAD AND FREQUENTLY CRIED.
LOOK WHO'S HERE.
MY MOTHER CALLED MY BEST FRIEND TO COME TO SEE ME.
HELLO...
ANDREA!
MOM ALSO SPOKE TO MY TEACHER, AND I WAS SEPARATED FROM PAULA DURING CLASS.
ALTHOUGH IT WASN'T A GOOD YEAR FOR PAULA EITHER... SHE GOT COMMITTED.
I ALSO DIDN'T LIKE TO BE STARED AT...
AND EVEN THOUGH MY BELLY WAS QUITE FLAT, I SHOWED IT LESS THAN EVER.
I WANTED TO GET BACK WITH THE BOY I HAD FALLEN FOR THE PREVIOUS YEAR, BUT...
HEY... HE TOLD ME HE DOESN'T LIKE YOU ANYMORE...
...THAT YOU'RE TOO THIN...
DIANA.
EH?
ALL THE EFFORT FOR NOTHING.

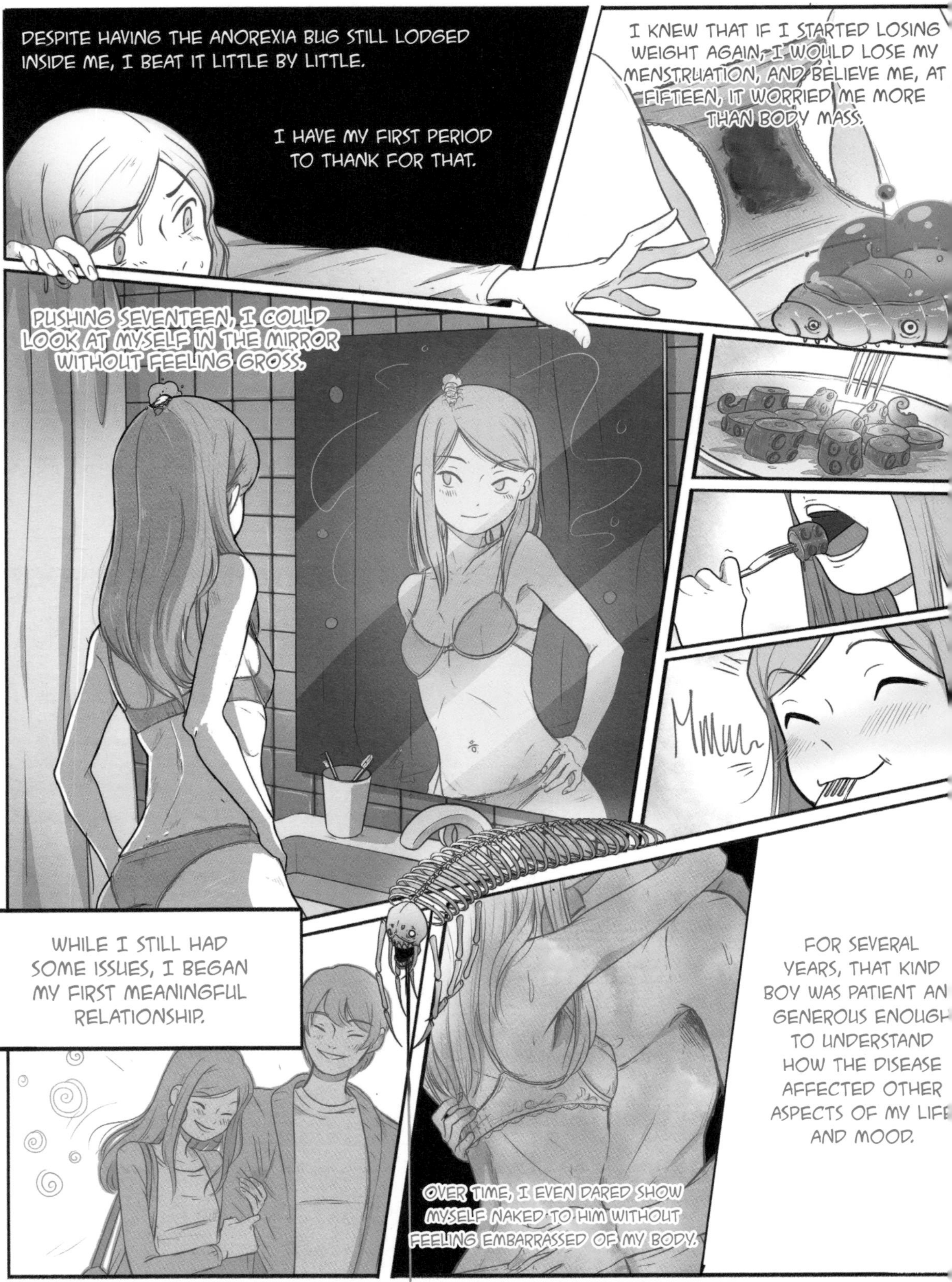
DESPITE HAVING THE ANOREXIA BUG STILL LODGED INSIDE ME, I BEAT IT LITTLE BY LITTLE.
I HAVE MY FIRST PERIOD TO THANK FOR THAT.
I KNEW THAT IF I STARTED LOSING WEIGHT AGAIN, I WOULD LOSE MY MENSTRUATION, AND BELIEVE ME, AT FIFTEEN, IT WORRIED ME MORE THAN BODY MASS.
PUSHING SEVENTEEN, I COULD LOOK AT MYSELF IN THE MIRROR WITHOUT FEELING GROSS.
Mmm
WHILE I STILL HAD SOME ISSUES, I BEGAN MY FIRST MEANINGFUL RELATIONSHIP.
FOR SEVERAL YEARS, THAT KIND BOY WAS PATIENT AN GENEROUS ENOUGH TO UNDERSTAND HOW THE DISEASE AFFECTED OTHER ASPECTS OF MY LIFE AND MOOD.
OVER TIME, I EVEN DARED SHOW MYSELF NAKED TO HIM WITHOUT FEELING EMBARRASSED OF MY BODY.

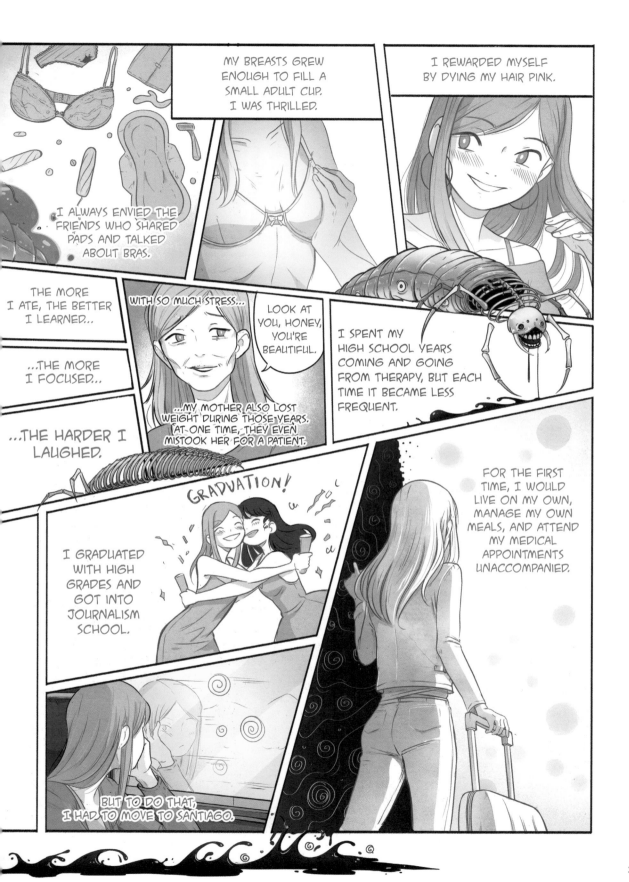

MY BREASTS GREW ENOUGH TO FILL A SMALL ADULT CUP. I WAS THRILLED.

I REWARDED MYSELF BY DYING MY HAIR PINK.

I ALWAYS ENVIED THE FRIENDS WHO SHARED PADS AND TALKED ABOUT BRAS.

THE MORE I ATE, THE BETTER I LEARNED...

WITH SO MUCH STRESS...

LOOK AT YOU, HONEY, YOU'RE BEAUTIFUL.

...THE MORE I FOCUSED...

...MY MOTHER ALSO LOST WEIGHT DURING THOSE YEARS. AT ONE TIME, THEY EVEN MISTOOK HER FOR A PATIENT.

...THE HARDER I LAUGHED.

I SPENT MY HIGH SCHOOL YEARS COMING AND GOING FROM THERAPY, BUT EACH TIME IT BECAME LESS FREQUENT.

GRADUATION!

I GRADUATED WITH HIGH GRADES AND GOT INTO JOURNALISM SCHOOL.

FOR THE FIRST TIME, I WOULD LIVE ON MY OWN, MANAGE MY OWN MEALS, AND ATTEND MY MEDICAL APPOINTMENTS UNACCOMPANIED.

BUT TO DO THAT, I HAD TO MOVE TO SANTIAGO.

DURING MY COLLEGE YEARS, I FOCUSED ON STUDYING AND HAVING A GOOD TIME.

I OVERINDULGED.

I FINALLY REACHED A HEALTHY WEIGHT FOR MY LITTLE BODY.

YOU'VE DONE GREAT.

MY PSYCHIATRIST, DOCTOR LADO, FINALLY DISCHARGED ME.

TAKE GOOD CARE OF YOURSELF.

I WILL!

I PROMISED HER I WOULD COME BACK TO VISIT HER AFTER THOSE YEARS THAT SAVED MY LIFE.

BY THE WAY, THAT KID WHO COMPLAINED ABOUT MY TUMMY DIDN'T PRECISELY AGE WELL, SO I'D CALL IT...

DIVINE JUSTICE.

10 WEIGHT LOSS TIPS

1. RUN AWAY FROM BAKERIES:
Not only is it good exercise but you will learn to control those cravings.
You'll end up feeling proud of yourself.

2. CLEAN-UP TIME:
Two factors at play here.
First cleaning your home burns lots of calories, and second, you will be rewarded for being a good daughter.

3. DANCING QUEEN:
...to your cleaning efforts, your folks will ...ke you out of the house for a night at the ...unity will you have a great time but it ...exercise.

RAG.
Keep your body IN CHECK.

EVEN AS AN ADULT WOMAN, I KEPT CATCHING EXTERNAL MESSAGES ON HOW TO STAY THIN.

DURING THOSE FIRST YEARS, I HAD A FEW EPISODES AND WAS TEMPTED TO FLIRT WITH ANOREXIA, LIKE A FORMER JUNKIE FLIRTS WITH THE IDEA OF SUBSTANCE ABUSE.

HOWEVER, THE MEMORY OF THOSE HAZY DAYS AND A GOOD SUPPORT NETWORK KEPT ME AWAY FROM DANGER.

BUT THE BUG NEVER TOTALLY LEFT...

...RATHER, IT MUTATED INTO NEW FORMS OVER THE YEARS.

YESTERDAY'S ANOREXIA IS TODAY'S...

IMPOSTOR SYNDROME...

ANXIETY...

DEPRESSION...

...GUILT AND FEAR OF NOT BEING WHAT'S EXPECTED OF ME.

THAT'S WHY I USUALLY FORGET
I SUFFERED FROM A DISEASE
I RARELY THINK ABOUT...

SOMETIMES I NEED TO REMIND
MYSELF THAT, IN SPITE OF IT, I
WAS CAPABLE OF ACHIEVING A
LOT--EVEN THOUGH I WAS JUST
A SCARED TEENAGER.

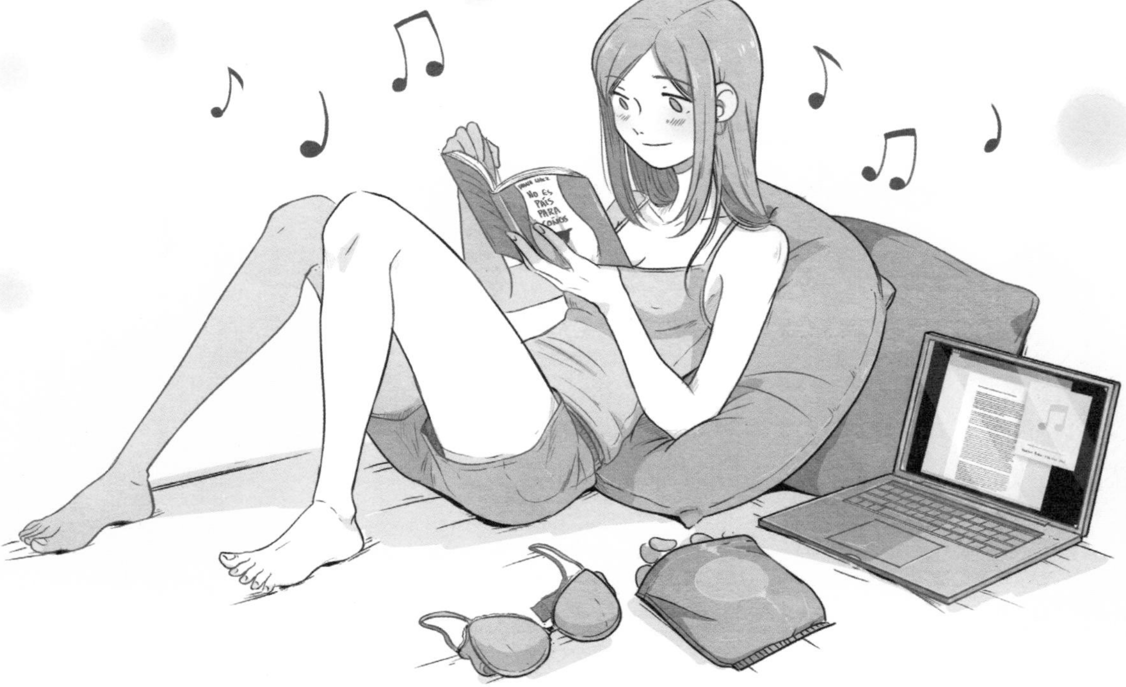
NO ES PAÍS PARA COÑOS

AND OTHER TIMES, I NEED TO GO BACK TO THE YEAR 2000,
WHEN EVERYTHING SEEMED IMPOSSIBLE, TO REMIND MYSELF I
CAN DO IT ONCE AND A THOUSAND TIMES OVER, AND THAT
WE ALL CAN WHEN WE TRUST OURSELVES.

BECAUSE IT DOESN'T MATTER HOW THIN, YOUNG, AND FERTILE
YOU ARE--THERE WILL ALWAYS BE A SCHMUCK WILLING TO
BREAK YOUR HEART AND DESTROY YOUR SELF-ESTEEM.

THAT'S WHY I TELL IT, AND TELL IT TO MYSELF.
BECAUSE WITHOUT WOMEN IN MY LIFE, WITHOUT FEMINISM,
THIS STORY WOULDN'T HAVE ENDED THE SAME WAY.

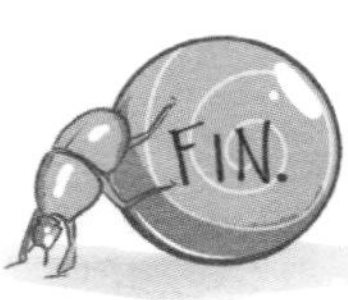
FIN.

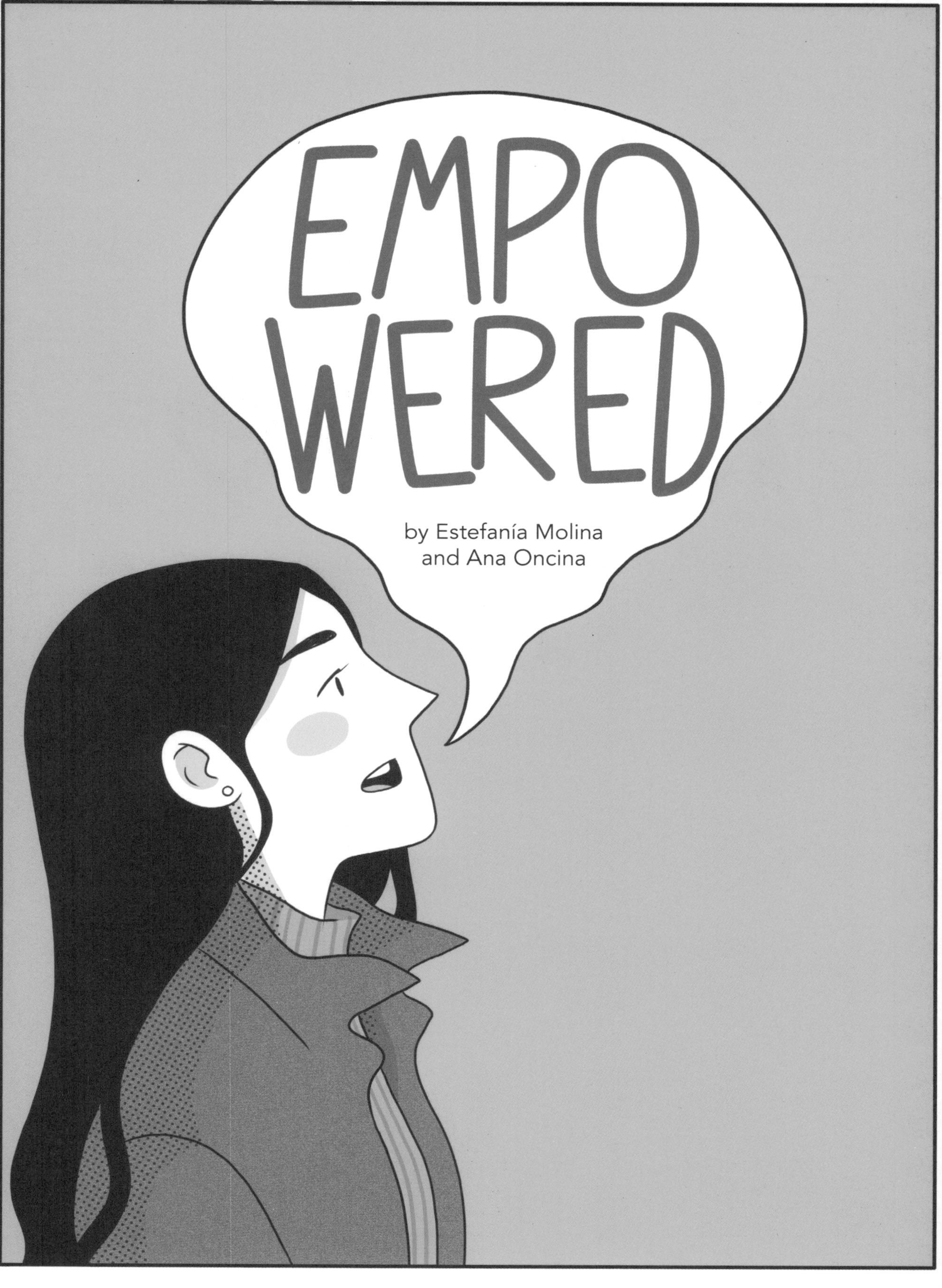
EMPO WERED
by Estefanía Molina
and Ana Oncina

Being "empowered" is the social prestige some citizens or professionals possess given their knowledge and good judgment. It is that moral authority that legitimizes their influential opinion on relevant subjects of public interest. Such repute isn't expected but built through life trajectory and brought about by the collective appreciation of the value of that person's reasoning.

The goal of this story isn't pointing out external factors, nor gender discrimination, but to reflect on why women self-impose on ourselves a series of limitations that prevent us from taking that extra step toward open empowerment, be it driven by bias, fear of external reactions, lack of role models, or simply lack of belief in oneself and the power our thoughts may have on the world.

From a young age I was always the curious child who asked lots of questions and gave her opinion about what happened around her.

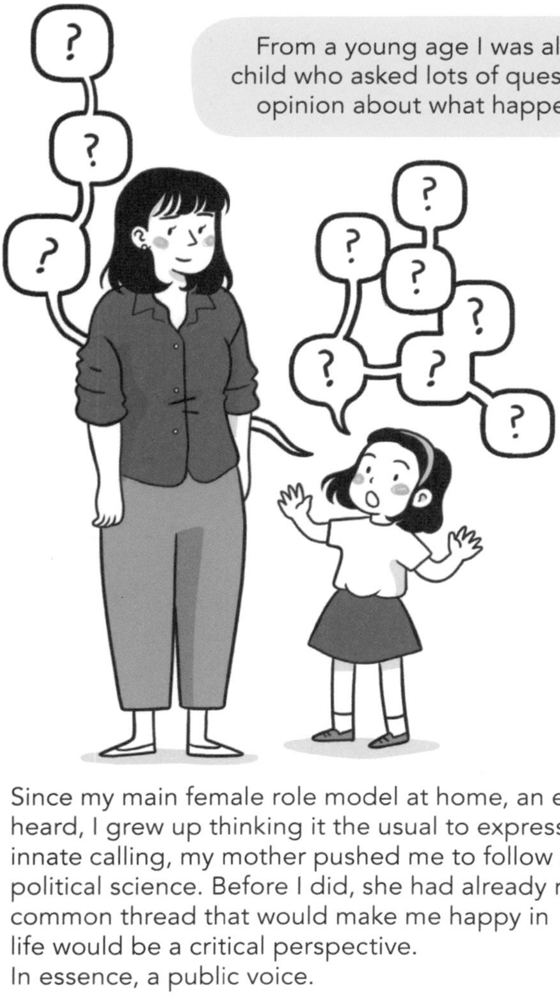
?
?
?
?
?
?
?
?
?
?

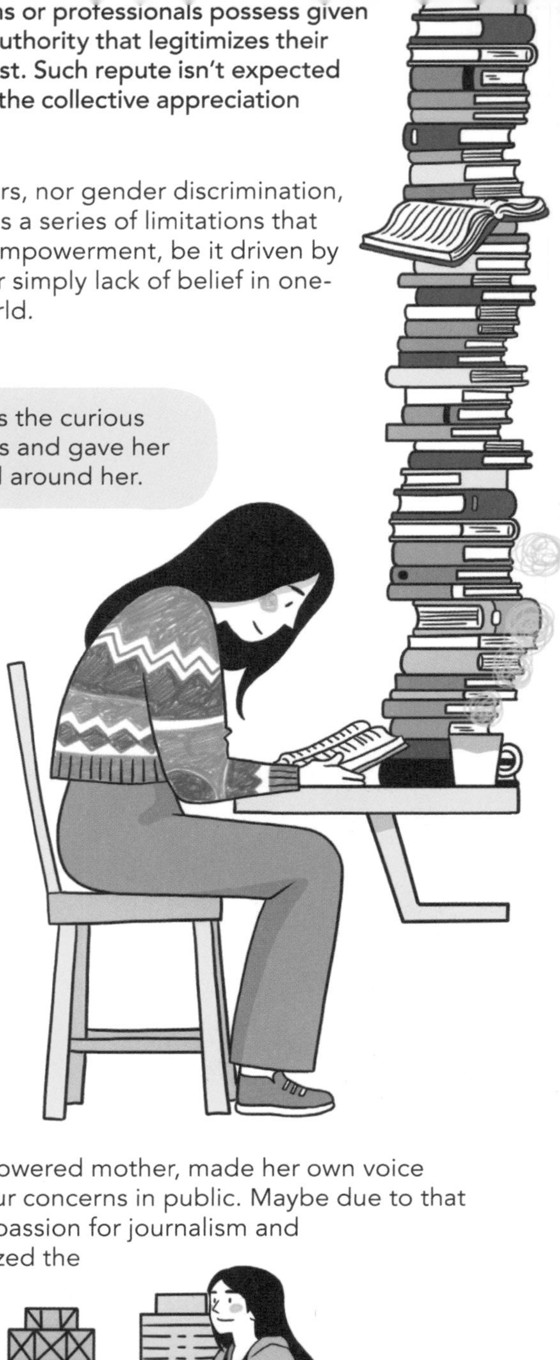

Since my main female role model at home, an empowered mother, made her own voice heard, I grew up thinking it the usual to express your concerns in public. Maybe due to that innate calling, my mother pushed me to follow my passion for journalism and political science. Before I did, she had already realized the common thread that would make me happy in life would be a critical perspective.
In essence, a public voice.

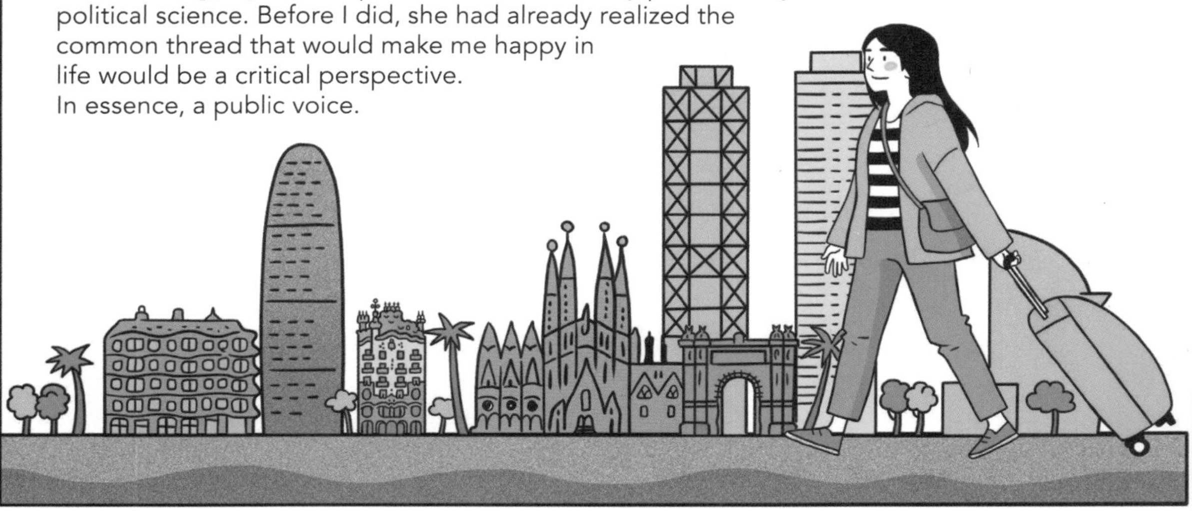

However, once I had left my hometown of Igualada, and once I had reached the Barcelona university, I was made aware of the landscape that went completely unnoticed through my years of childhood and school.

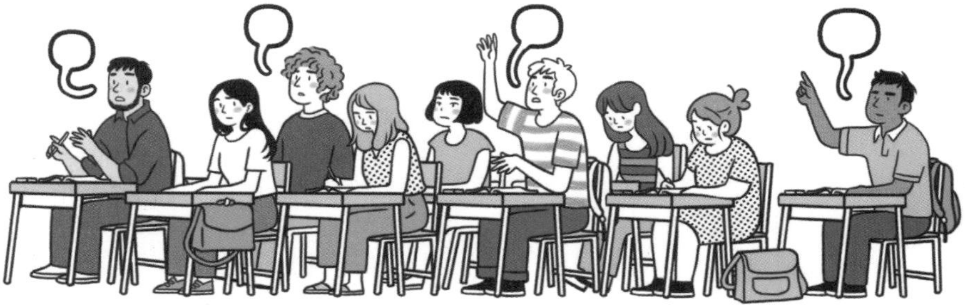

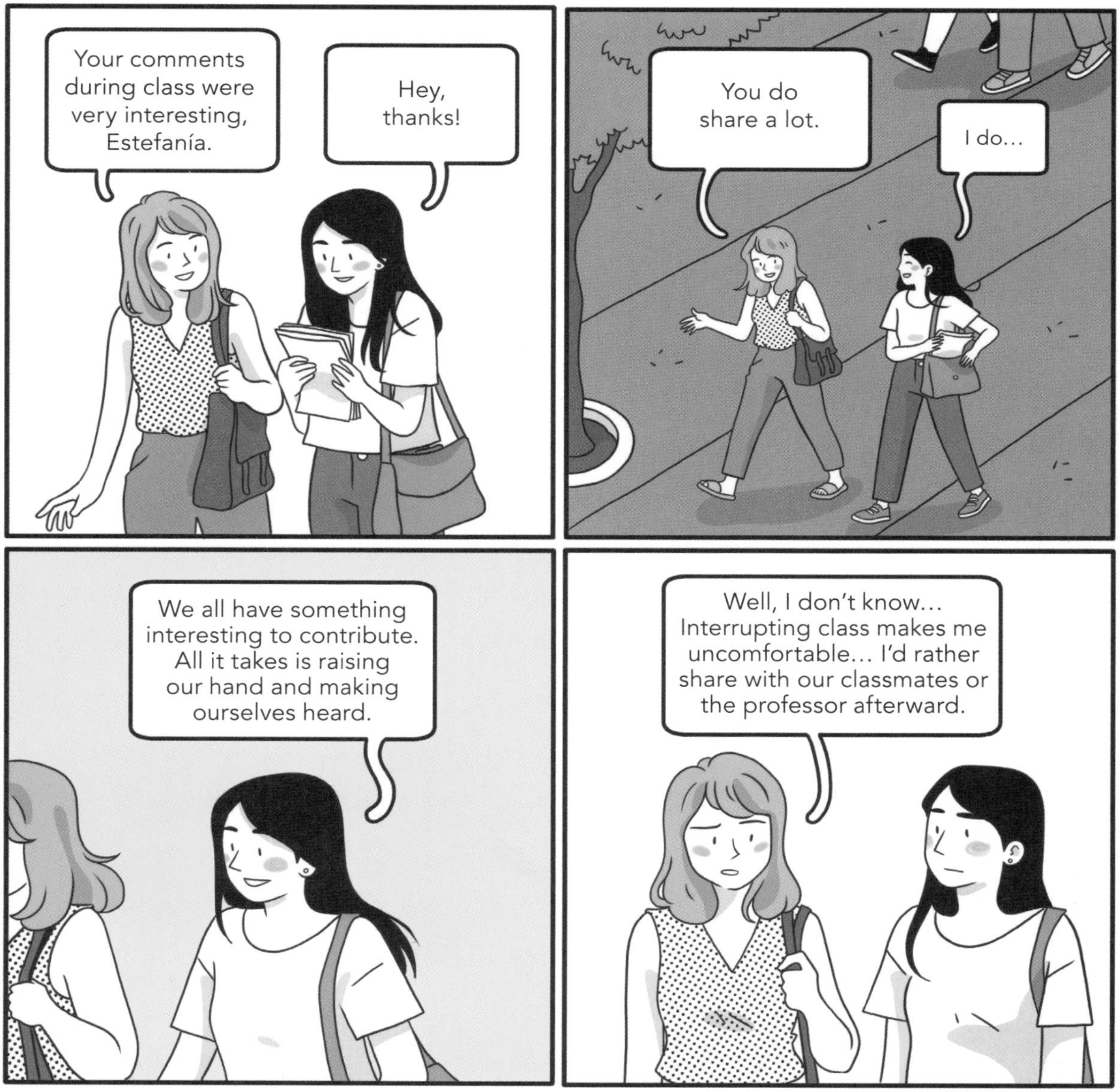
Your comments during class were very interesting, Estefanía.
Hey, thanks!
You do share a lot.
I do...
We all have something interesting to contribute. All it takes is raising our hand and making ourselves heard.
Well, I don't know... Interrupting class makes me uncomfortable... I'd rather share with our classmates or the professor afterward.

Arriving in Madrid and having set roots there, I got involved in the debate of ideas. These instances usually gather young people from the fields of law, management, politics, and economics, which means they have multiple interests and a desire to influence public policy and exchange views with others of their generation.

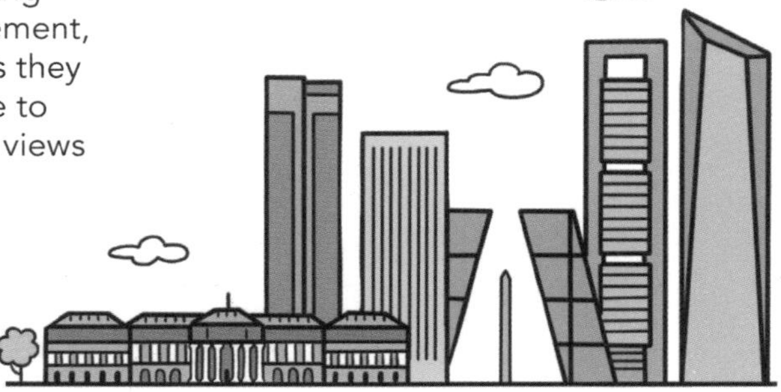

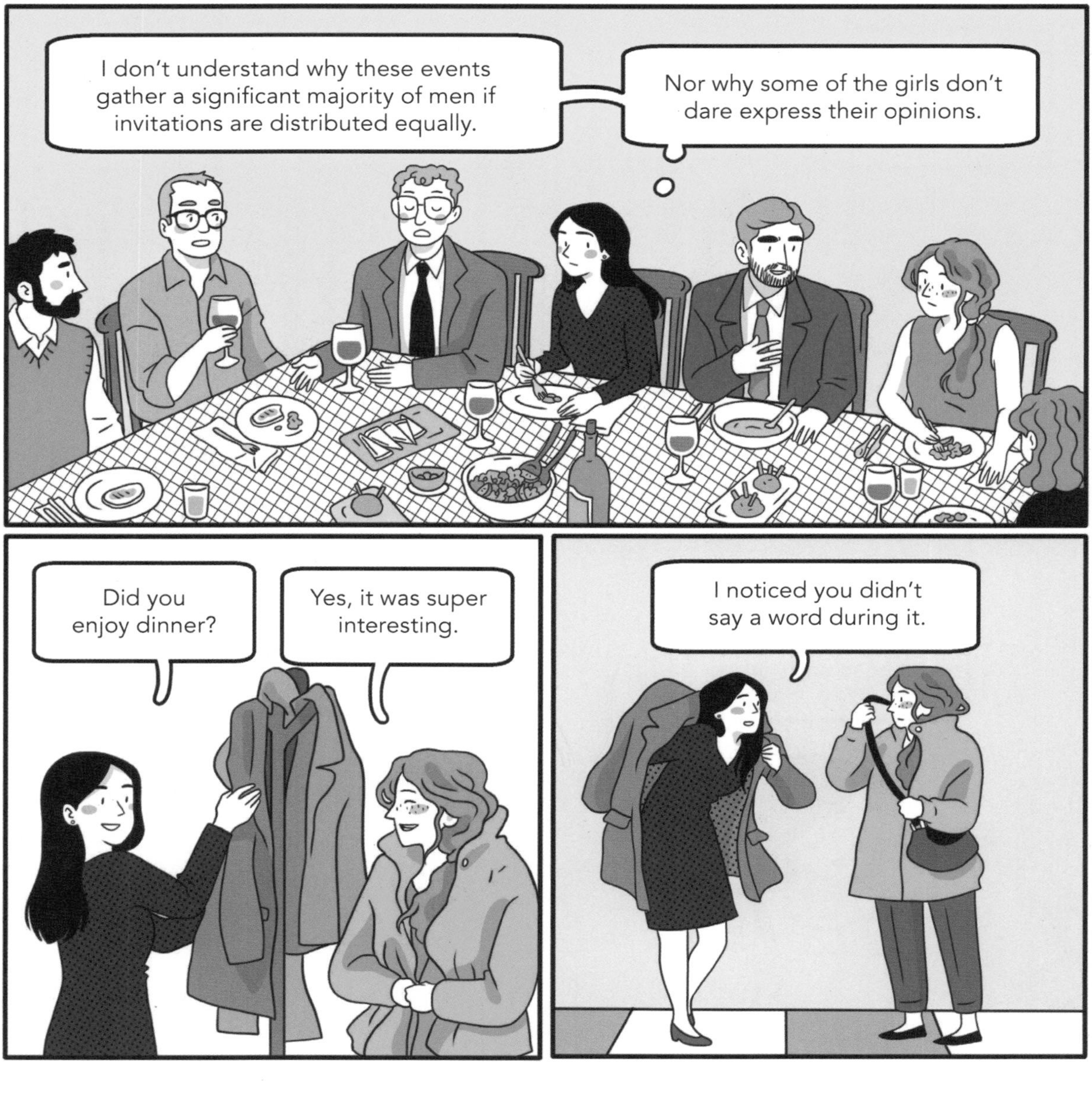
I don't understand why these events gather a significant majority of men if invitations are distributed equally.
Nor why some of the girls don't dare express their opinions.
Did you enjoy dinner?
Yes, it was super interesting.
I noticed you didn't say a word during it.

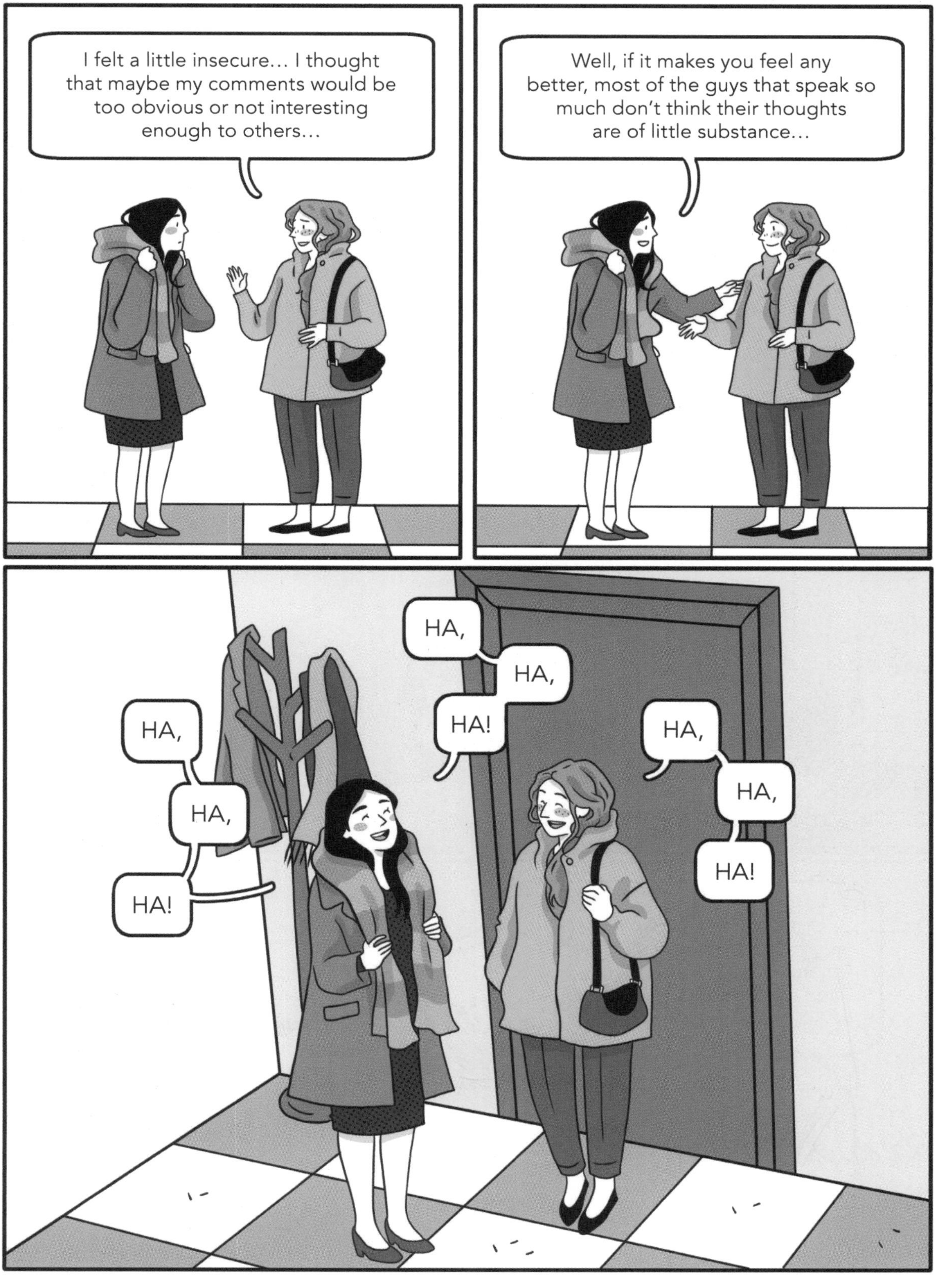
I felt a little insecure… I thought that maybe my comments would be too obvious or not interesting enough to others…
Well, if it makes you feel any better, most of the guys that speak so much don't think their thoughts are of little substance…
HA, HA, HA!
HA, HA, HA!
HA, HA, HA!

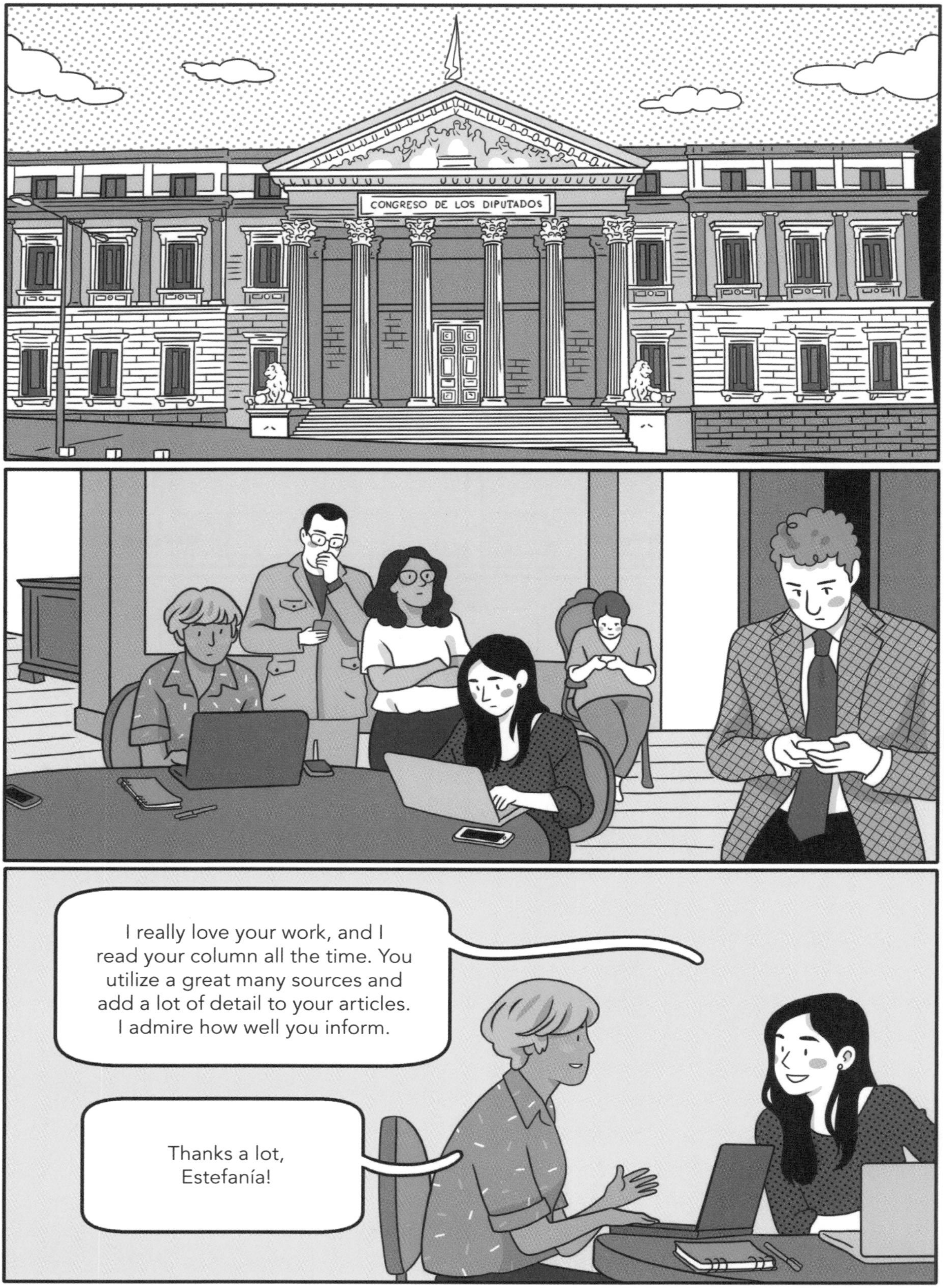
CONGRESO DE LOS DIPUTADOS
I really love your work, and I read your column all the time. You utilize a great many sources and add a lot of detail to your articles. I admire how well you inform.
Thanks a lot, Estefanía!

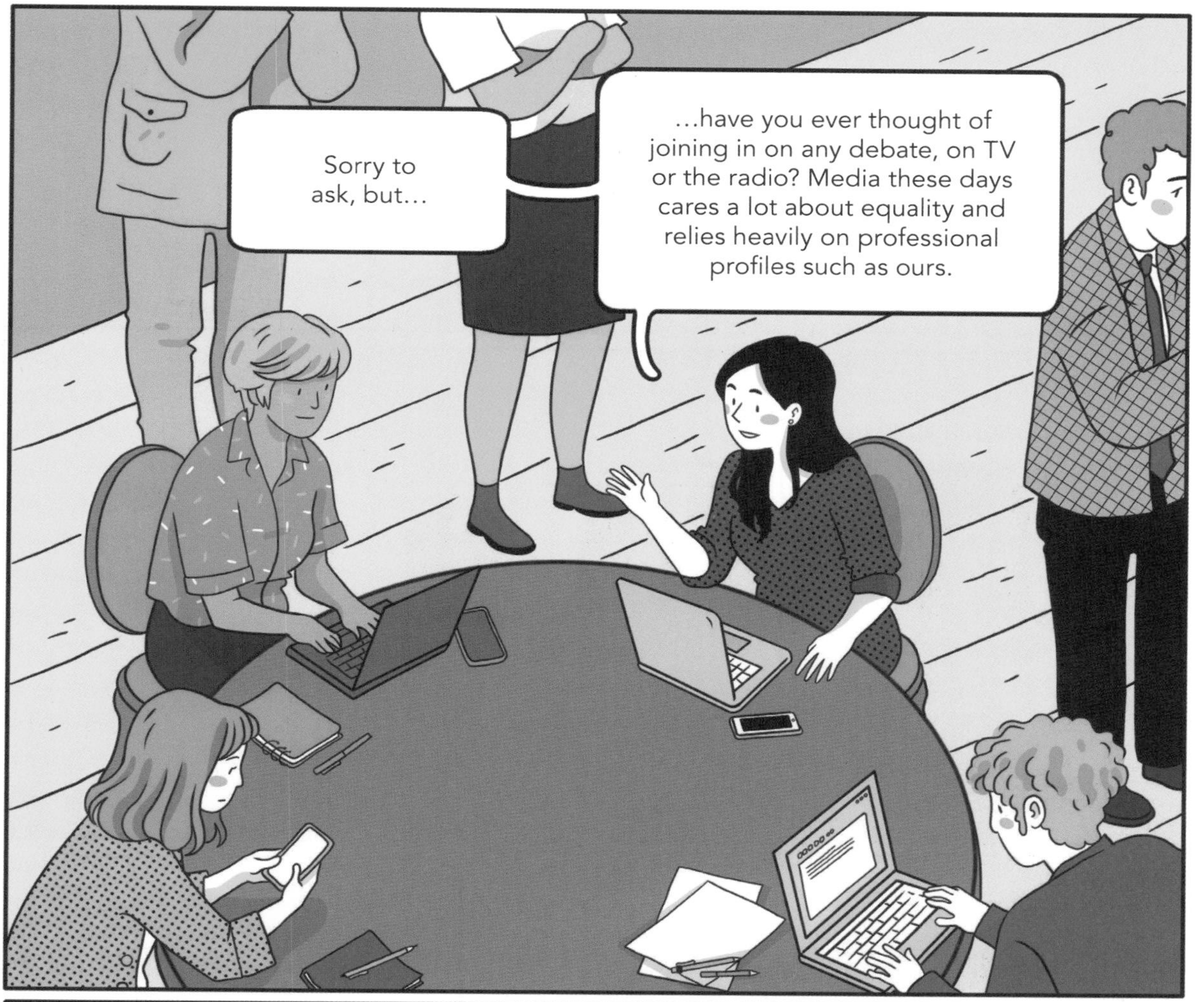
Sorry to ask, but…
…have you ever thought of joining in on any debate, on TV or the radio? Media these days cares a lot about equality and relies heavily on professional profiles such as ours.

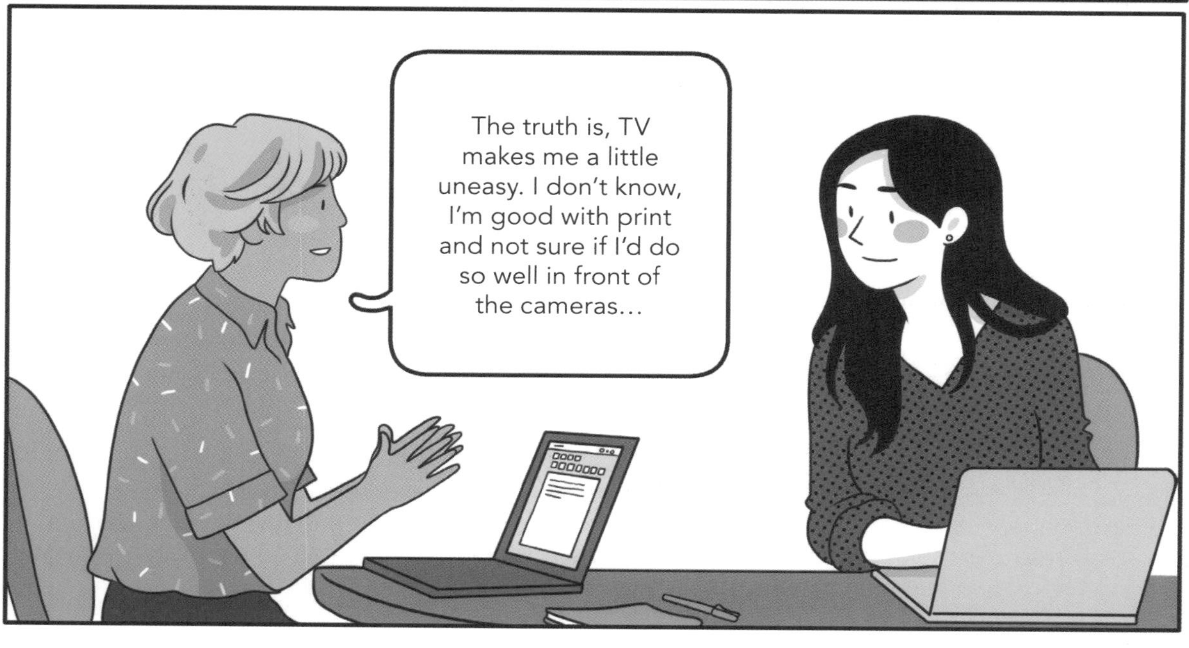
The truth is, TV makes me a little uneasy. I don't know, I'm good with print and not sure if I'd do so well in front of the cameras…

Even though there is a significant number of female journalists in the printed press and information fields, and well-regarded female journalists in mass media (radio and television) running poignant shows, there is still a huge gap when it comes to writers of political opinion columns, where male journalists continue to outnumber female ones.

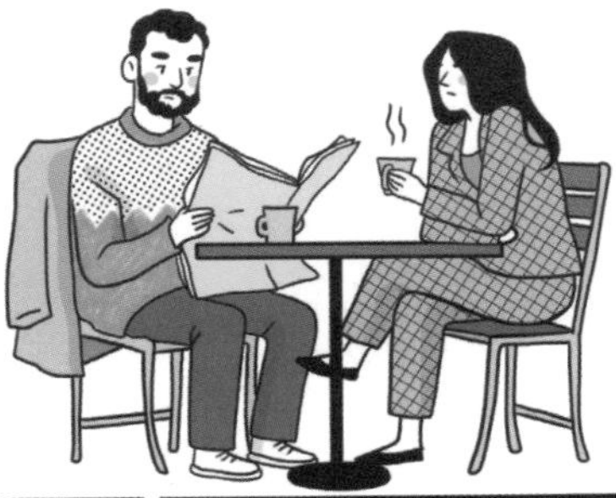

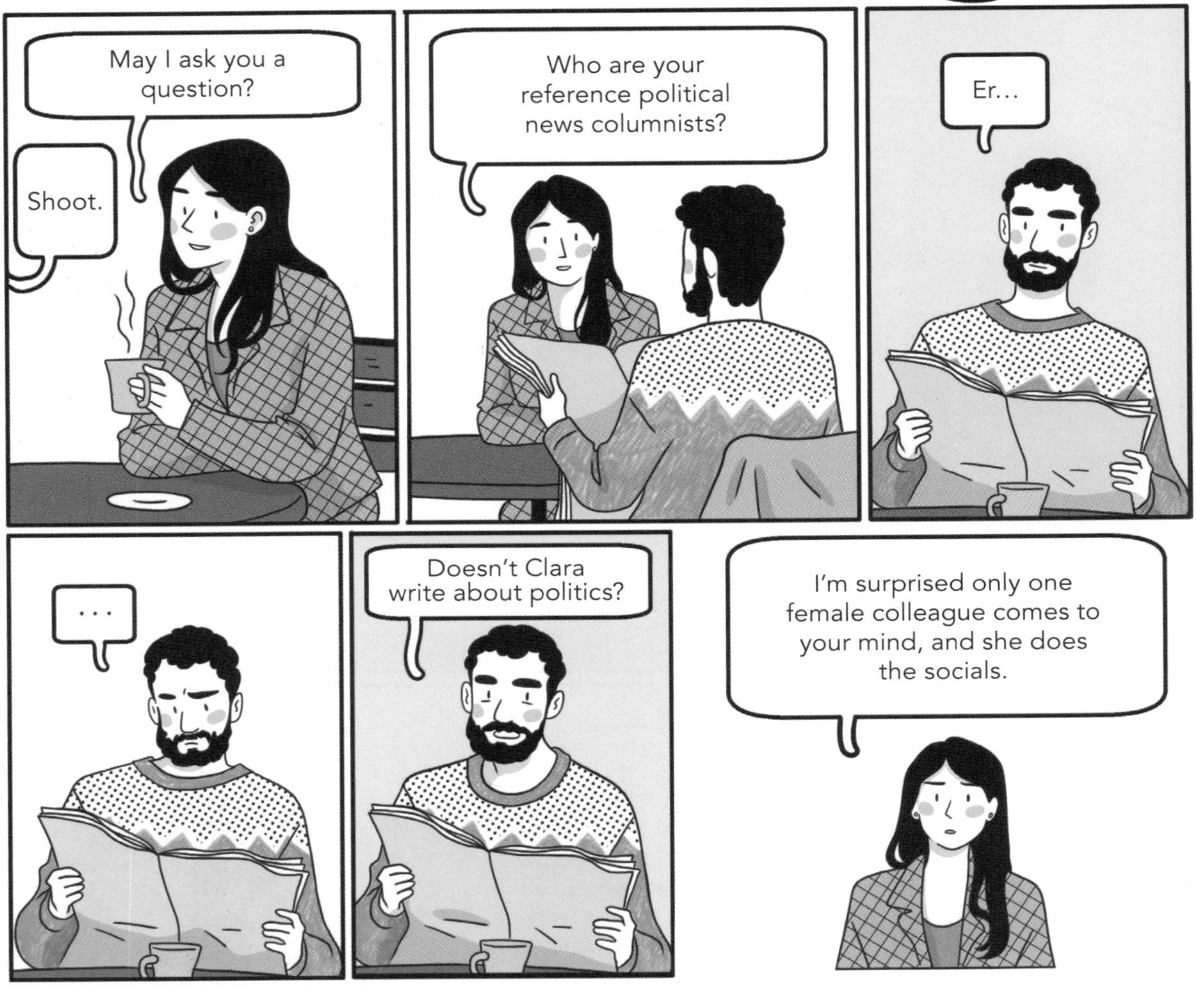

May I ask you a question?
Shoot.
Who are your reference political news columnists?
Er...
...
Doesn't Clara write about politics?
I'm surprised only one female colleague comes to your mind, and she does the socials.

The great "political pens" of this country are still mostly men. So much so that this friend of mine, a newspaper junkie, couldn't name one female journalist, despite being a young guy with an open mentality and who is supposedly less influenced by gender bias.

However, the moral of this story is to show that this is due to a years-long accumulation process. "Empowerment" is also built by helping women find early role models and giving them courage to speak their minds publicly, because what they have to say matters--a lot--to politics, to society, and to the women that will come next.

"LONELINESS"

WRITTEN BY EVA AMARAL

DRAWN BY MARÍA HESSE

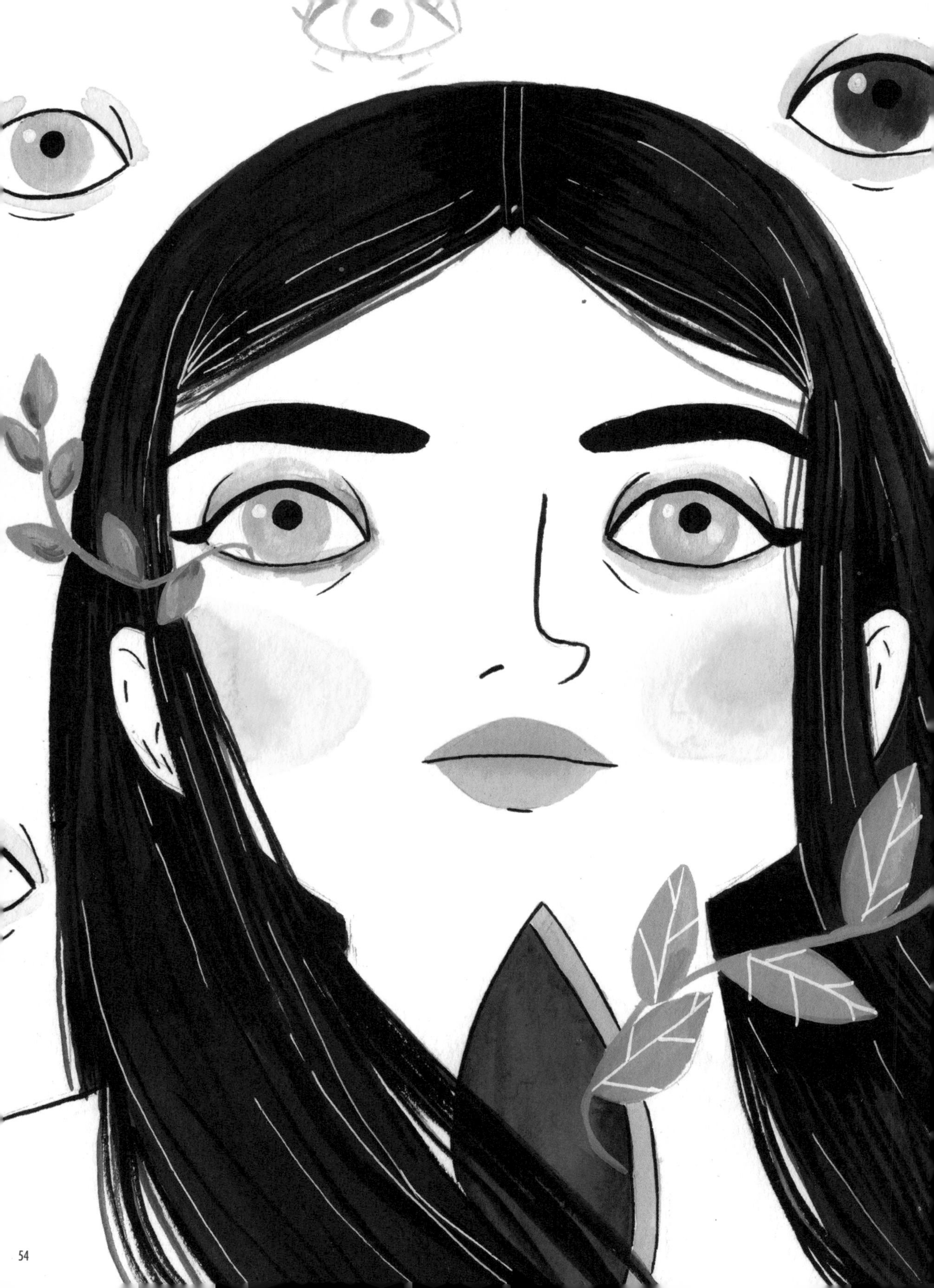

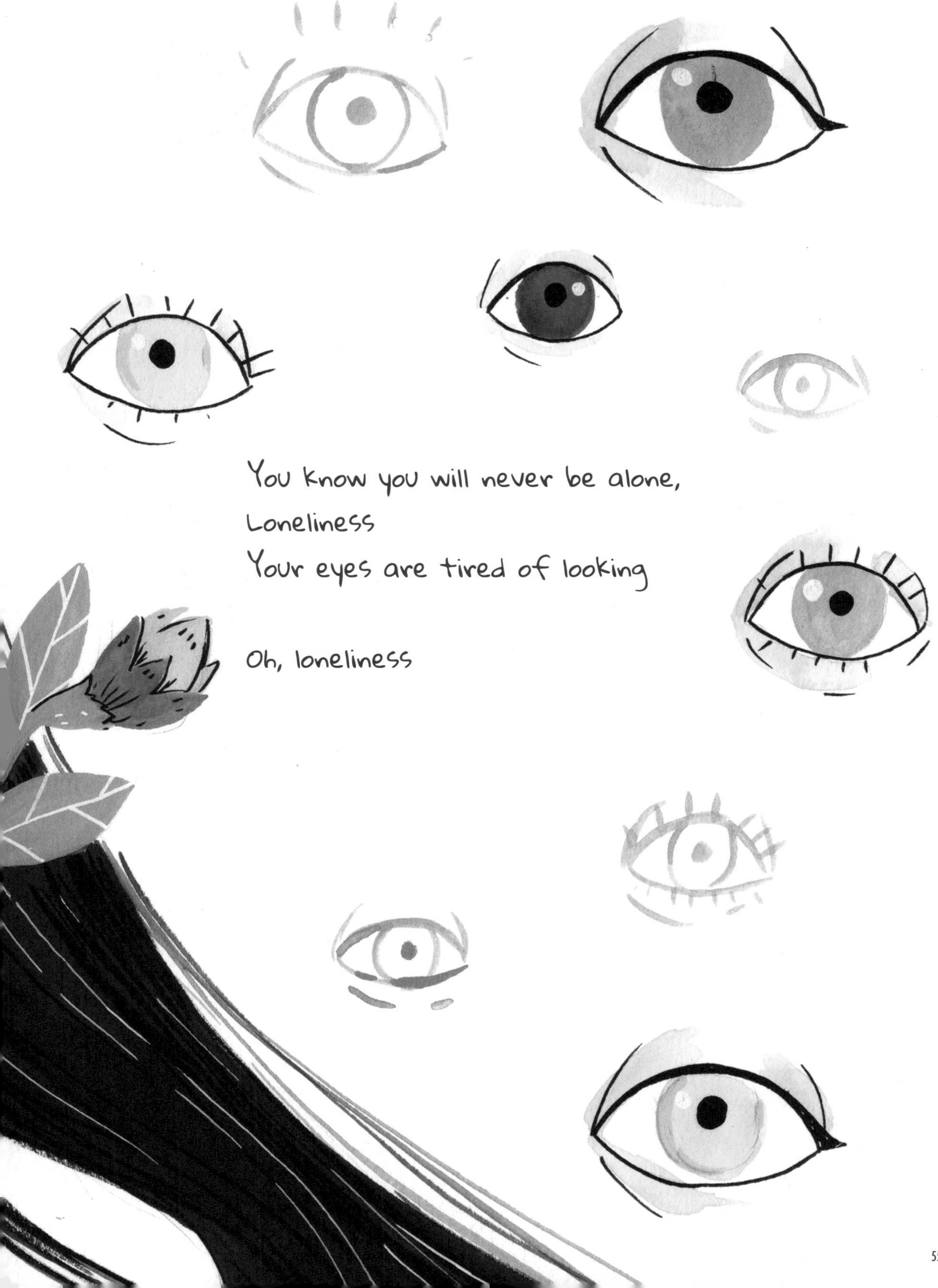

You know you will never be alone,
Loneliness
Your eyes are tired of looking

Oh, loneliness

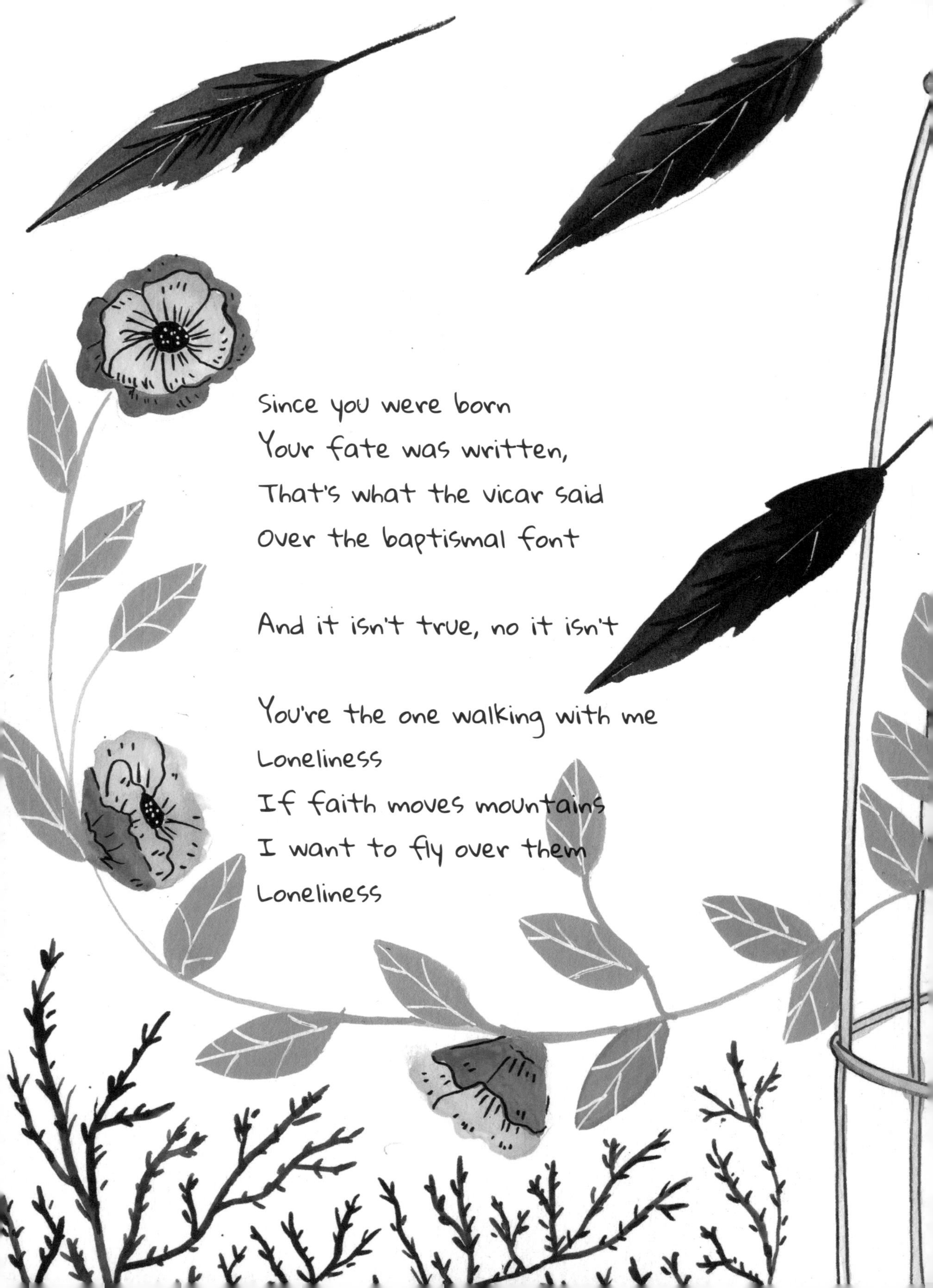

Since you were born
Your fate was written,
That's what the vicar said
Over the baptismal font

And it isn't true, no it isn't

You're the one walking with me
Loneliness
If faith moves mountains
I want to fly over them
Loneliness

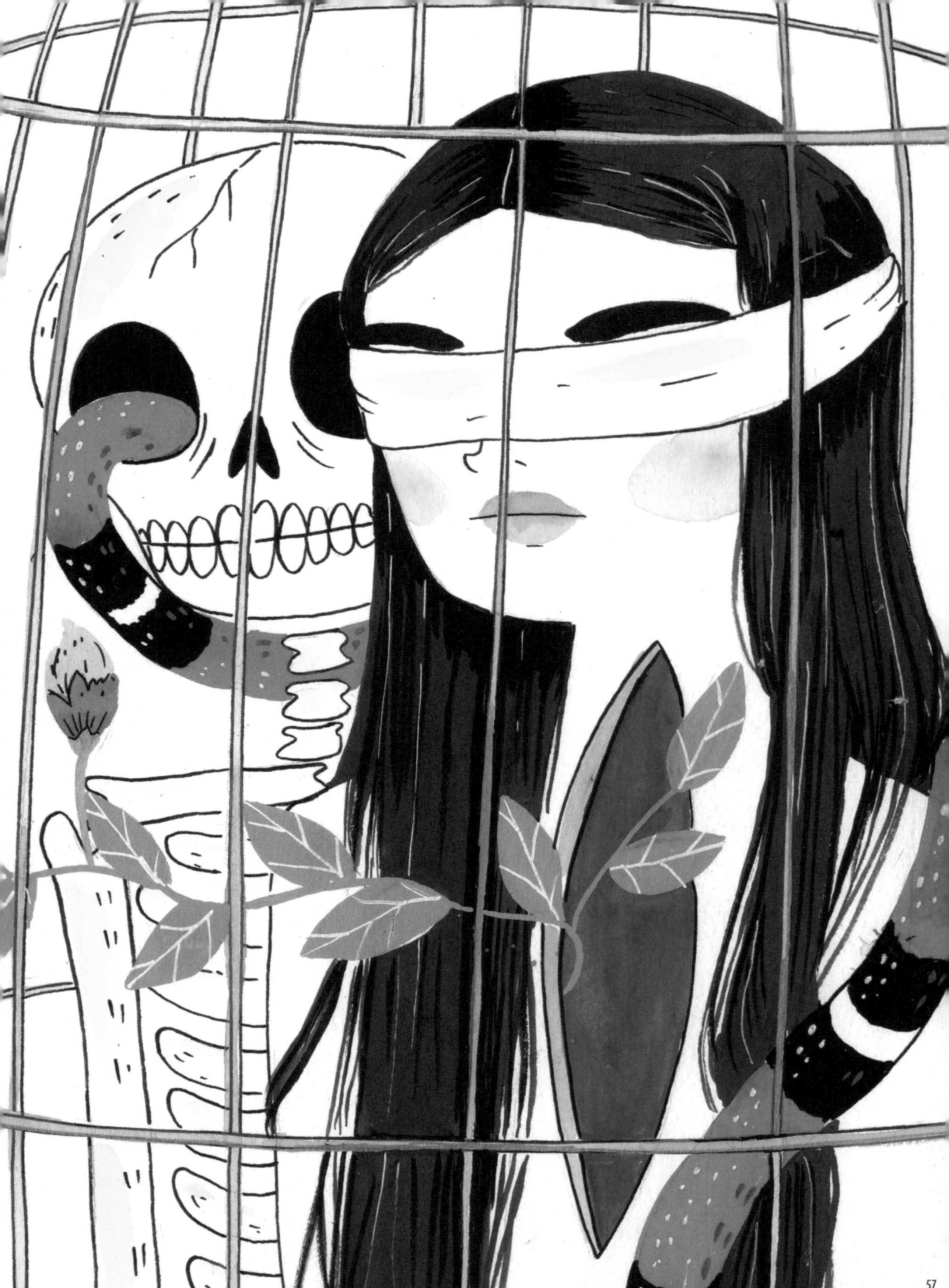

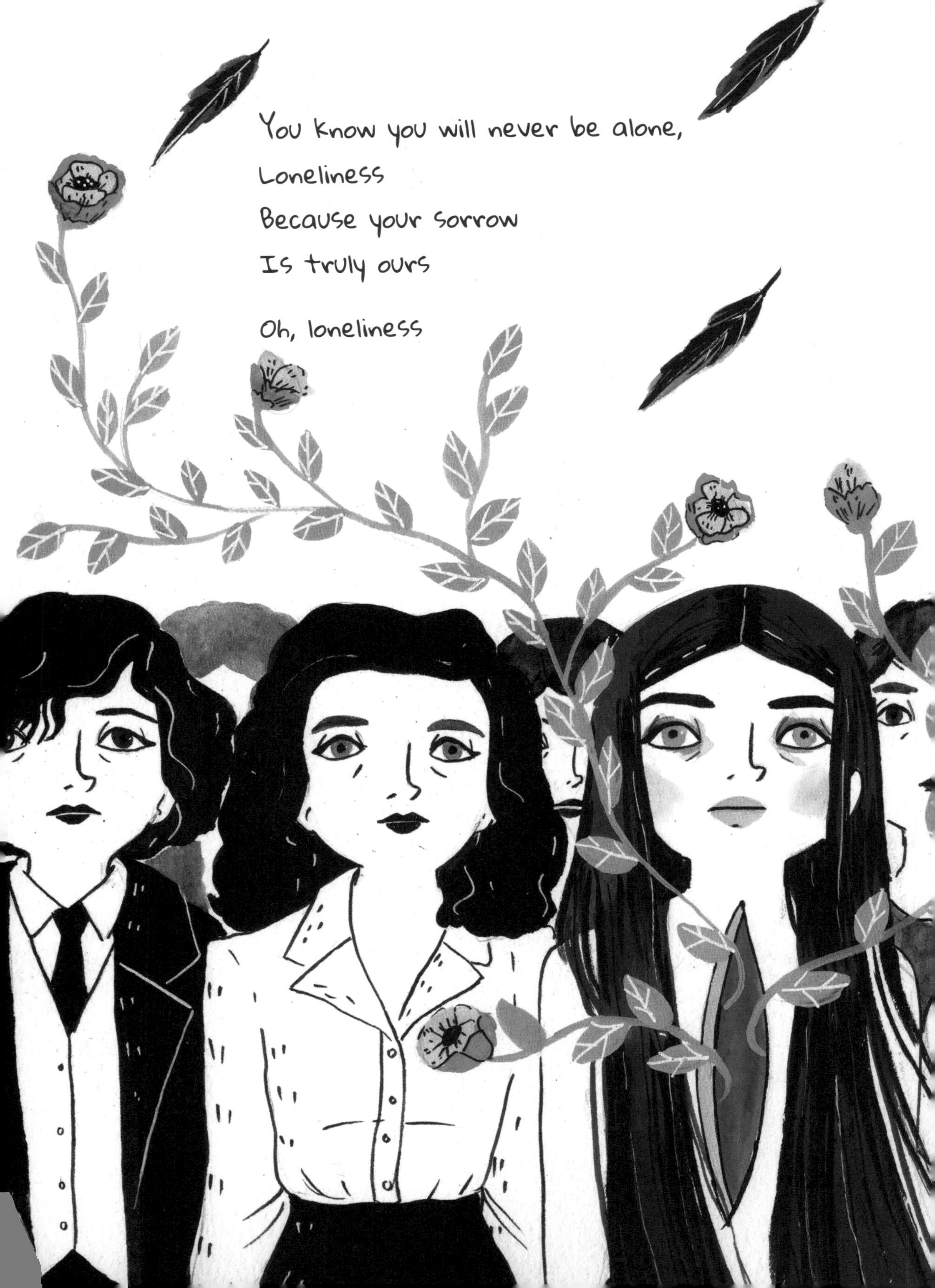
You know you will never be alone,
Loneliness
Because your sorrow
Is truly ours
Oh, loneliness

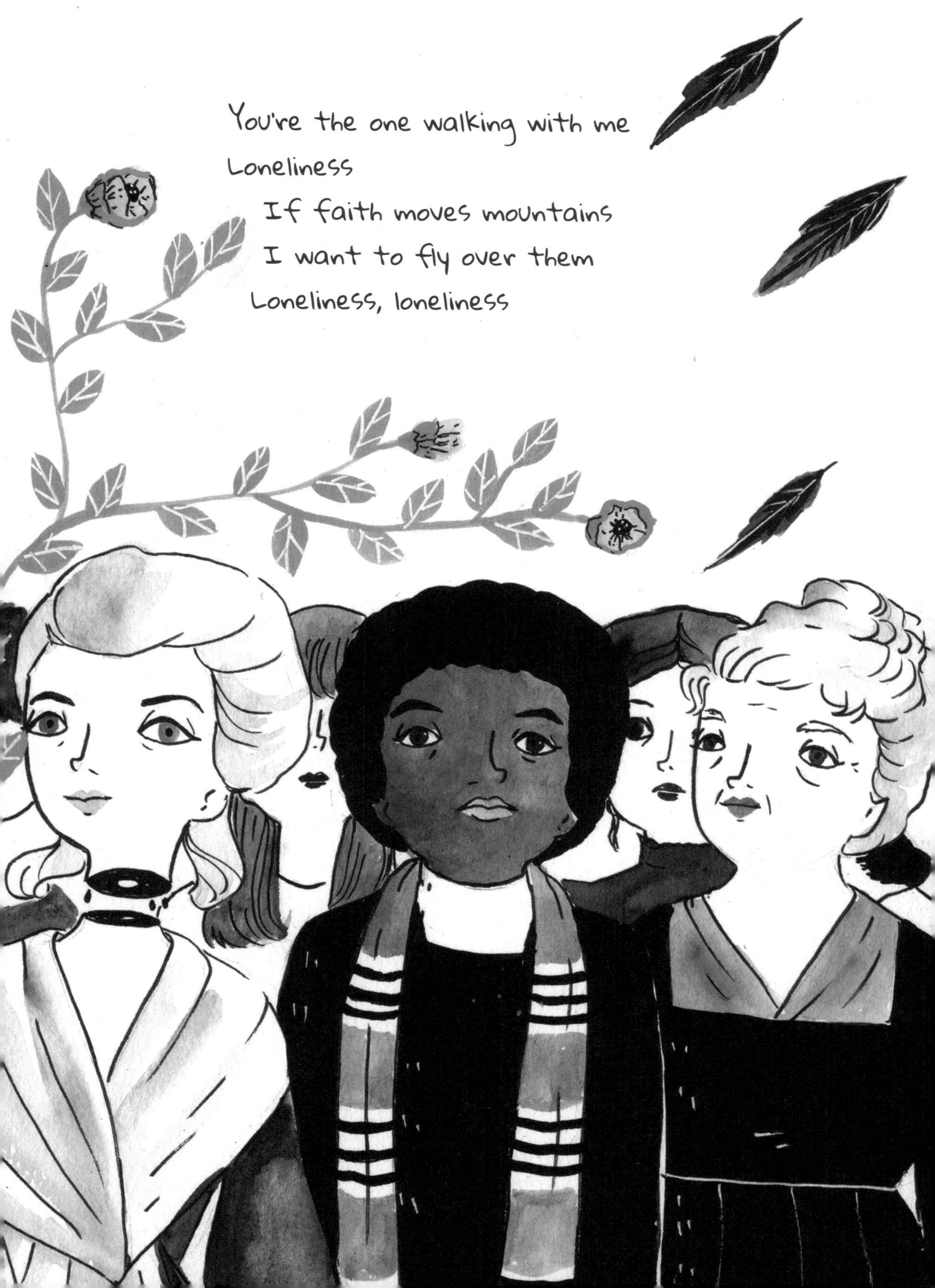
You're the one walking with me
Loneliness
If faith moves mountains
I want to fly over them
Loneliness, loneliness

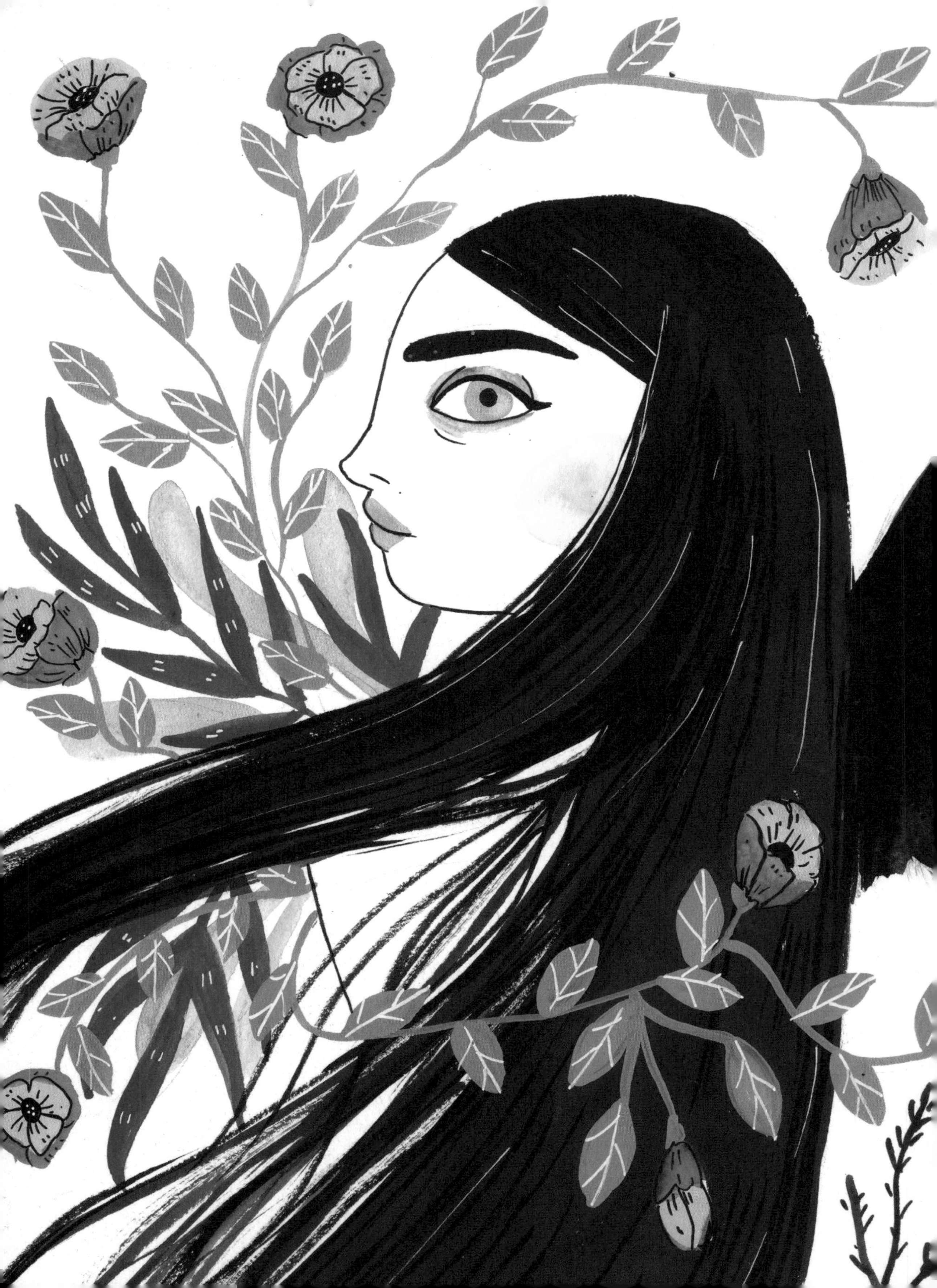

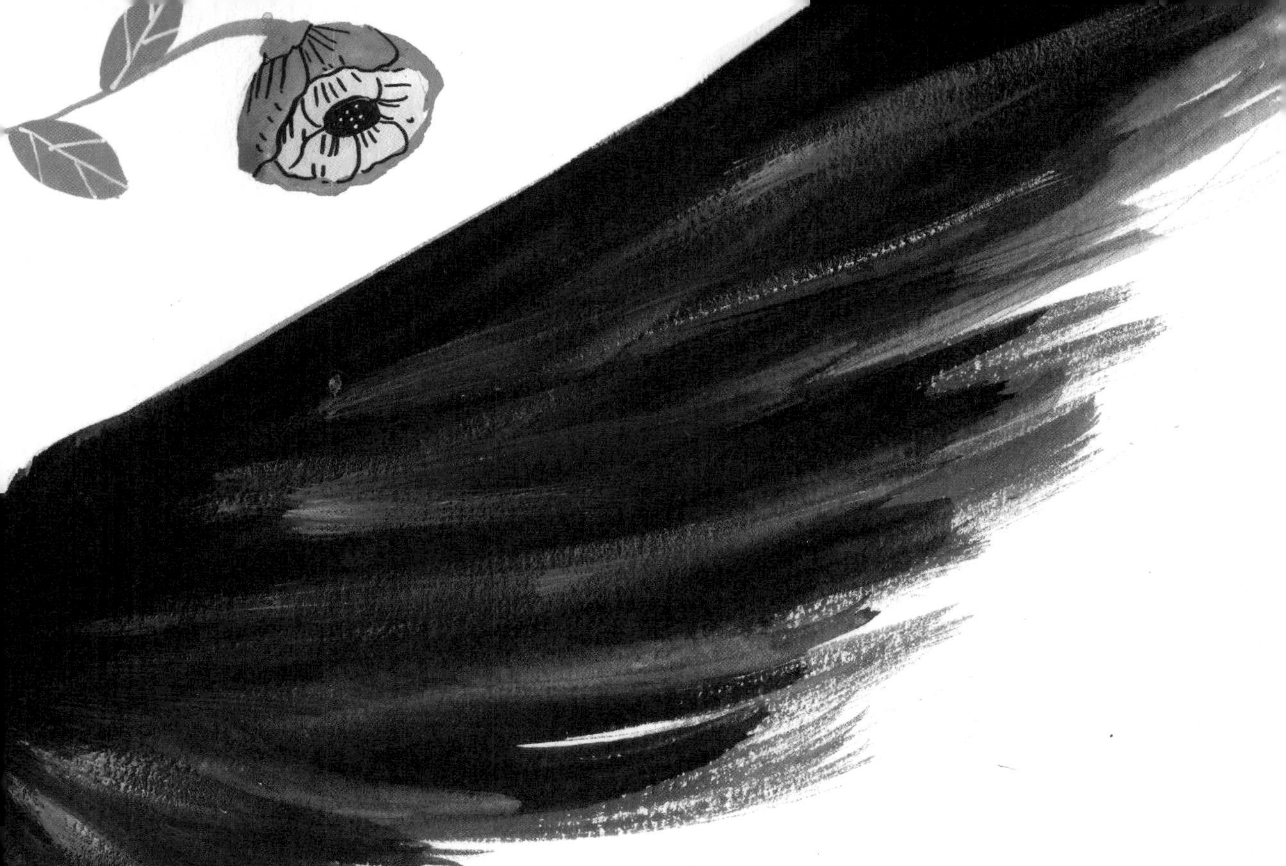

Holy patience has abandoned me,
Mother of all the neglected
This road covered in thorns,
Becomes shortened if you walk it with me

You're the one walking with me
Loneliness
If faith moves mountains
I want to fly over them
Loneliness, loneliness

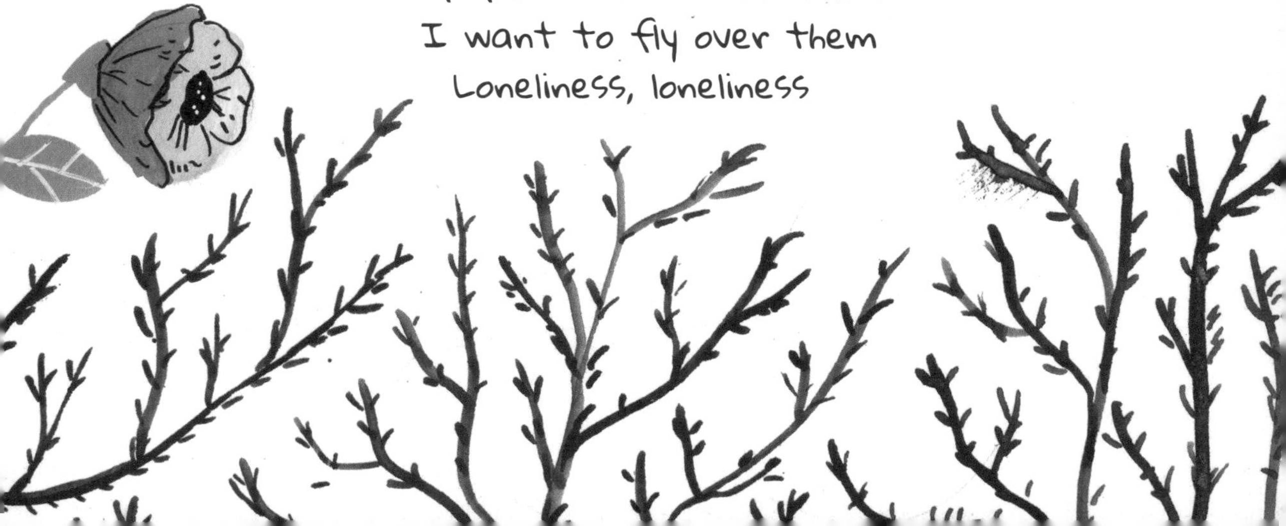

SEXIER

A fragment from

Biting the Apple

WRITTEN BY LETICIA DOLERA

DRAWN BY RAQUEL RIBA ROSSY

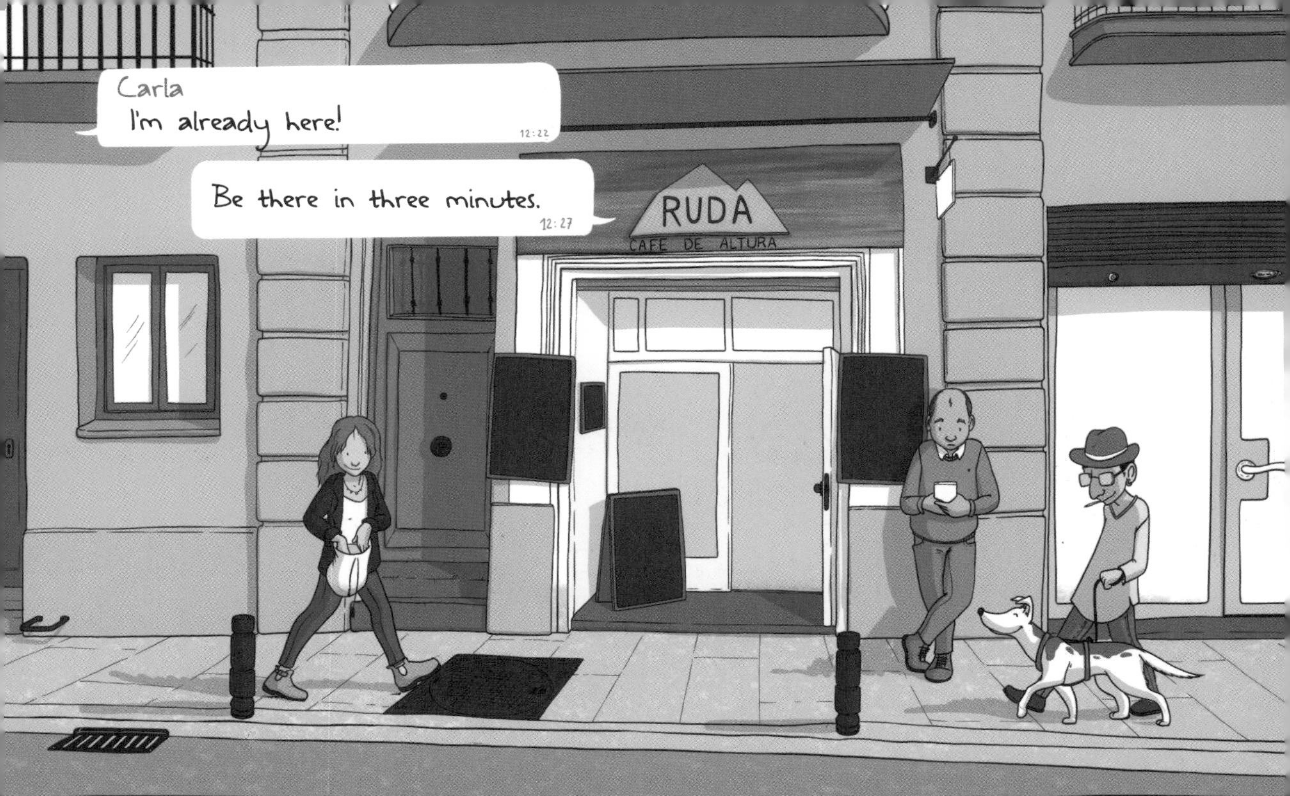
Carla
I'm already here!
12:22
Be there in three minutes.
12:27
RUDA
CAFE DE ALTURA

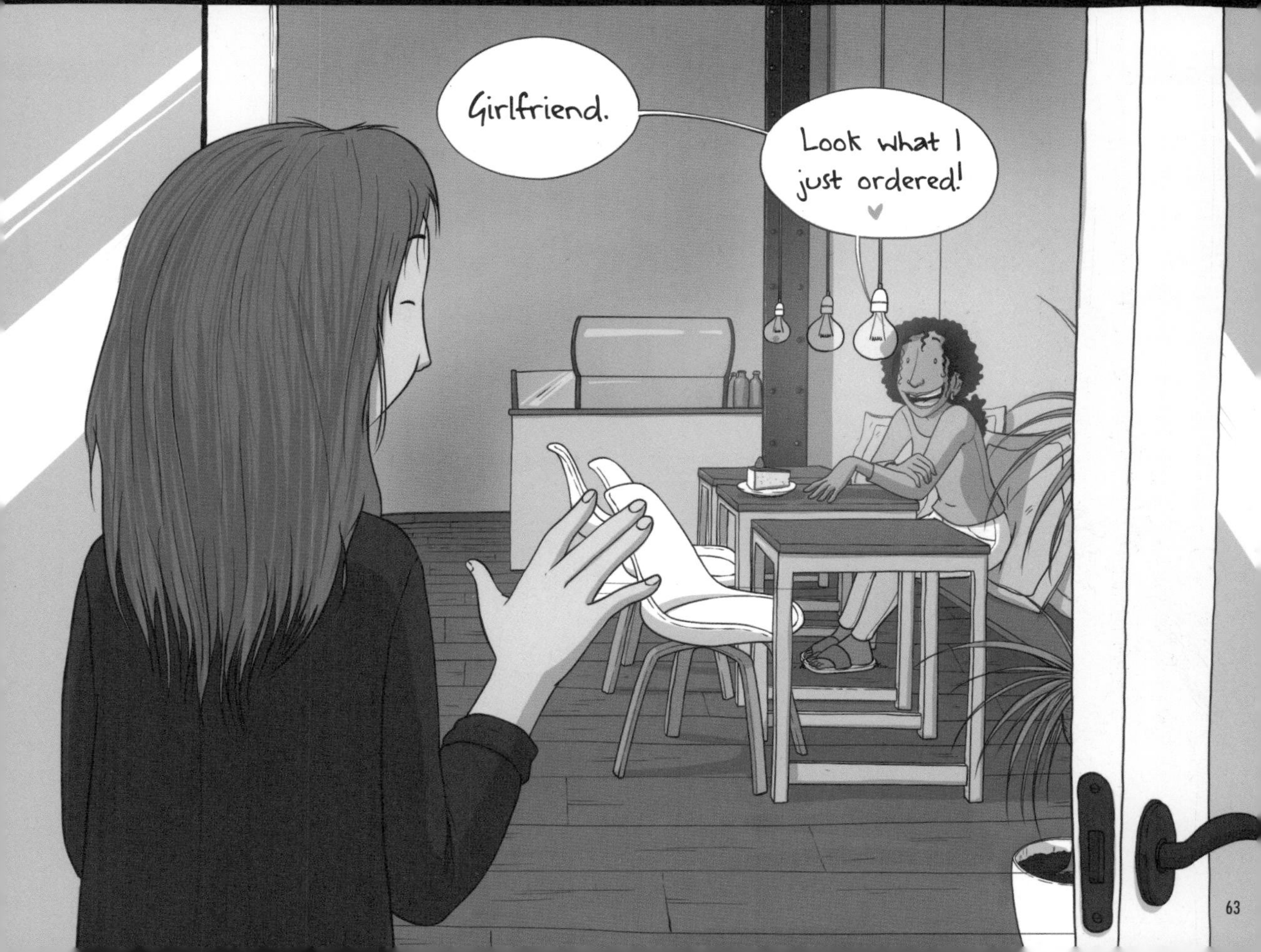
Girlfriend.
Look what I just ordered!

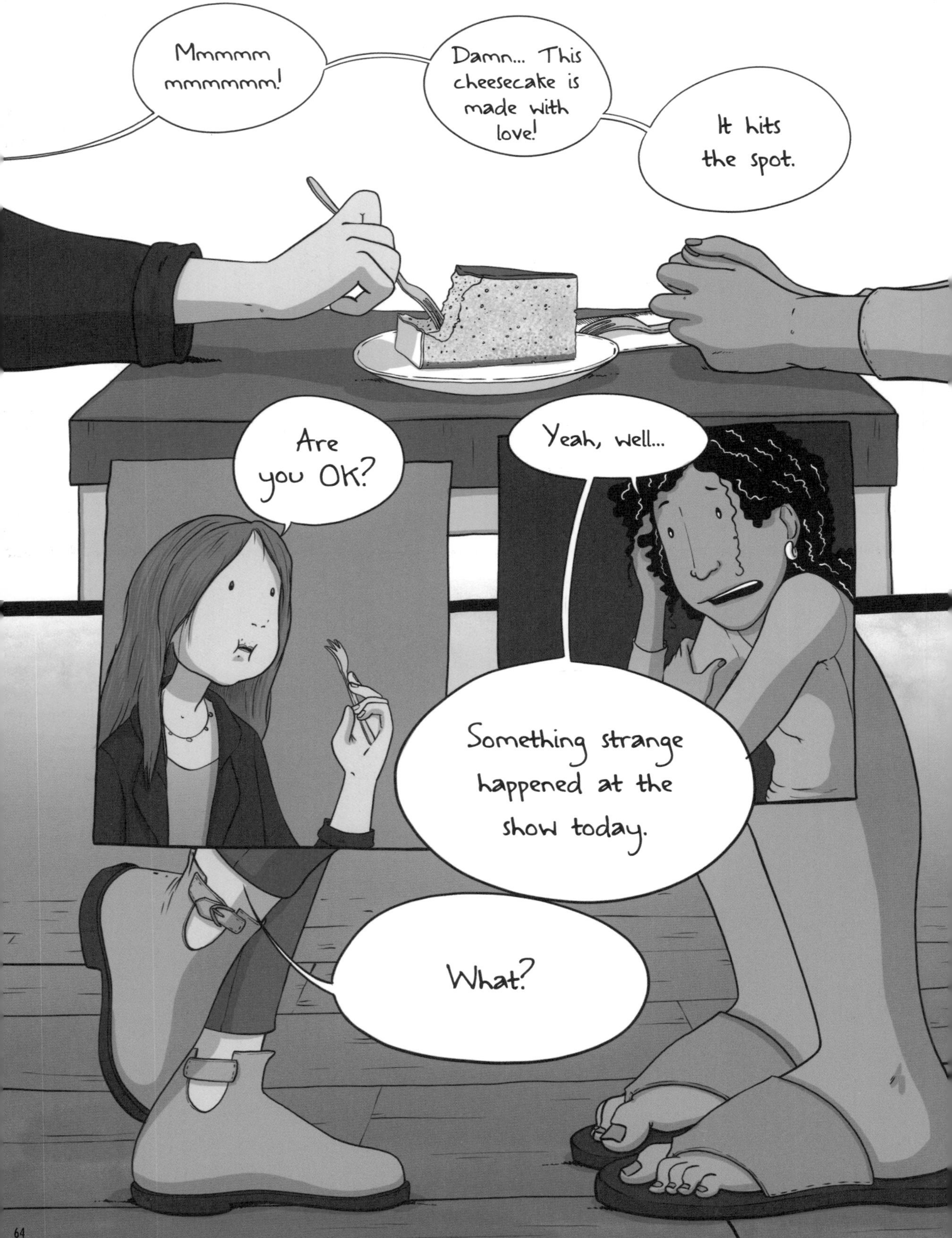
Mmmmm mmmmmm!
Damn... This cheesecake is made with love!
It hits the spot.
Are you OK?
Yeah, well...
Something strange happened at the show today.
What?

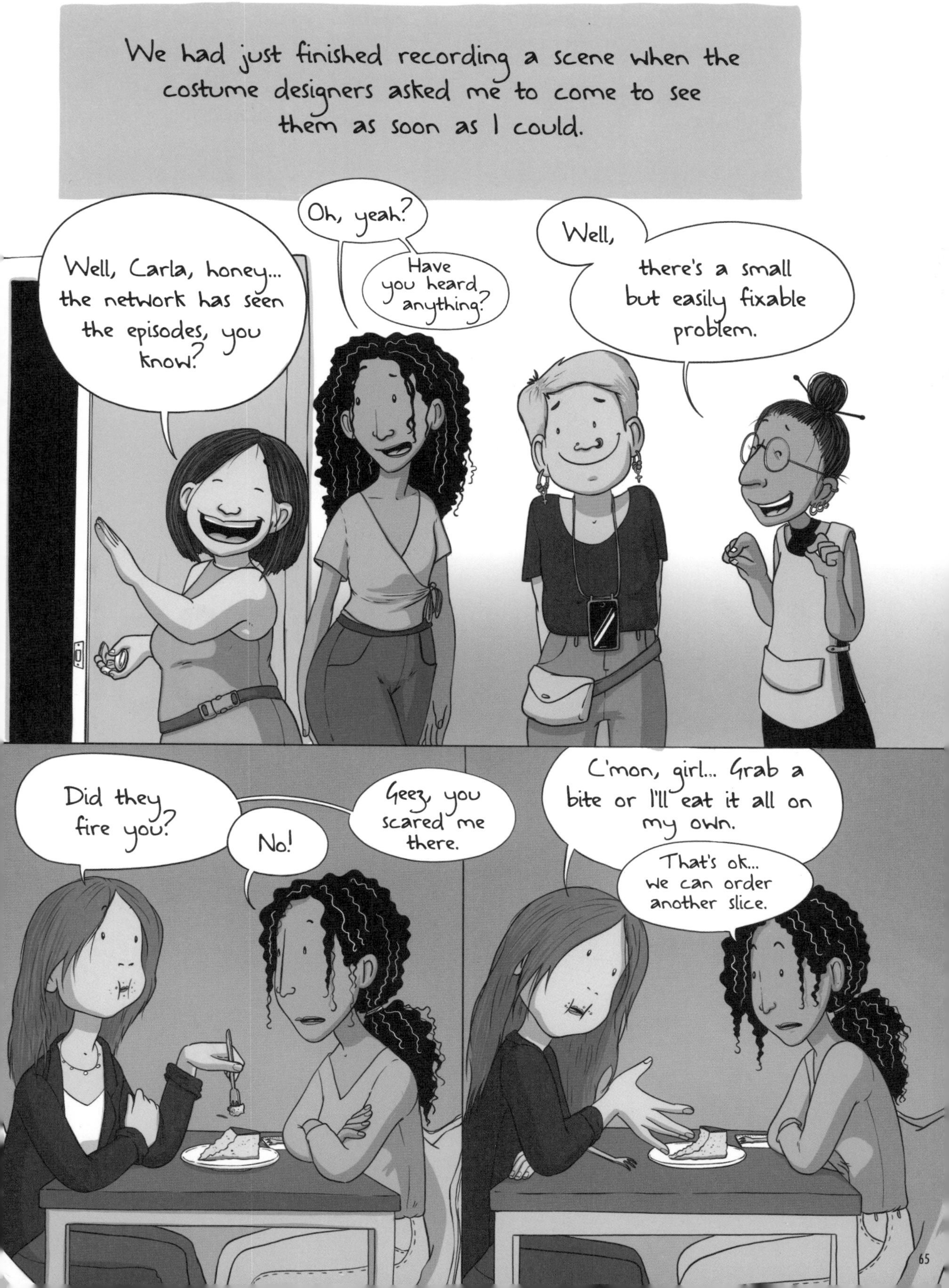
We had just finished recording a scene when the costume designers asked me to come to see them as soon as I could.
Well, Carla, honey... the network has seen the episodes, you know?
Oh, yeah?
Have you heard anything?
Well,
there's a small but easily fixable problem.
Did they fire you?
No!
Geez, you scared me there.
C'mon, girl... Grab a bite or I'll eat it all on my own.
That's ok... we can order another slice.

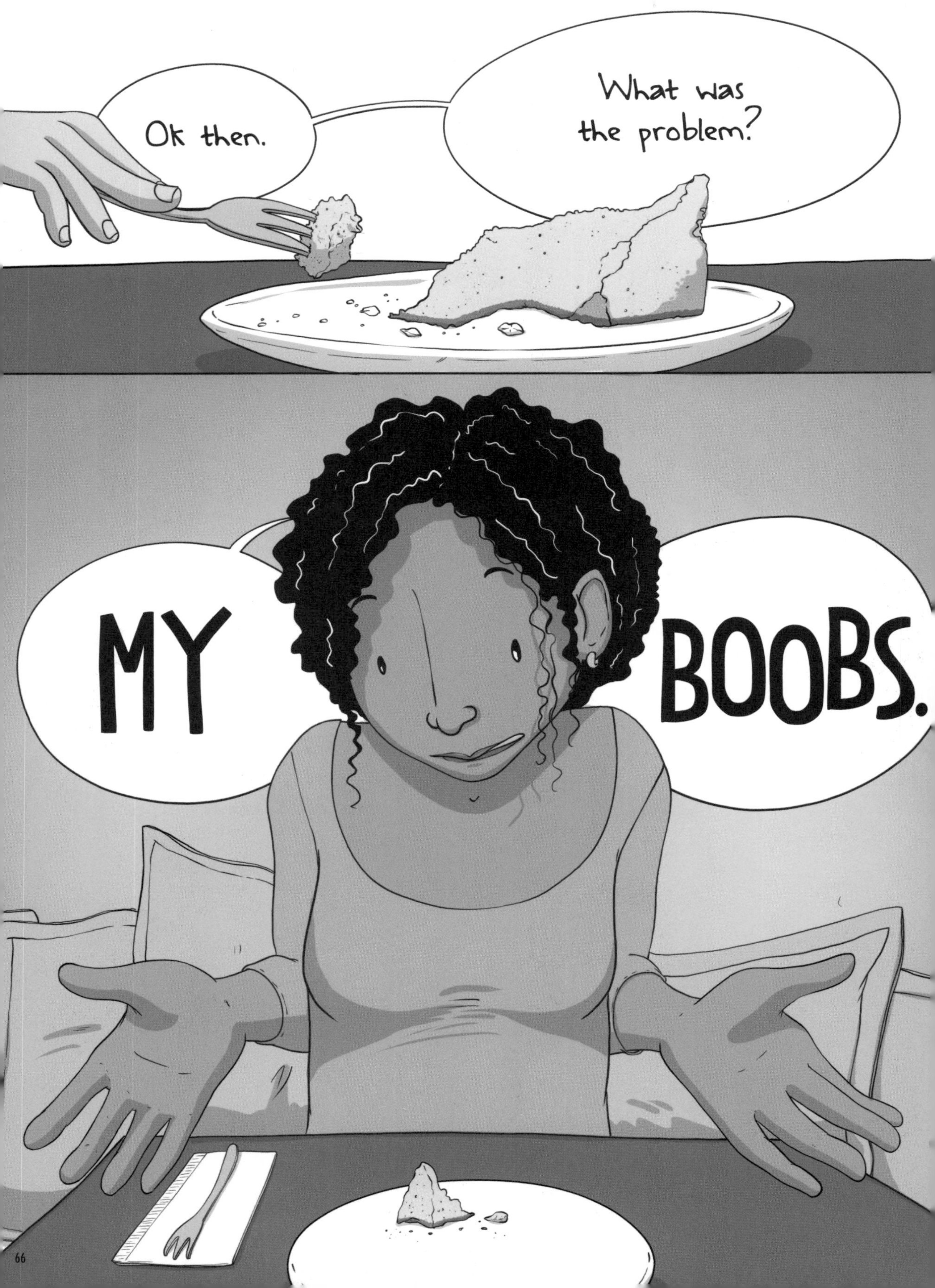
Ok then.
What was the problem?
MY
BOOBS.

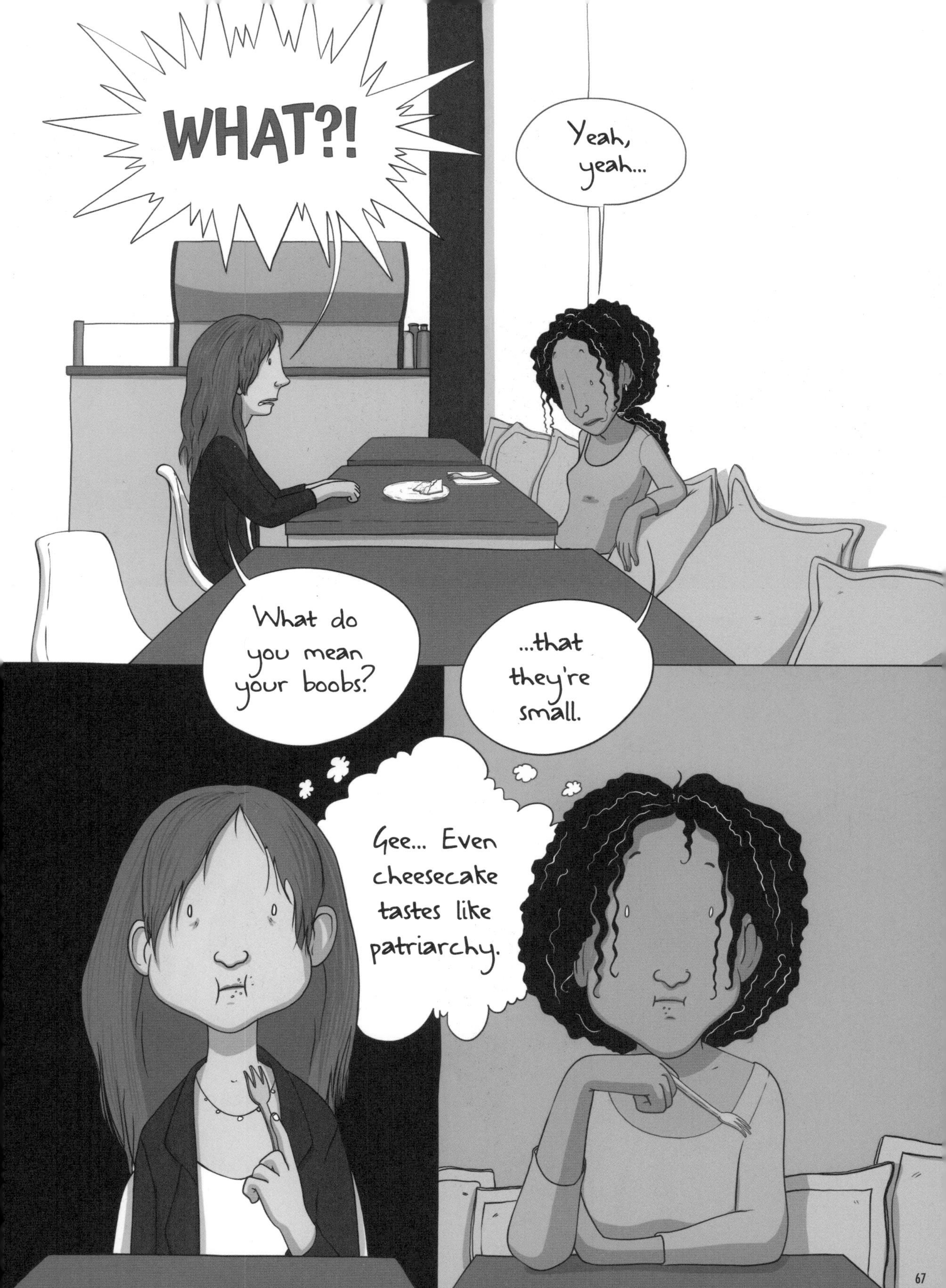
WHAT?!
Yeah, yeah...
What do you mean your boobs?
...that they're small.
Gee... Even cheesecake tastes like patriarchy.

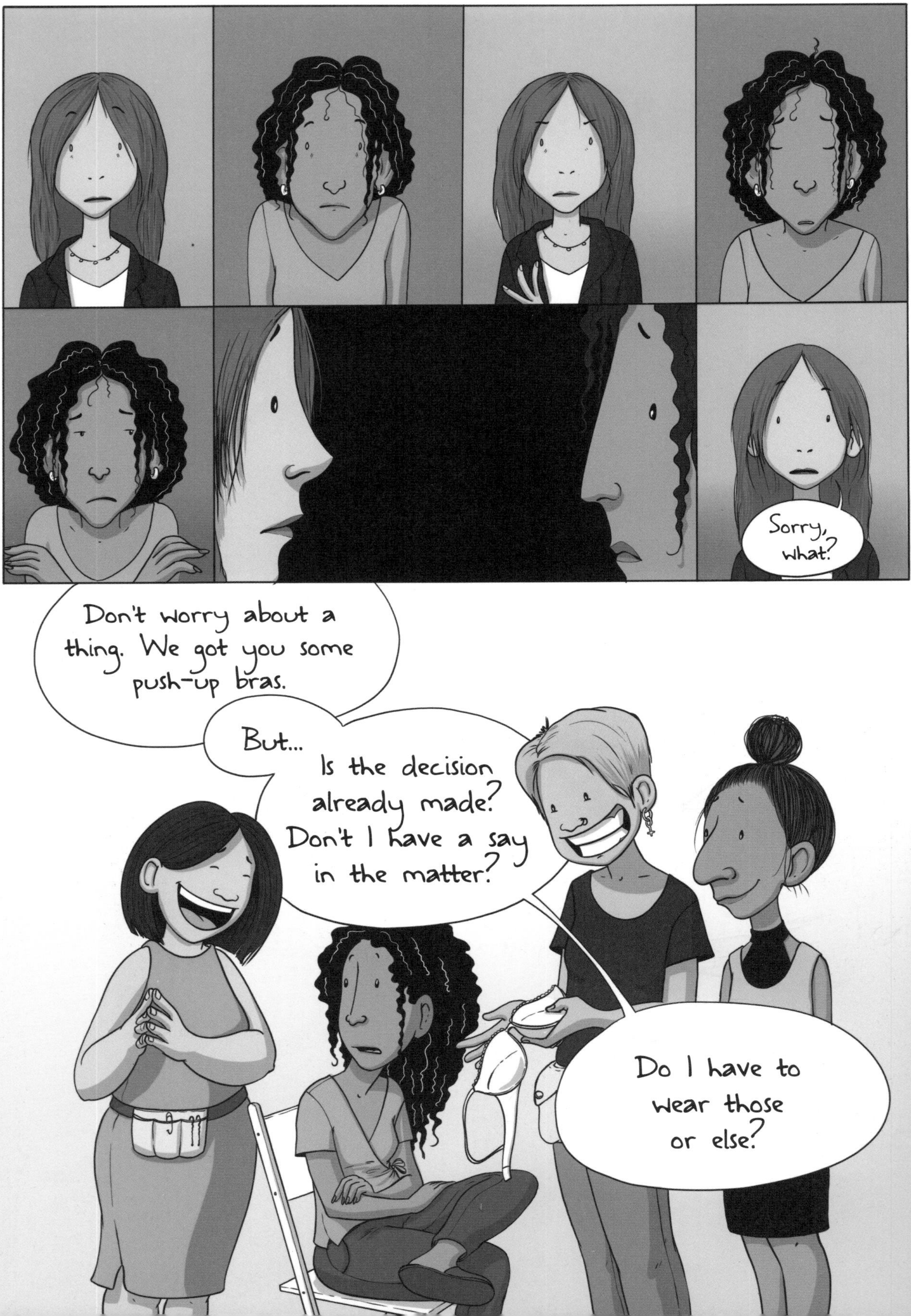
Sorry, what?
Don't worry about a thing. We got you some push-up bras.
But...
Is the decision already made? Don't I have a say in the matter?
Do I have to wear those or else?

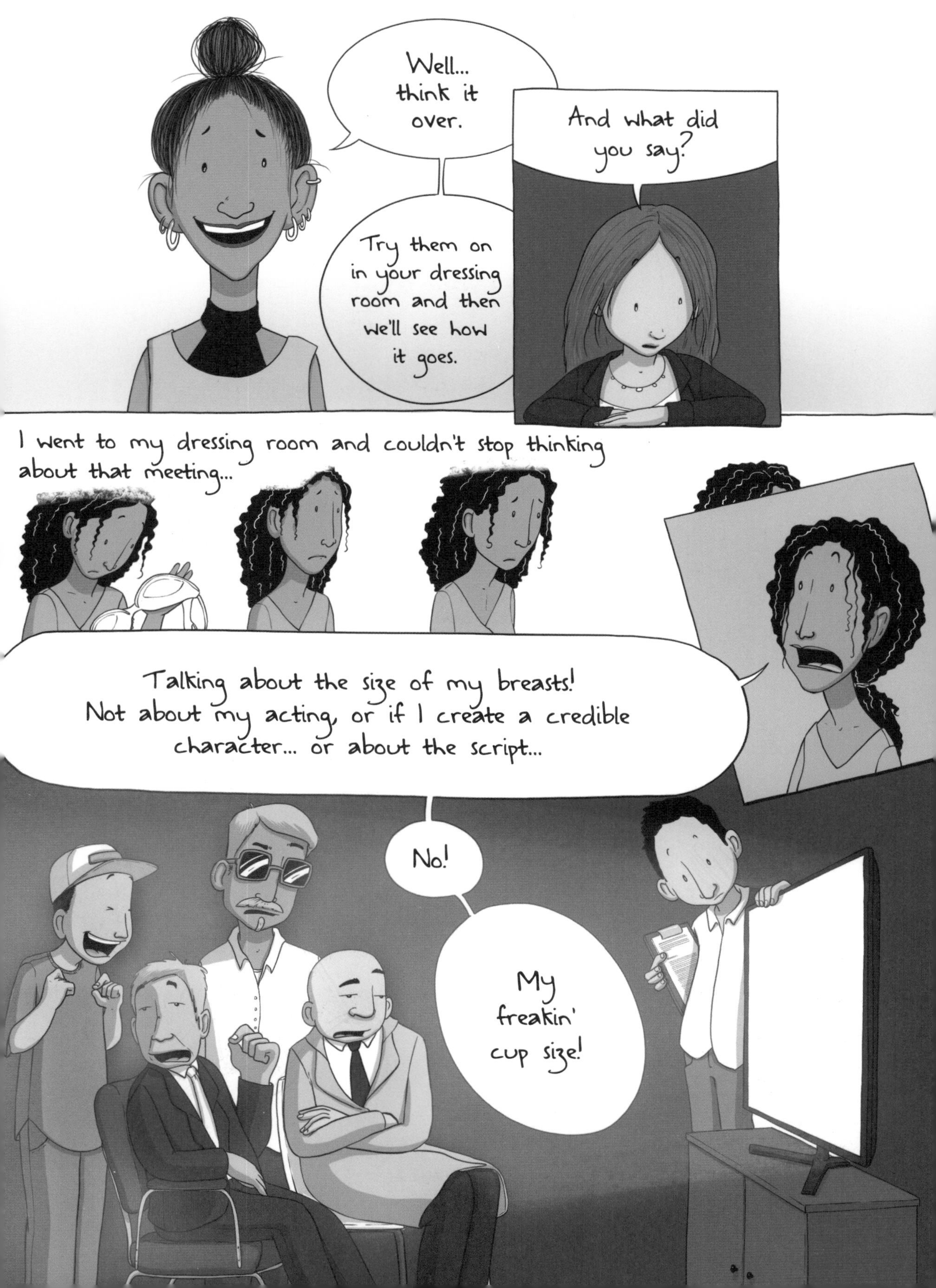
Well... think it over.
Try them on in your dressing room and then we'll see how it goes.
And what did you say?
I went to my dressing room and couldn't stop thinking about that meeting...
Talking about the size of my breasts! Not about my acting, or if I create a credible character... or about the script...
No!
My freakin' cup size!

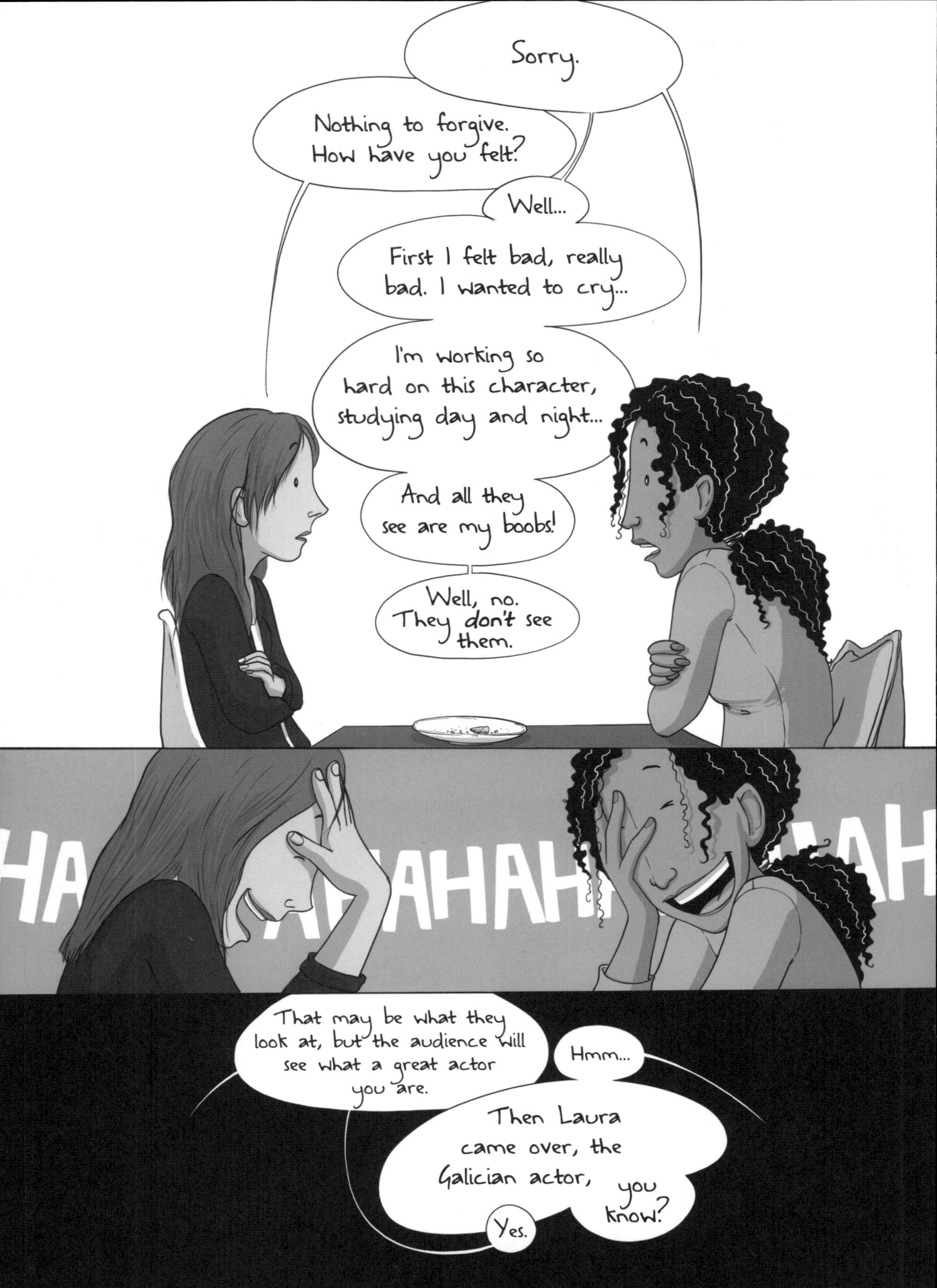

Sorry.
Nothing to forgive. How have you felt?
Well...
First I felt bad, really bad. I wanted to cry...
I'm working so hard on this character, studying day and night...
And all they see are my boobs!
Well, no. They *don't* see them.
HAHAHAHAHAHAH
That may be what they look at, but the audience will see what a great actor you are.
Hmm...
Then Laura came over, the Galician actor,
you know?
Yes.

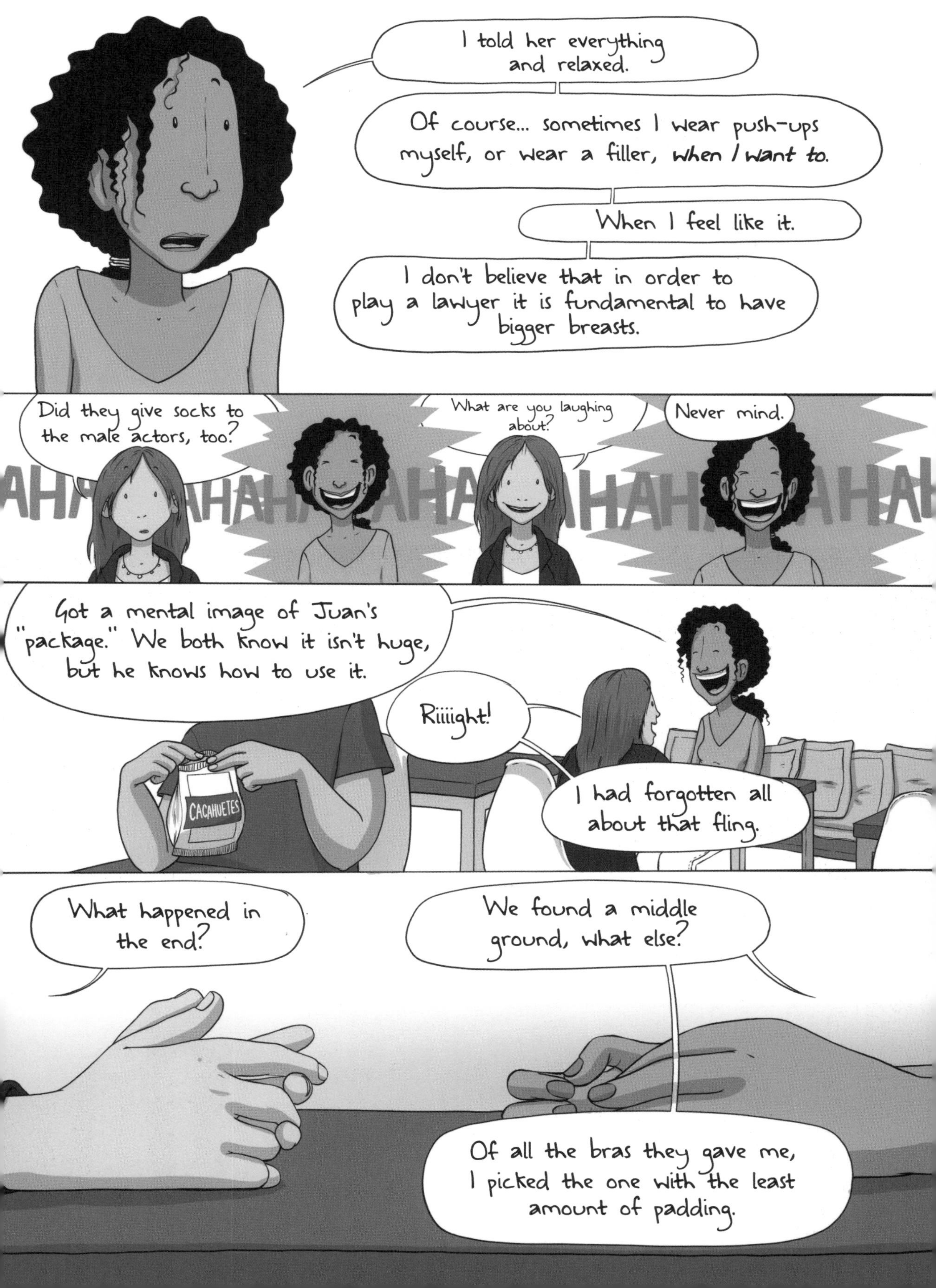
I told her everything and relaxed.
Of course... sometimes I wear push-ups myself, or wear a filler, **when I want to.**
When I feel like it.
I don't believe that in order to play a lawyer it is fundamental to have bigger breasts.
Did they give socks to the male actors, too?
AHAHAHAHAHAHAHAHAHAHAHA
What are you laughing about?
Never mind.
Got a mental image of Juan's "package." We both know it isn't huge, but he knows how to use it.
Riiiight!
I had forgotten all about that fling.
CACAHUETES
What happened in the end?
We found a middle ground, what else?
Of all the bras they gave me, I picked the one with the least amount of padding.

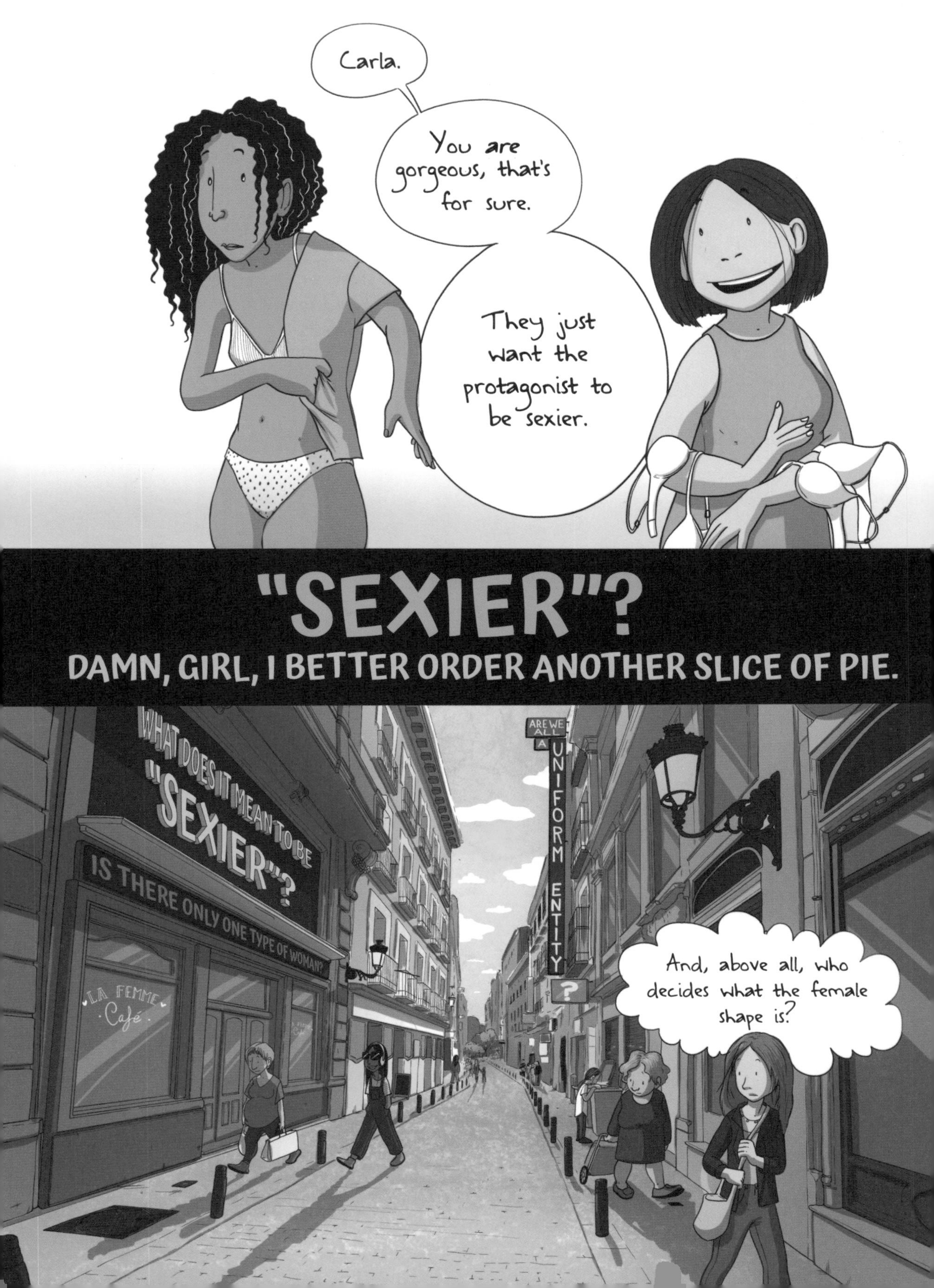
Carla.
You are gorgeous, that's for sure.
They just want the protagonist to be sexier.
"SEXIER"?
DAMN, GIRL, I BETTER ORDER ANOTHER SLICE OF PIE.
WHAT DOES IT MEAN TO BE "SEXIER"?
IS THERE ONLY ONE TYPE OF WOMAN?
LA FEMME Café
ARE WE ALL A UNIFORM ENTITY ?
And, above all, who decides what the female shape is?

TURTLE STEPS

WRITTEN BY SANDRA SABATÉS

DRAWN BY SANDRA CARDONA

SANDRA SABATÉS   SANDRA CARDONA

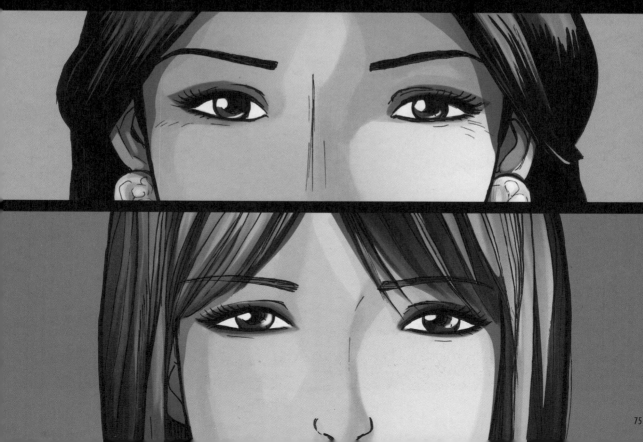

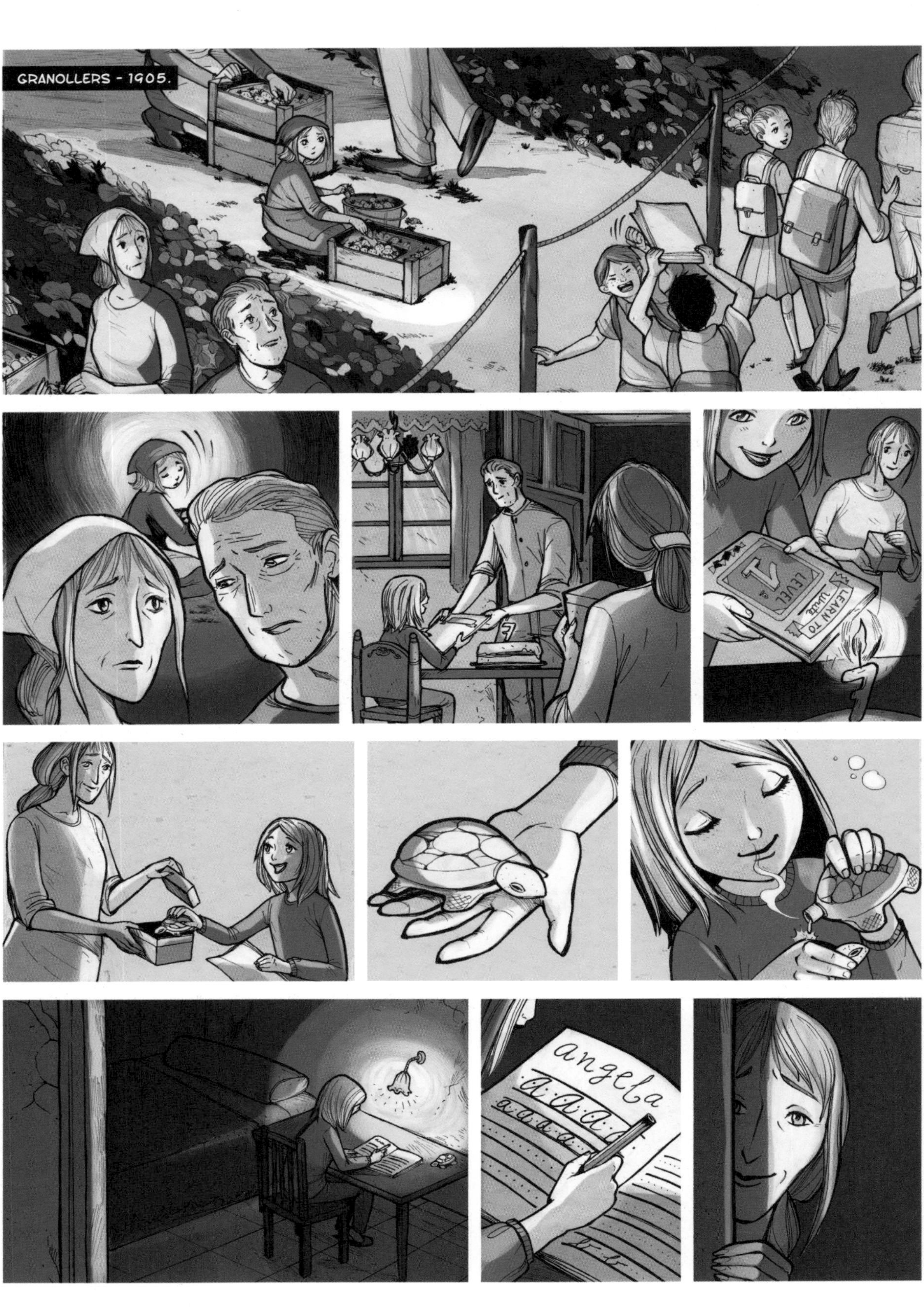
GRANOLLERS - 1905.
LEVEL 1
LEARN TO WRITE
angela

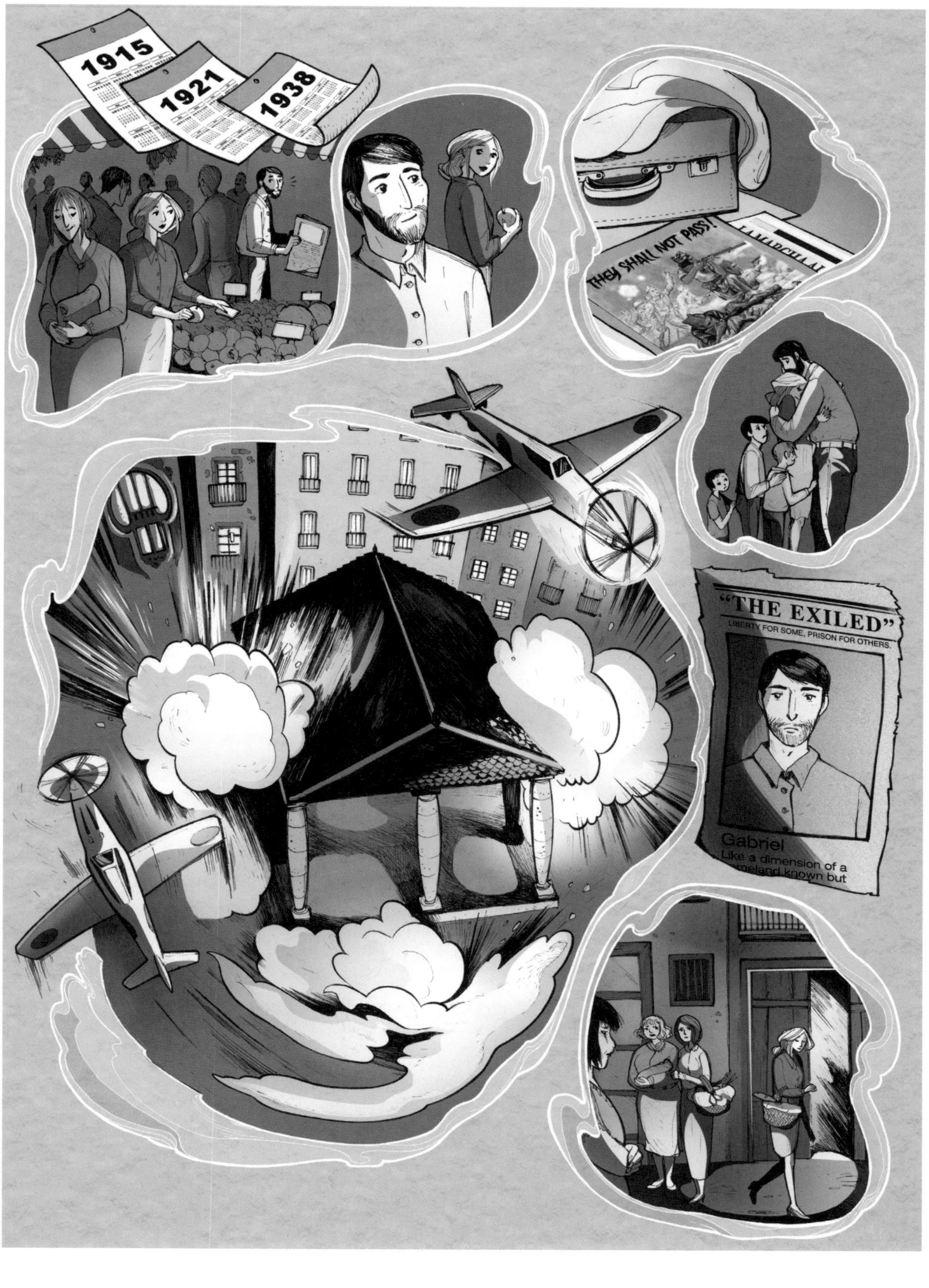
1915
1921
1938
THEY SHALL NOT PASS!
"THE EXILED"
LIBERTY FOR SOME, PRISON FOR OTHERS.
Gabriel
Like a dimension of a
meland known but

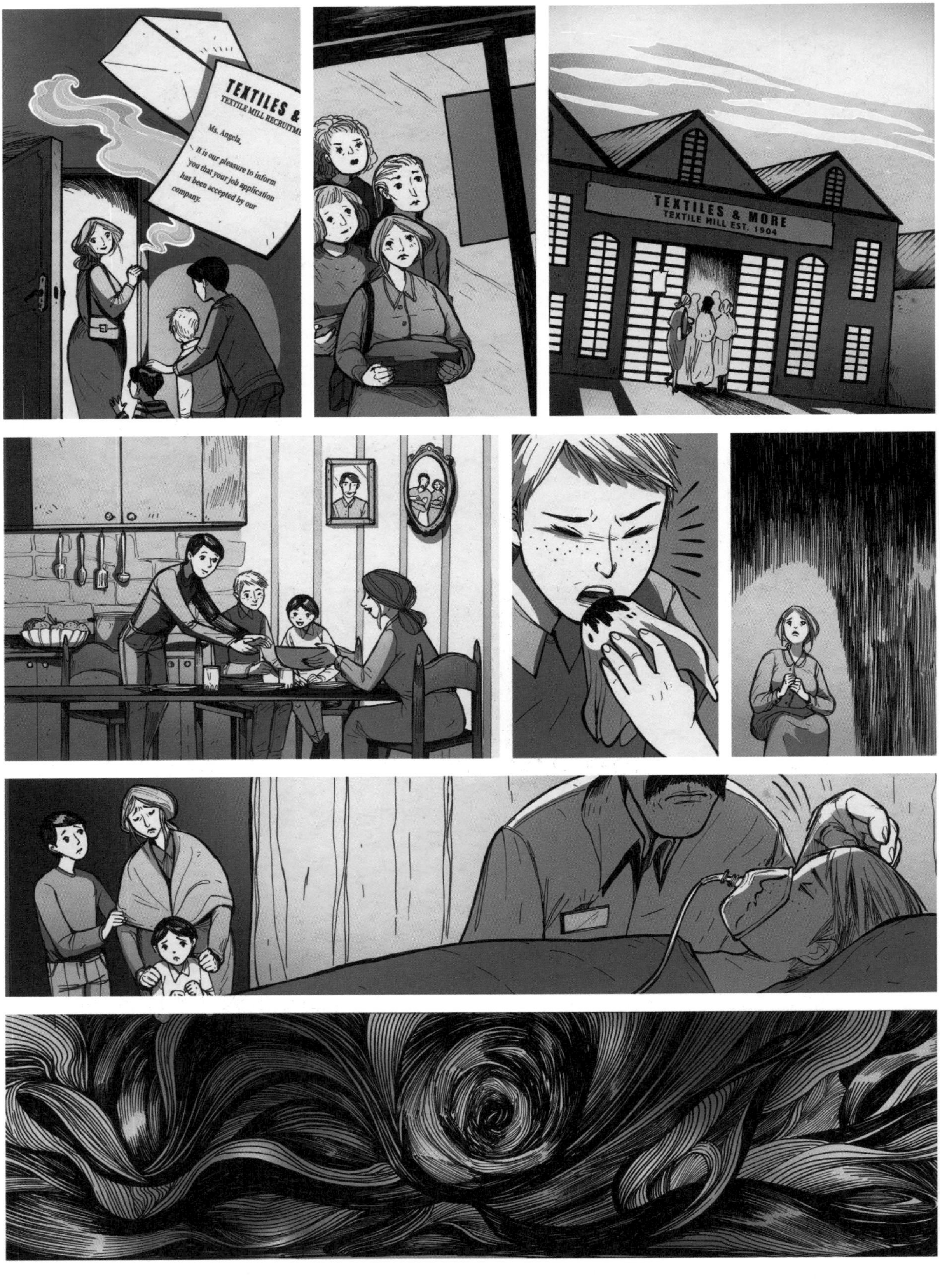
TEXTILES &
TEXTILE MILL RECRUITM
Ms. Angela,
It is our pleasure to inform you that your job application has been accepted by our company.
TEXTILES & MORE
TEXTILE MILL EST. 1904

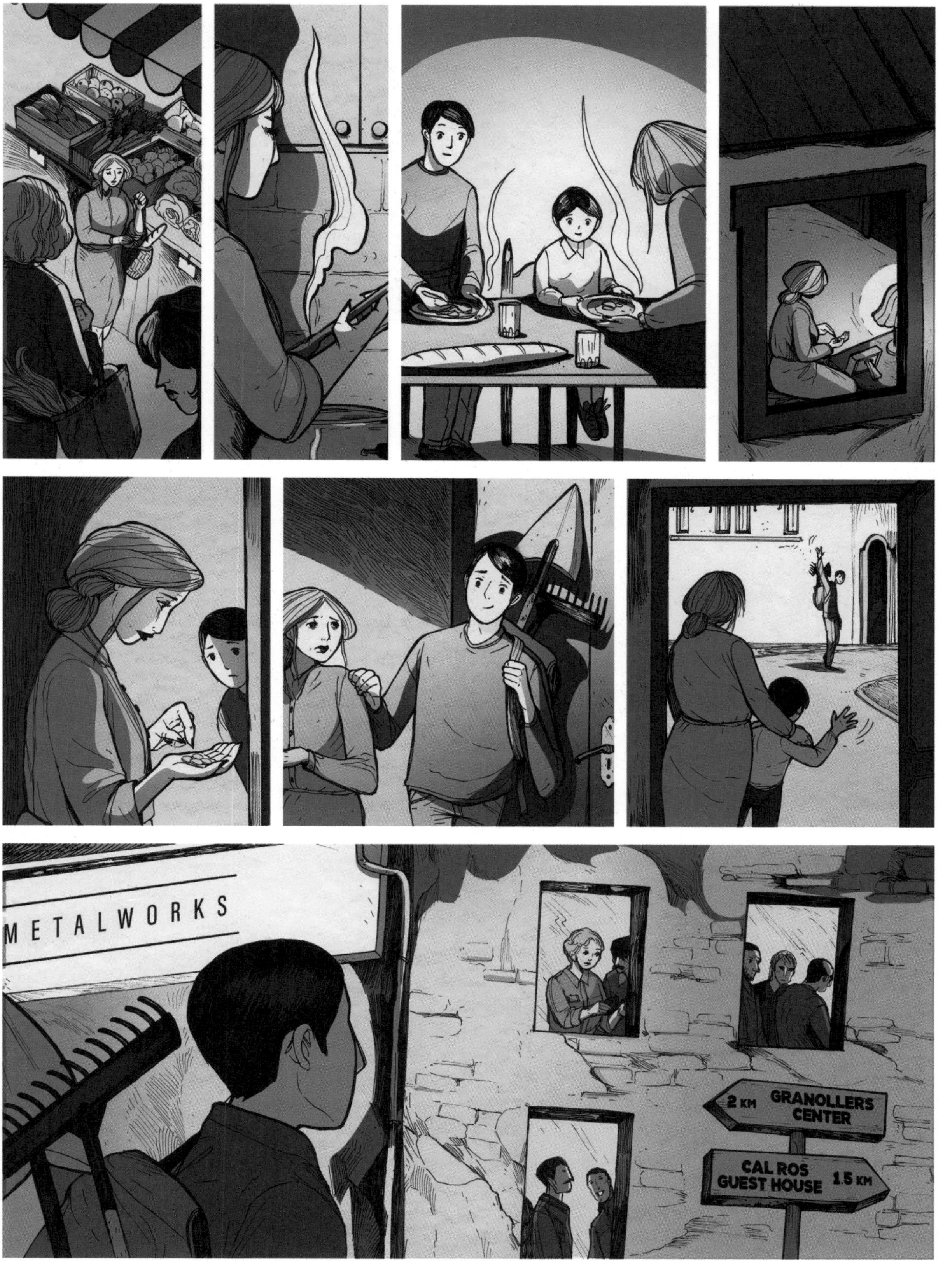
METALWORKS
2 KM GRANOLLERS CENTER
CAL ROS GUEST HOUSE 1.5 KM

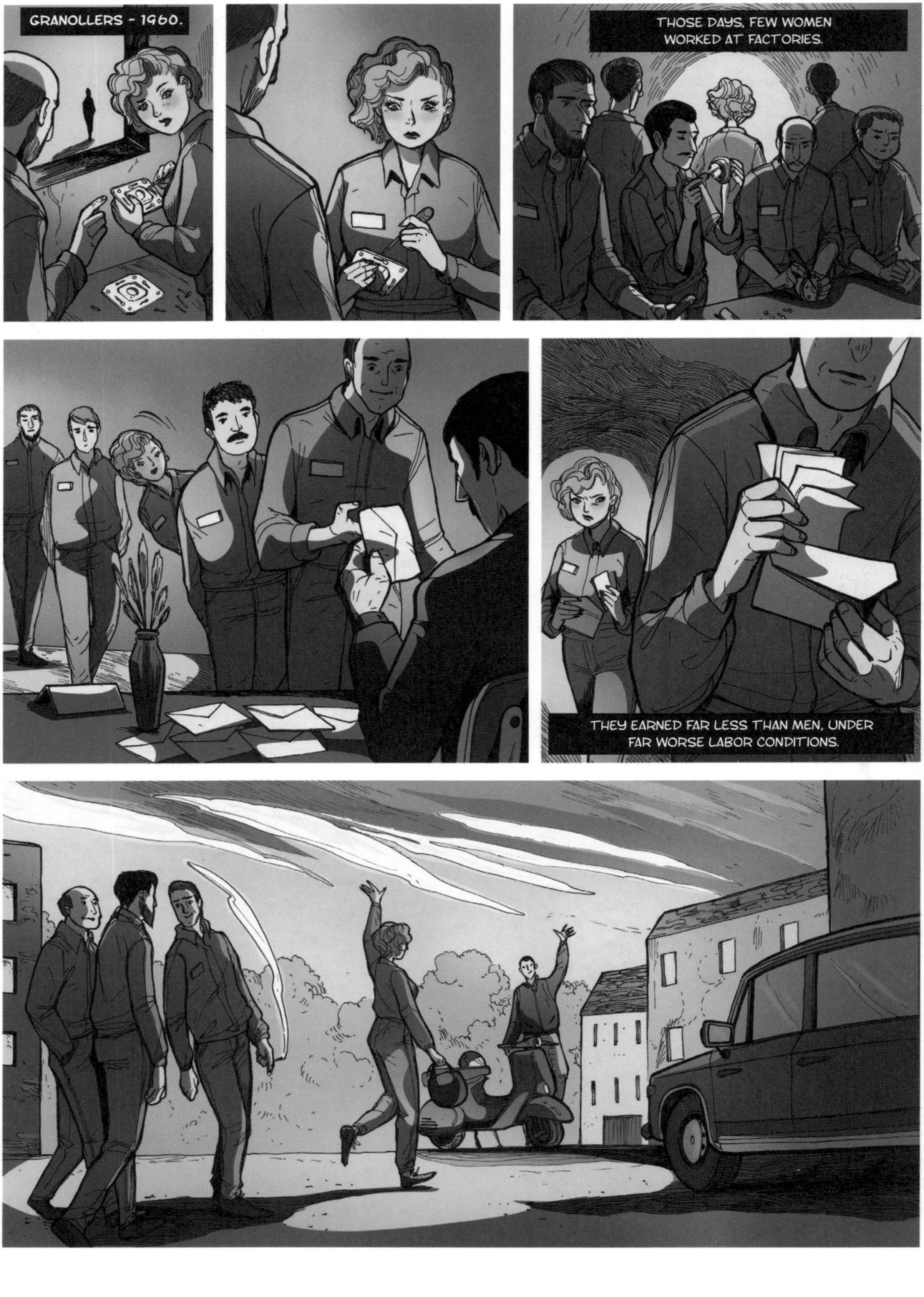
GRANOLLERS - 1960.
THOSE DAYS, FEW WOMEN WORKED AT FACTORIES.
THEY EARNED FAR LESS THAN MEN, UNDER FAR WORSE LABOR CONDITIONS.

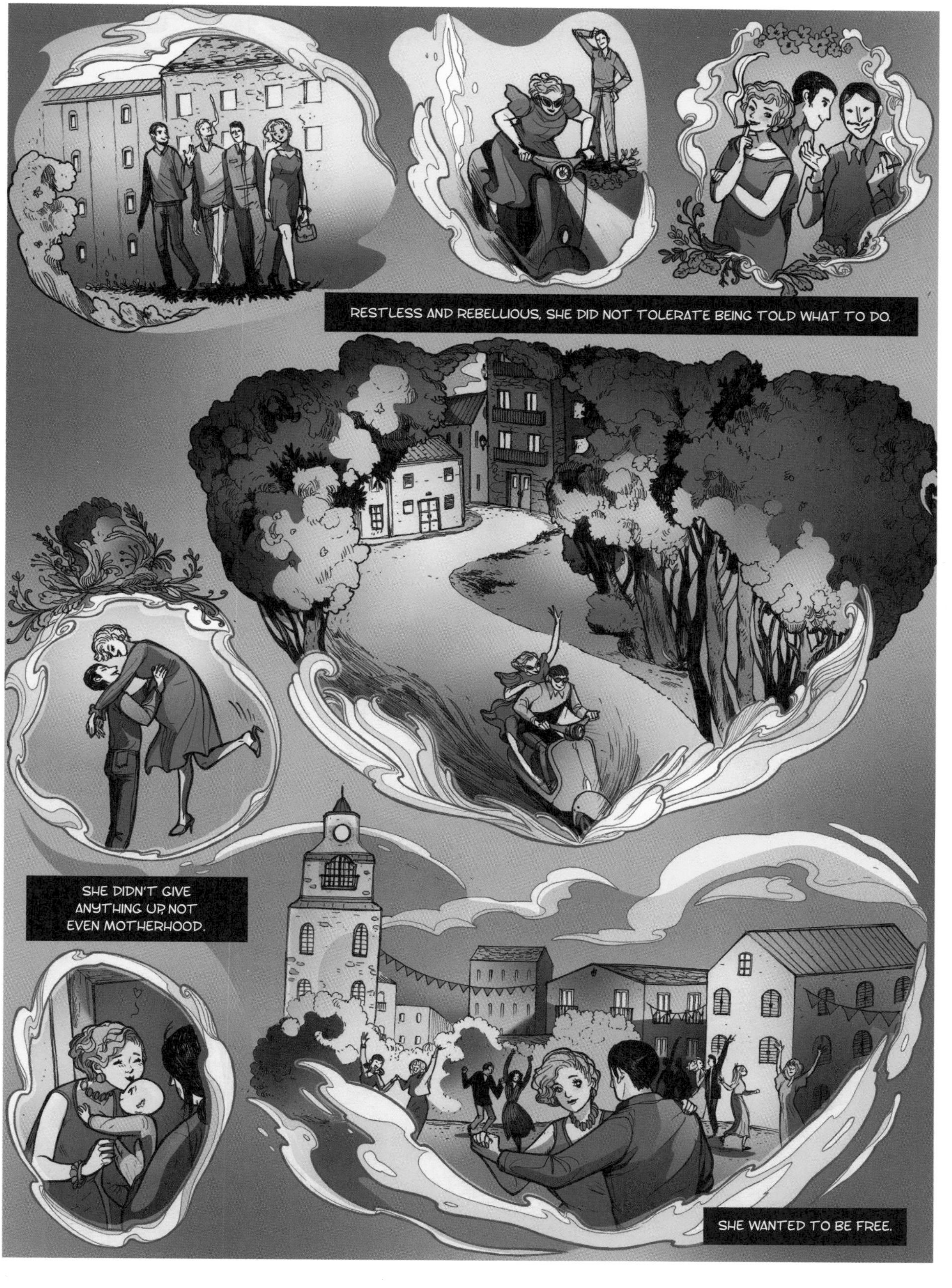
RESTLESS AND REBELLIOUS, SHE DID NOT TOLERATE BEING TOLD WHAT TO DO.
SHE DIDN'T GIVE ANYTHING UP, NOT EVEN MOTHERHOOD.
SHE WANTED TO BE FREE.

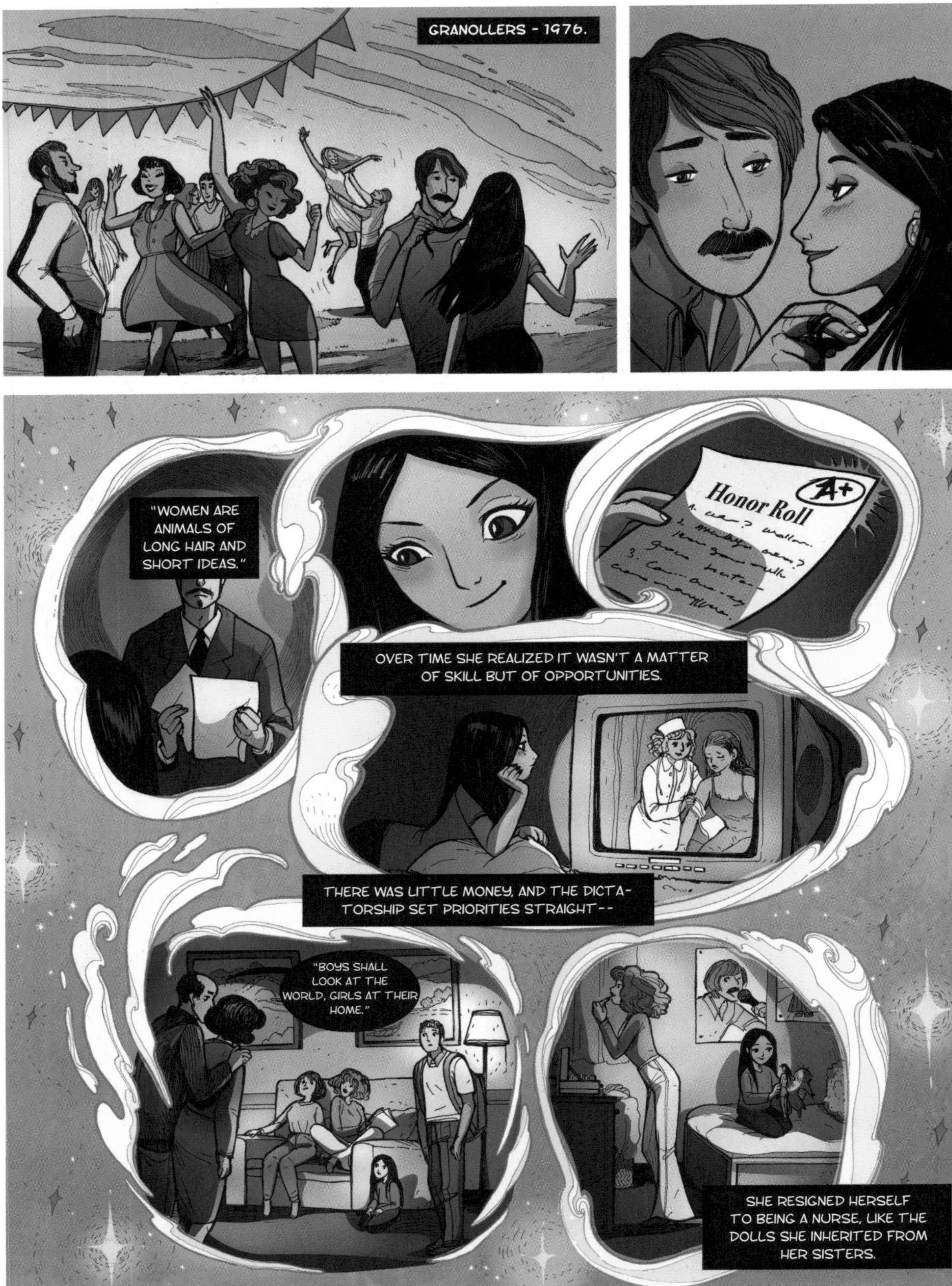
GRANOLLERS - 1976.
"WOMEN ARE ANIMALS OF LONG HAIR AND SHORT IDEAS."
Honor Roll
A+
OVER TIME SHE REALIZED IT WASN'T A MATTER OF SKILL BUT OF OPPORTUNITIES.
THERE WAS LITTLE MONEY, AND THE DICTATORSHIP SET PRIORITIES STRAIGHT--
"BOYS SHALL LOOK AT THE WORLD, GIRLS AT THEIR HOME."
SHE RESIGNED HERSELF TO BEING A NURSE, LIKE THE DOLLS SHE INHERITED FROM HER SISTERS.

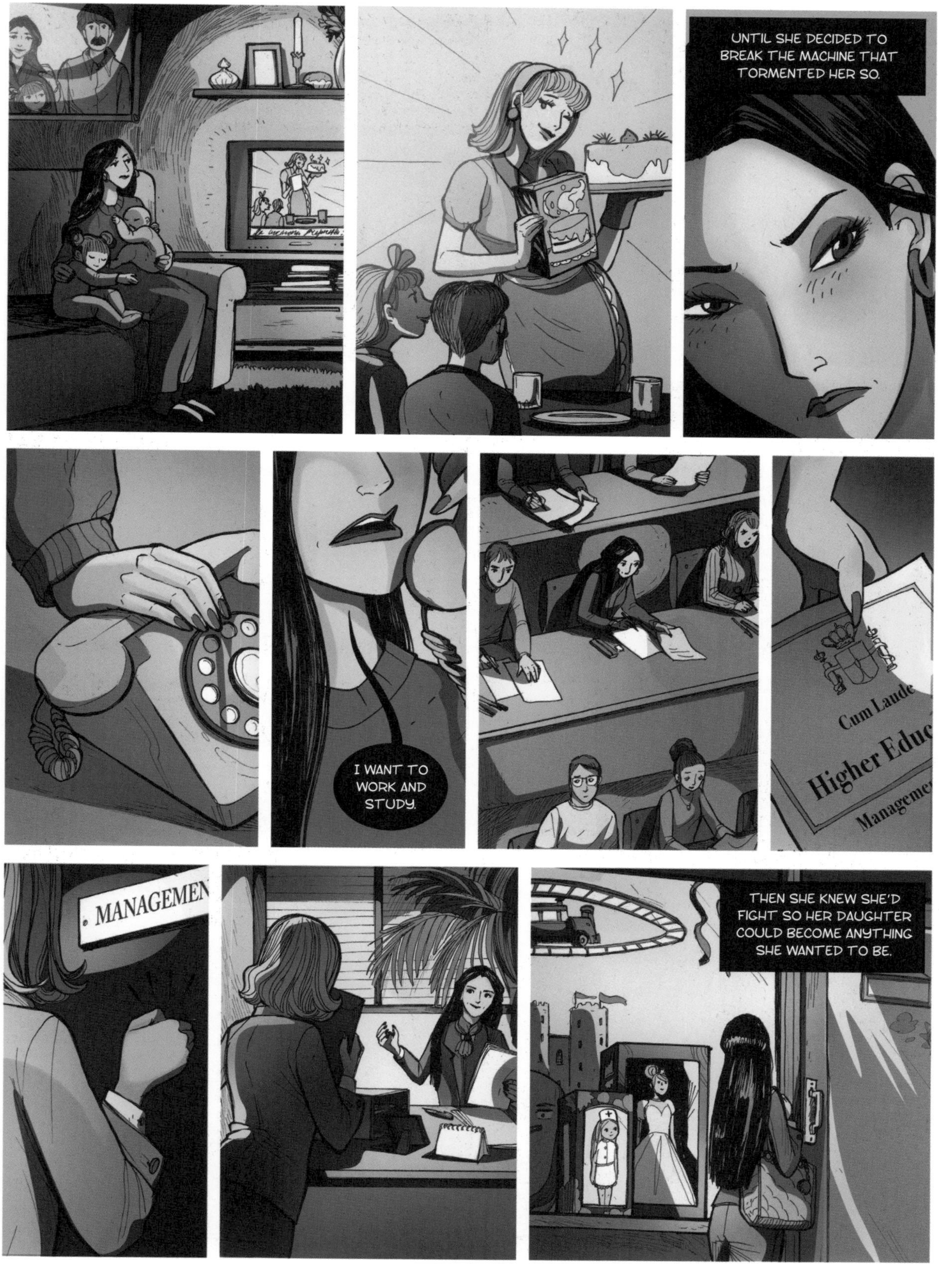

UNTIL SHE DECIDED TO BREAK THE MACHINE THAT TORMENTED HER SO.
I WANT TO WORK AND STUDY.
Cum Laude
Higher Educ
Managemen
MANAGEMEN
THEN SHE KNEW SHE'D FIGHT SO HER DAUGHTER COULD BECOME ANYTHING SHE WANTED TO BE.

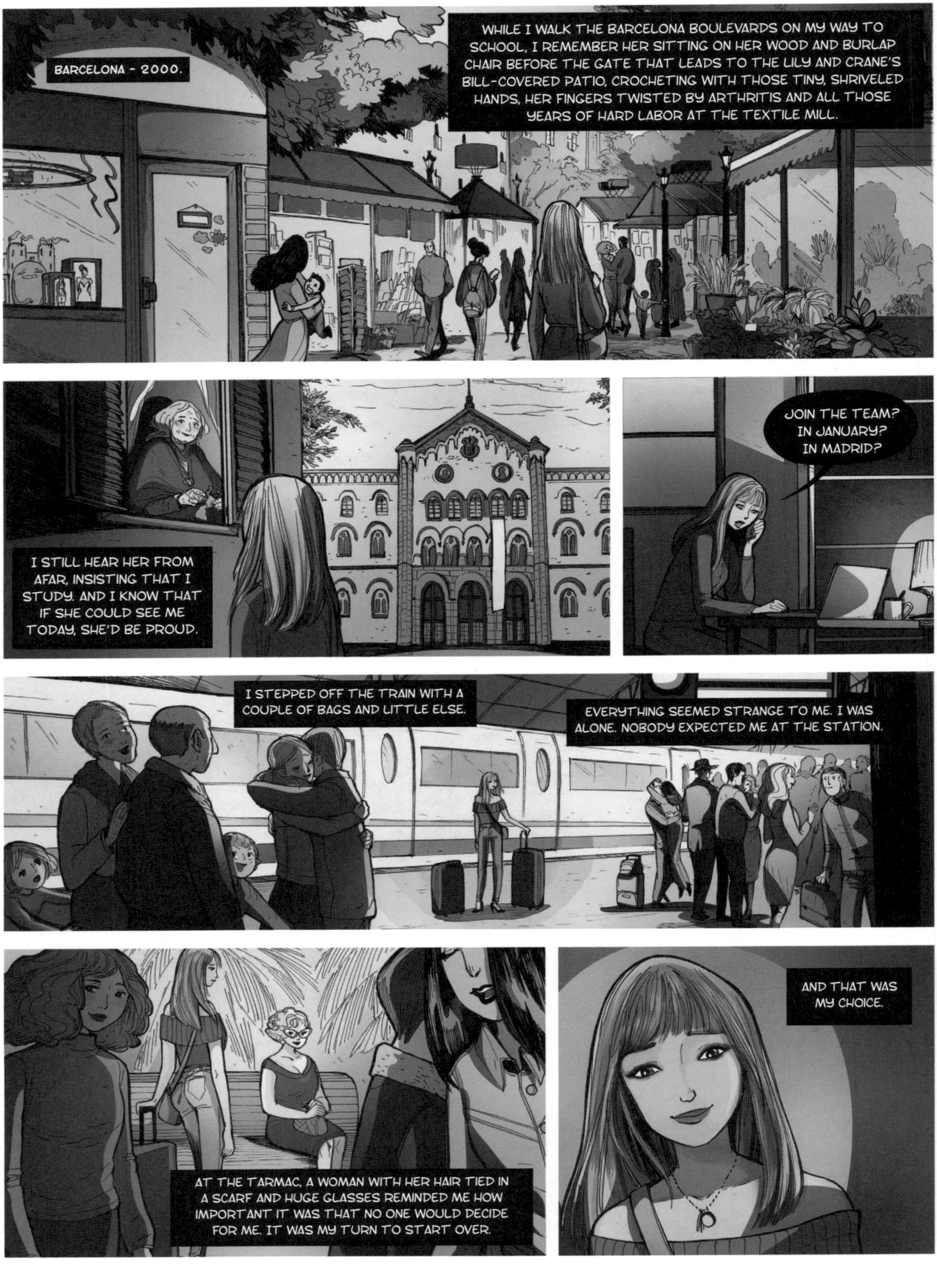
BARCELONA - 2000.
WHILE I WALK THE BARCELONA BOULEVARDS ON MY WAY TO SCHOOL, I REMEMBER HER SITTING ON HER WOOD AND BURLAP CHAIR BEFORE THE GATE THAT LEADS TO THE LILY AND CRANE'S BILL-COVERED PATIO, CROCHETING WITH THOSE TINY, SHRIVELED HANDS, HER FINGERS TWISTED BY ARTHRITIS AND ALL THOSE YEARS OF HARD LABOR AT THE TEXTILE MILL.
I STILL HEAR HER FROM AFAR, INSISTING THAT I STUDY. AND I KNOW THAT IF SHE COULD SEE ME TODAY, SHE'D BE PROUD.
JOIN THE TEAM? IN JANUARY? IN MADRID?
I STEPPED OFF THE TRAIN WITH A COUPLE OF BAGS AND LITTLE ELSE.
EVERYTHING SEEMED STRANGE TO ME. I WAS ALONE. NOBODY EXPECTED ME AT THE STATION.
AT THE TARMAC, A WOMAN WITH HER HAIR TIED IN A SCARF AND HUGE GLASSES REMINDED ME HOW IMPORTANT IT WAS THAT NO ONE WOULD DECIDE FOR ME. IT WAS MY TURN TO START OVER.
AND THAT WAS MY CHOICE.

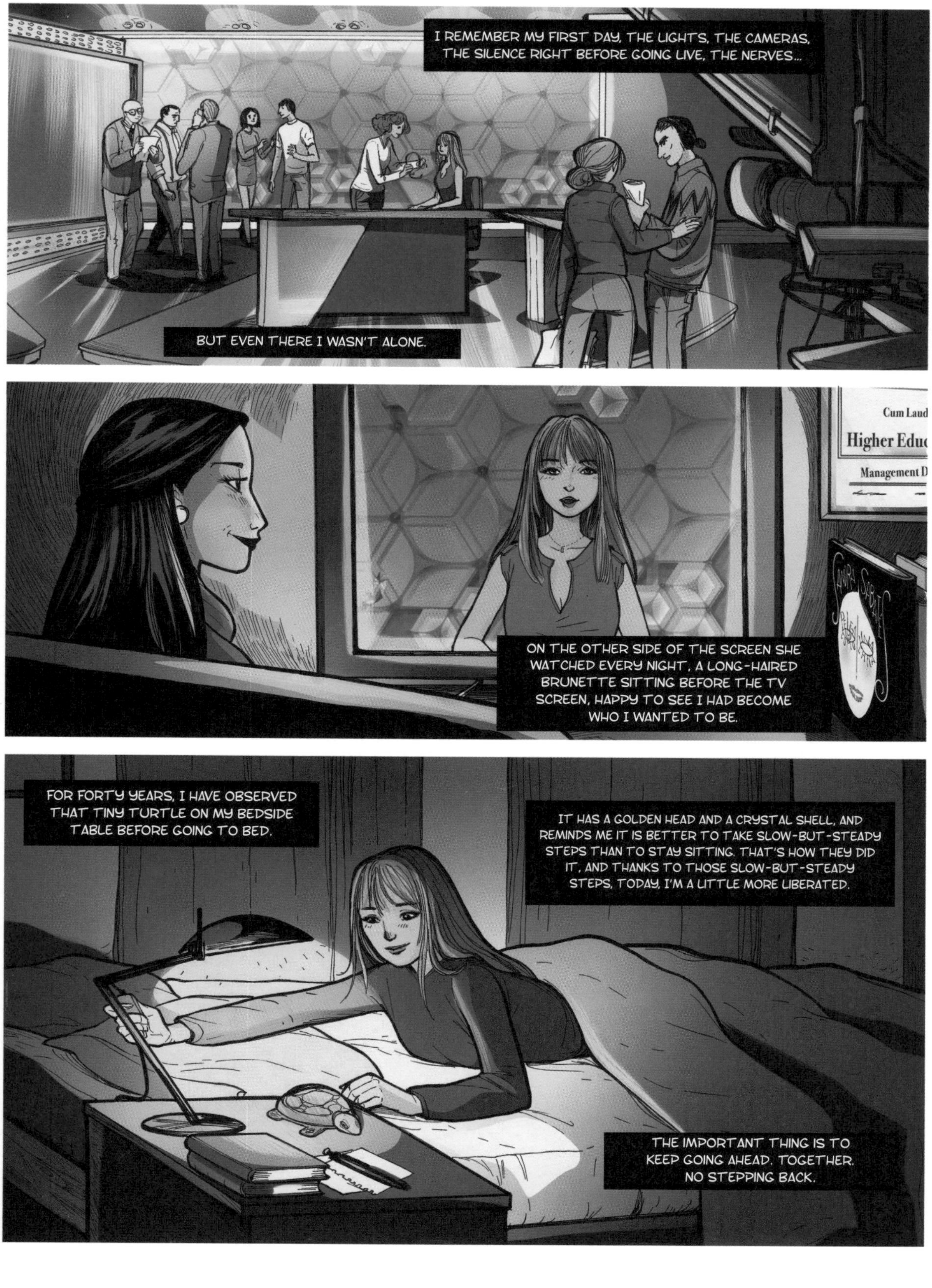
I REMEMBER MY FIRST DAY, THE LIGHTS, THE CAMERAS, THE SILENCE RIGHT BEFORE GOING LIVE, THE NERVES...
BUT EVEN THERE I WASN'T ALONE.
Cum Laud
Higher Educ
Management D
ON THE OTHER SIDE OF THE SCREEN SHE WATCHED EVERY NIGHT, A LONG-HAIRED BRUNETTE SITTING BEFORE THE TV SCREEN, HAPPY TO SEE I HAD BECOME WHO I WANTED TO BE.
FOR FORTY YEARS, I HAVE OBSERVED THAT TINY TURTLE ON MY BEDSIDE TABLE BEFORE GOING TO BED.
IT HAS A GOLDEN HEAD AND A CRYSTAL SHELL, AND REMINDS ME IT IS BETTER TO TAKE SLOW-BUT-STEADY STEPS THAN TO STAY SITTING. THAT'S HOW THEY DID IT, AND THANKS TO THOSE SLOW-BUT-STEADY STEPS, TODAY, I'M A LITTLE MORE LIBERATED.
THE IMPORTANT THING IS TO KEEP GOING AHEAD. TOGETHER. NO STEPPING BACK.

OVER A
BANANA SKIRT

WRITTEN BY ALMUDENA GRANDES

DRAWN BY SARA HERRANZ

"What I learned cooking with my mother when I was twelve, maybe thirteen, years old has given me a foundation for one of the main pillars of my literary work."

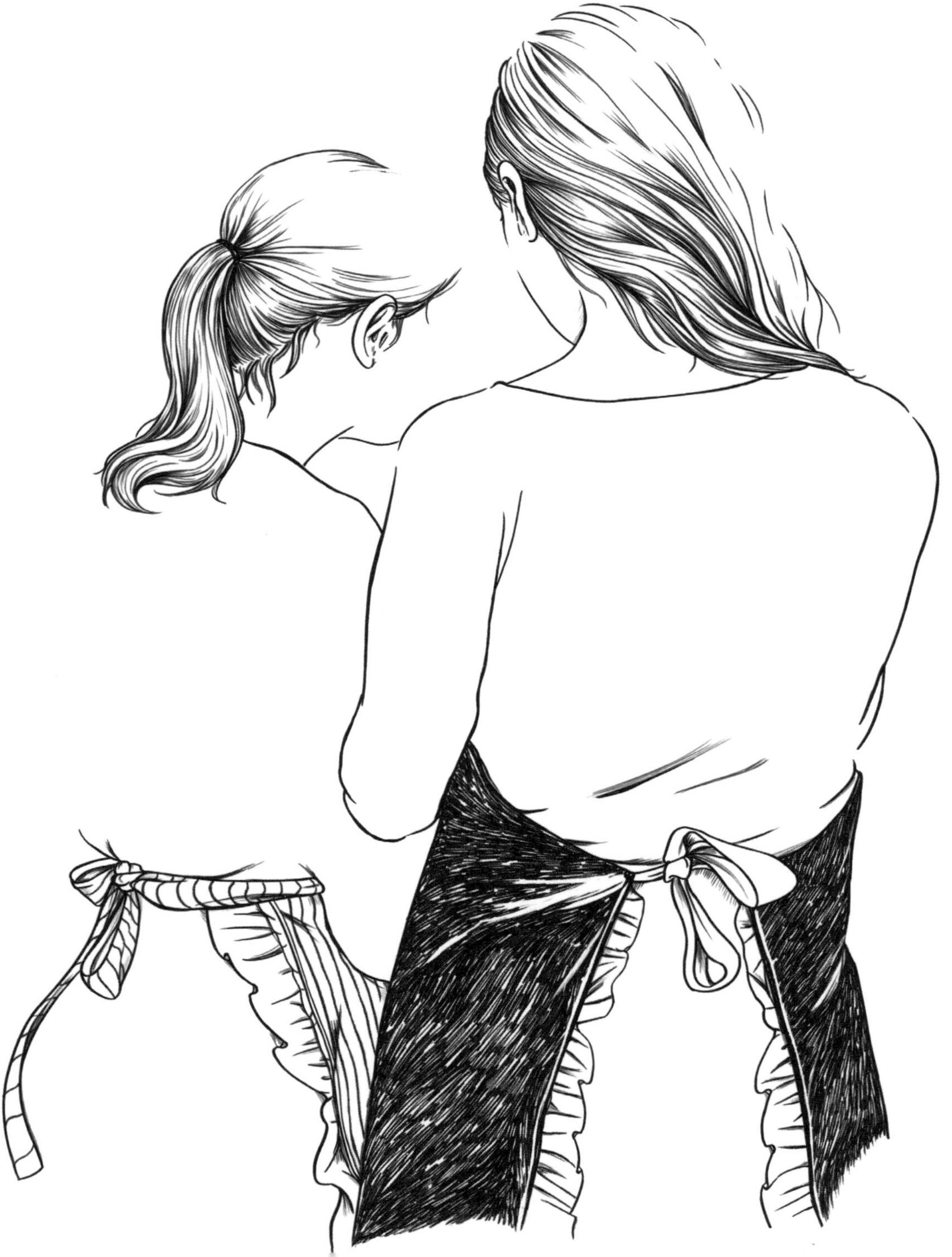

I began to acquire agency over my own destiny that afternoon in 1972, or perhaps 1973, in the kitchen where my mother let me help her, giving me small tasks like peeling and slicing the hard-boiled eggs, cutting up veggies, or stirring the fried onions with a wooden spoon. She was a great cook, and I've sought to follow in her footsteps. I have always enjoyed cooking--today it remains part of my skill set, one of my main delights--and I love kitchens, but the question that triggered that scene had nothing to do with spices, ingredients, or cooking times. Nor do I remember what we were making.

Since I can remember, my mother used to buy a magazine named *Hello!*, which back then already was a venerable institution of Spanish life…

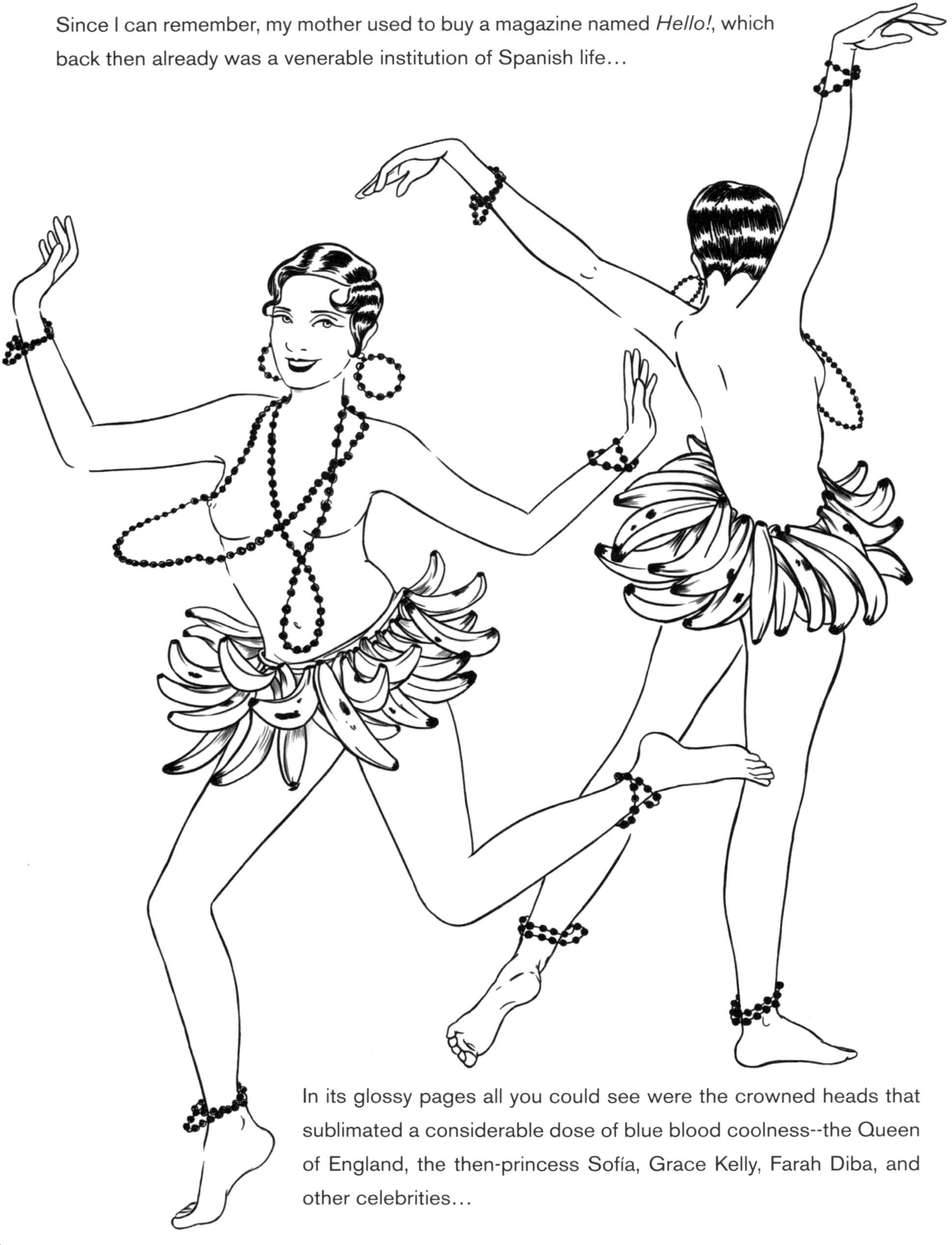

In its glossy pages all you could see were the crowned heads that sublimated a considerable dose of blue blood coolness--the Queen of England, the then-princess Sofía, Grace Kelly, Farah Diba, and other celebrities…

"--She was a variety show star, or did cabaret. Your grandma saw her perform."

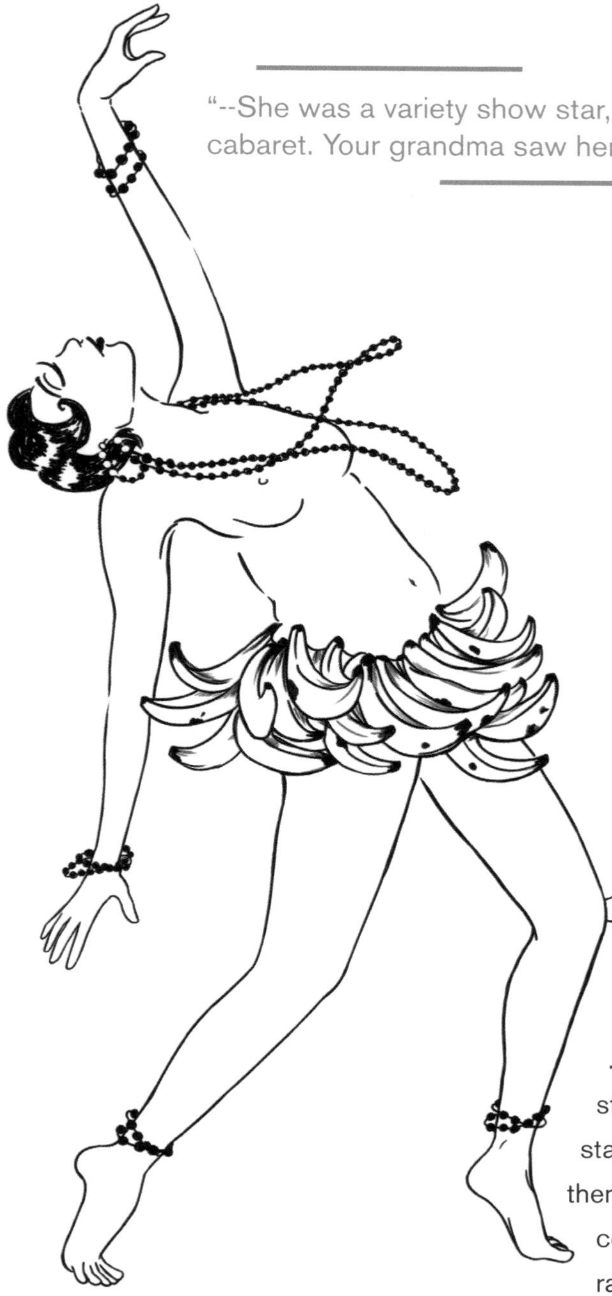

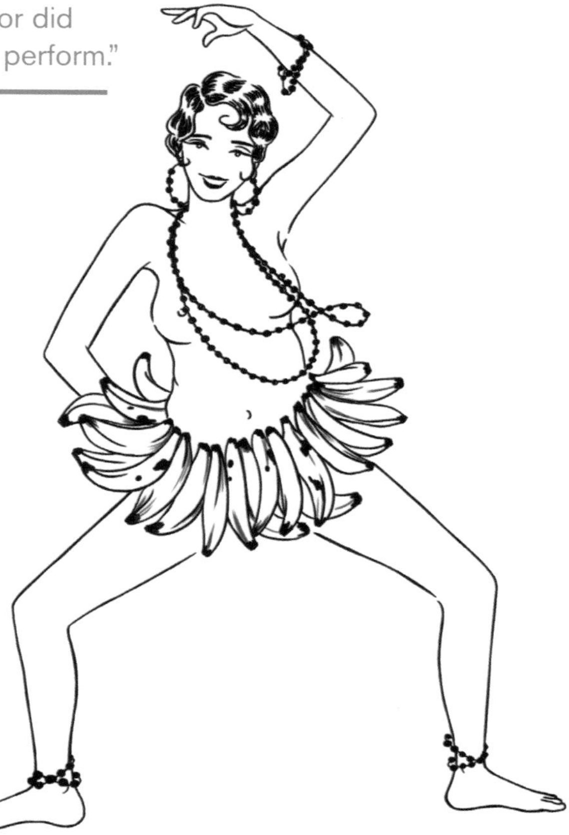

...of the sort--Hollywood starlets, and a strict selection of singers, bullfighters, and stage performers who mainly distinguished themselves through personal elegance or considerable contacts among the nobility rather than by the quality of their work. But, every now and then, a mysterious woman squeezed through its pages.

She was an incredibly young and cute café au lait model. Her hair trimmed in the garçon style, well greased with a big curl on her forehead, and appearing naked from the waist up, although the magazine's editorial department had censored her by placing two big, opaque stars over her nipples. Even so, her terse, shiny skin glowed like hot chocolate glazing, and the beauty of her body was heightened by the grace of a skirt, or rather a loincloth, made with bananas.

It was beyond weird and, of course, a rarity of such an incomparably superior magnitude that they managed to include all Josephine Baker's photos. That my grandma Paca, a theoretically--as far as I could grasp--decent, apostolic, Roman, and Catholic lady, had gone with her husband, Grandpa Manuel, a career military man, to see a naked woman dance in a theater was as unbelievable to me as a green-skinned Martian with yellow eyes and two trumpets instead of ears. Furthermore, how was I to believe that, if I had been born in Spain in 1960; if I was attending the Sacred Hearts of Mary and Jesus High School; if I watched zarzuelas and live theater plays on Spanish TV; if I had learned by osmosis, as naturally as breathing, that people going to strip clubs was necessarily **French**, like cabaret and variety shows in general?

It may seem frivolous, but the picture of both my grandparents, young and trusting, seeing Josephine Baker dance in a Madrid theater, applauding and quietly walking back home afterward, was the tip of the iceberg, the end of the yarn ball, a clear and bright image that took me many years to unravel. Now, on the other side of the road, I have managed to decode that mysterious lack-of-gravity feeling, the fear and the astonishment of walking on air, that I felt that afternoon with my feet trampling my mother's kitchen tiles. Because that seemingly trivial anecdote, apparently unimportant, taught me two fundamental things: first, that progress isn't a straight line, and second, the kind of country I chanced to be living in.

"My grandmother was dead, but I would devote my-self to rebuilding the threads that had been cut with a single stroke, repair by any means necessary the bonds no one should have dared destroy."

The role writing has played in my concern for memory goes way beyond anything I could have developed under another calling or job, because *memory* is, in itself, the most important concept involved in literary creation and, first and foremost, the starting point of all fiction. Writing is looking at the world, publishing, and communicating to readers the result of that outlook.

A lot of different people may look at the same scenery and see landscapes as differently from one another as they themselves are, because their viewpoints do not end in their eyes. In order to elaborate on what they are witnessing, they would have to compare their memory with the images they have seen.

"A lot of different people may look at the same scenery and see landscapes as differently from one another as they themselves are, because their viewpoints do not end in their eyes."

"Everything comes from memory. I can't invent a story I don't know about, nor can I give a voice to a character alien to me."

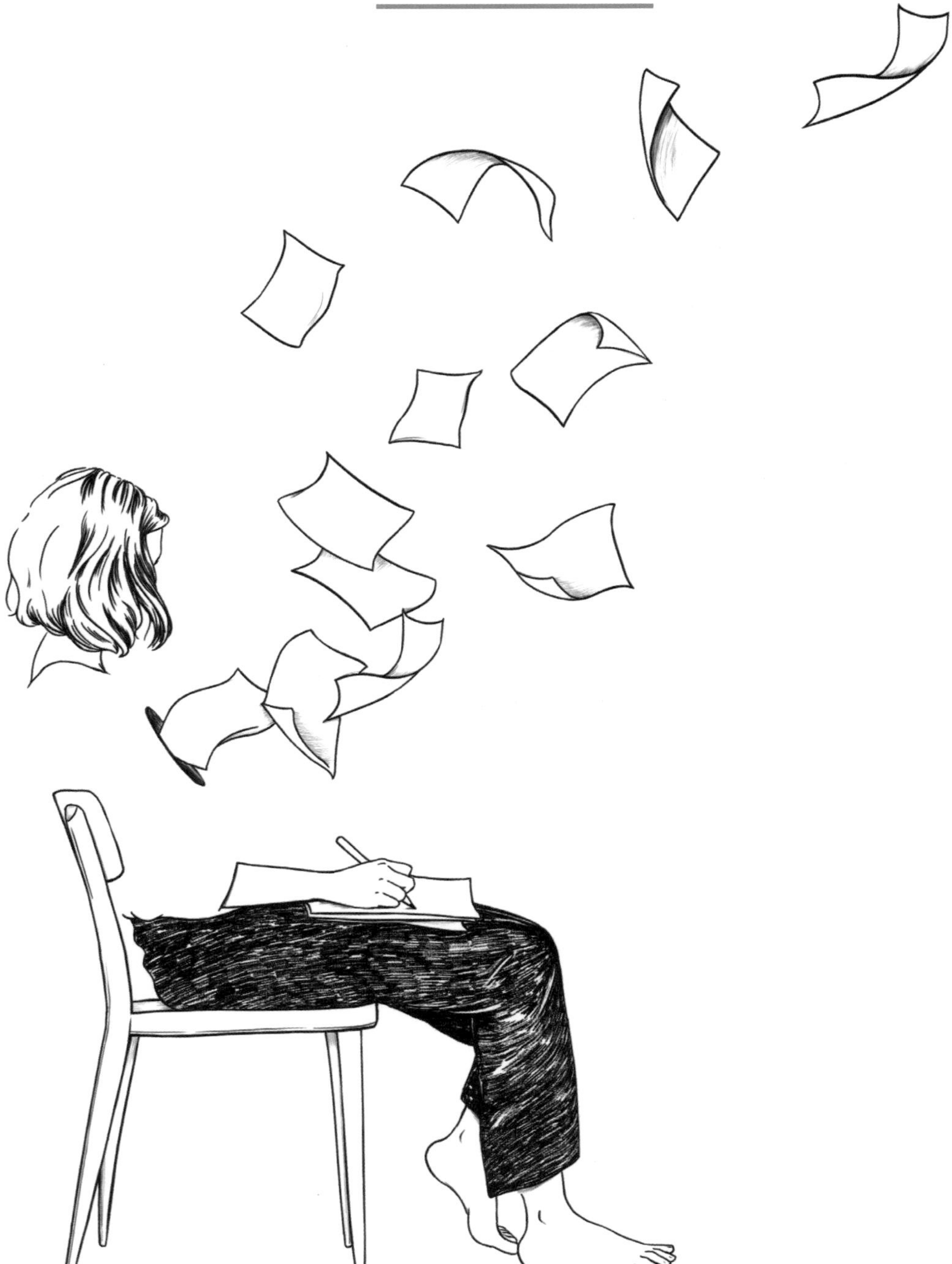

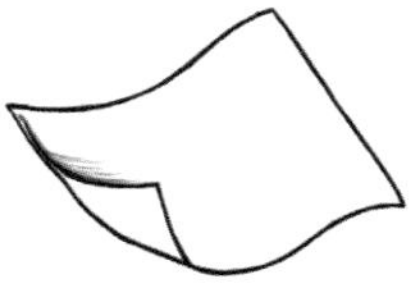

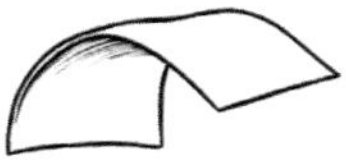

Inside a writer's memory resides, of course, her biographic experience, but it doesn't need to be more important than that of others. The lives she wishes she had lived are many, the ones she would have feared, also. Dreamed lives count in the metaphorical sense but also in the literal--hated lives and all those forks in the road that would have meant possible different outcomes if at a given moment she had decided to switch lanes. Lives that are read about count too, of course, because literature has to **do** with life, and reading **is** living, an experience that modifies the reader's conscience to fabricate its own memories. Human feelings and the infinite combinations they give birth to pose constant challenges in the life of anybody, but the writer's imagination is capable of developing full trajectories with very little. And all of them, absolutely all of them, are necessary, because we can only write about that which we remember. If we constrained ourselves to our real lives, the one unfolding in the time marked by clocks and calendars, most of our books would be very boring.

A writer's everyday life looks, more than any other thing, like the everyday life of any other person.

Memory is also the key concept of a whole generation of Spaniards--my own generation.

We were told to close our eyes and jump forward, and when we opened them everything had changed. Spain had been a dictatorship but was now a democracy; where once had been a general was now a king; where once no political parties existed, now there were many to pick from; in Spain women did not dance naked, but now grannies could go with their husbands to see them dance, and it worked. Why make inquiries, why question reality, why look underneath the carpet, if it worked? It seemed like it worked, and even that it would **always** work. But it didn't.

The leaders of "the movement" of the eighties grew old, like everybody else, in every time, in every era, almost without realizing it. And one day, on the verge of turning forty, we looked in and around us, and didn't understand what we were looking at, nor the country we were living in. It was then that a conversation half listened to behind a closed door, a deck of cards, or a photo of Josephine Baker in the pages of a 1972, maybe 1973 issue of *Hello!* recovered their meaning, acquiring a value we never, until then, were able to give them.

"Many Spaniards of my generation…have strived during the last ten years to connect their personal memory to that of other people, creating little by little a social fabric of a magnitude that's hard to grasp, which has begun to repair the collective memory."

MZUNGU

WRITTEN BY PATRICIA CAMPOS

DRAWN BY SARA SOLER

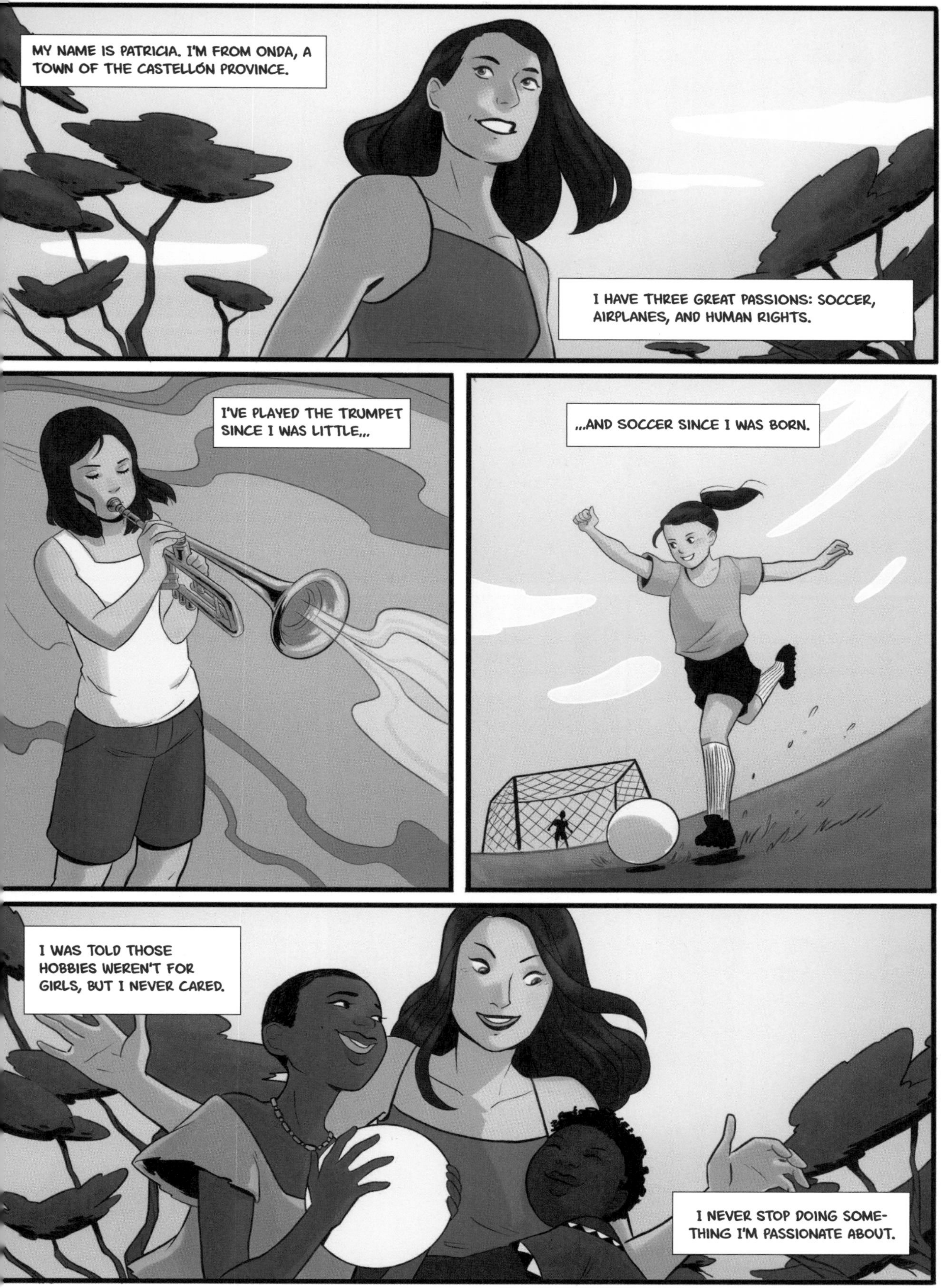
MY NAME IS PATRICIA. I'M FROM ONDA, A TOWN OF THE CASTELLÓN PROVINCE.
I HAVE THREE GREAT PASSIONS: SOCCER, AIRPLANES, AND HUMAN RIGHTS.
I'VE PLAYED THE TRUMPET SINCE I WAS LITTLE...
...AND SOCCER SINCE I WAS BORN.
I WAS TOLD THOSE HOBBIES WEREN'T FOR GIRLS, BUT I NEVER CARED.
I NEVER STOP DOING SOME-THING I'M PASSIONATE ABOUT.

IN 2005, I BECAME THE FIRST AND ONLY FEMALE JET PILOT IN THE SPANISH NAVY.

I WAS STATIONED AT THE ROTA BASE.

YOU PROBABLY REALIZE THE KIND OF TROUBLE I WAS IN IF NO OTHER WOMAN HAS JOINED SINCE. MY PATH THROUGH THE ARMED FORCES WAS HARD.

PIONEER WOMEN ARE RARELY APPRECIATED. OUR PROFESSIONALISM IS PUT INTO QUESTION.

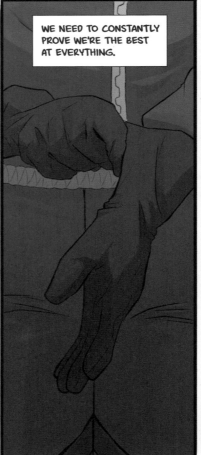

WE NEED TO CONSTANTLY PROVE WE'RE THE BEST AT EVERYTHING.

WE'RE ALWAYS IN THE EYE OF THE STORM.

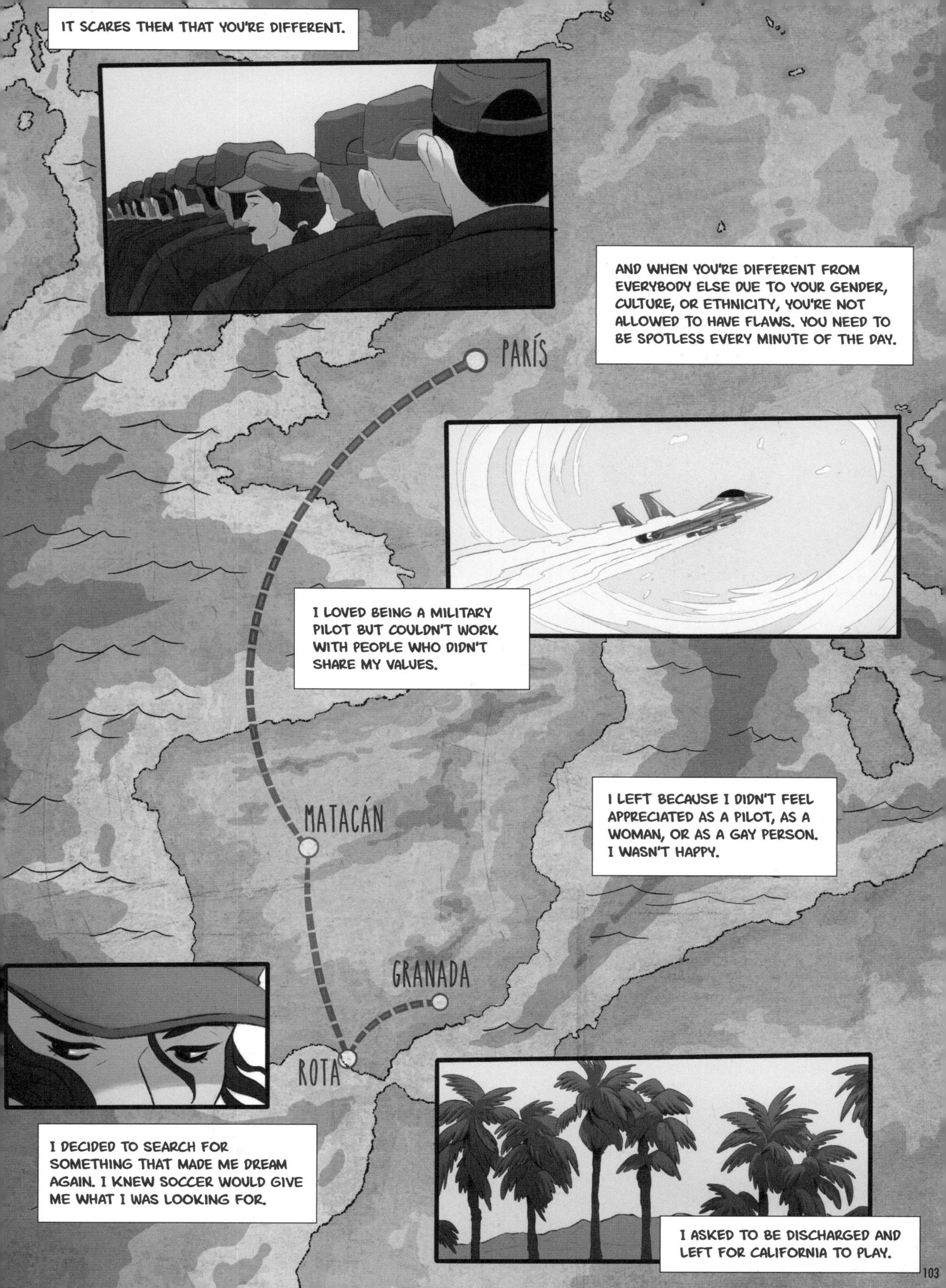
IT SCARES THEM THAT YOU'RE DIFFERENT.
AND WHEN YOU'RE DIFFERENT FROM EVERYBODY ELSE DUE TO YOUR GENDER, CULTURE, OR ETHNICITY, YOU'RE NOT ALLOWED TO HAVE FLAWS. YOU NEED TO BE SPOTLESS EVERY MINUTE OF THE DAY.
PARÍS
I LOVED BEING A MILITARY PILOT BUT COULDN'T WORK WITH PEOPLE WHO DIDN'T SHARE MY VALUES.
MATACÁN
I LEFT BECAUSE I DIDN'T FEEL APPRECIATED AS A PILOT, AS A WOMAN, OR AS A GAY PERSON. I WASN'T HAPPY.
GRANADA
ROTA
I DECIDED TO SEARCH FOR SOMETHING THAT MADE ME DREAM AGAIN. I KNEW SOCCER WOULD GIVE ME WHAT I WAS LOOKING FOR.
I ASKED TO BE DISCHARGED AND LEFT FOR CALIFORNIA TO PLAY.

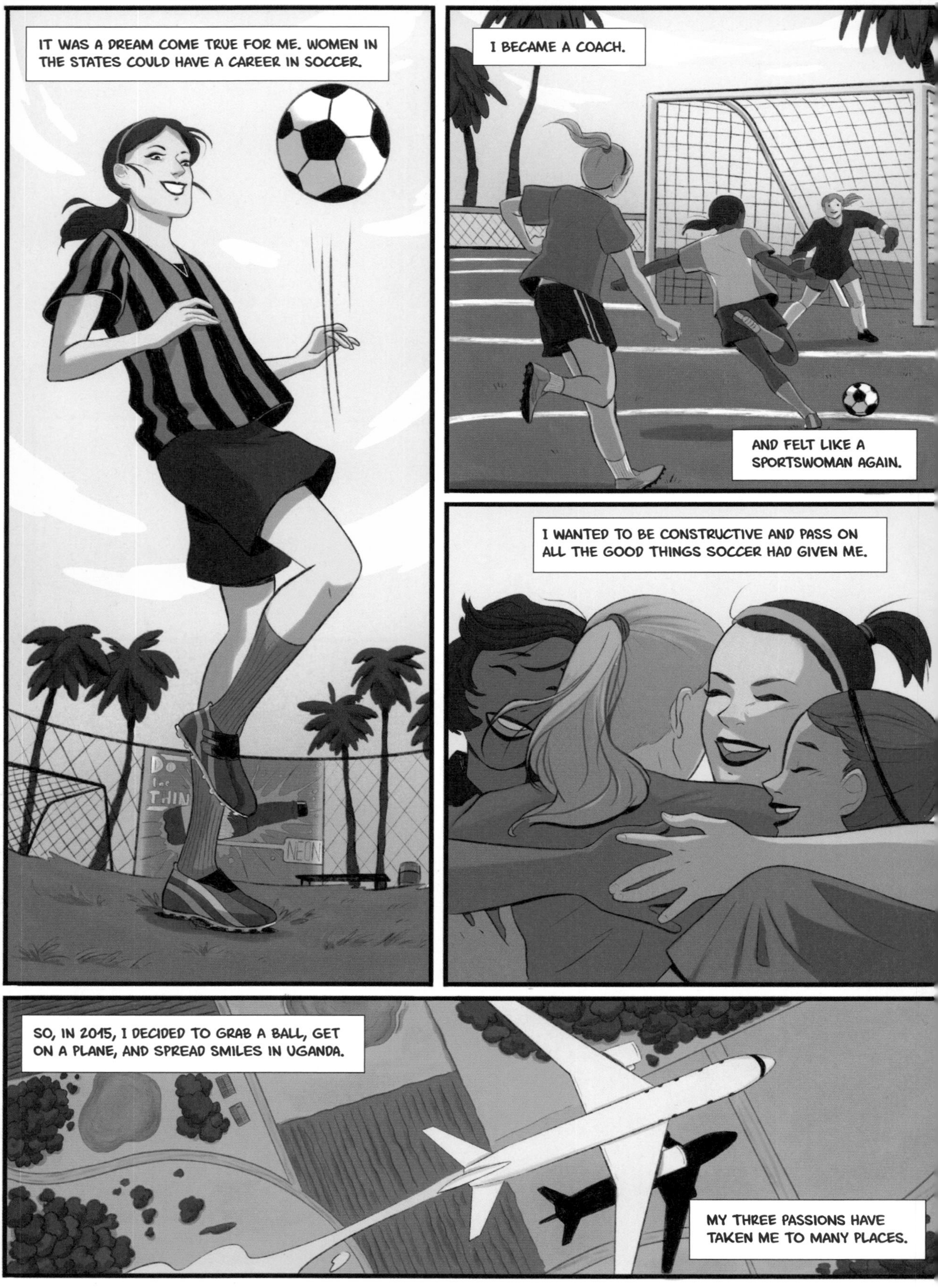
IT WAS A DREAM COME TRUE FOR ME. WOMEN IN THE STATES COULD HAVE A CAREER IN SOCCER.
NEON
I BECAME A COACH.
AND FELT LIKE A SPORTSWOMAN AGAIN.
I WANTED TO BE CONSTRUCTIVE AND PASS ON ALL THE GOOD THINGS SOCCER HAD GIVEN ME.
SO, IN 2015, I DECIDED TO GRAB A BALL, GET ON A PLANE, AND SPREAD SMILES IN UGANDA.
MY THREE PASSIONS HAVE TAKEN ME TO MANY PLACES.

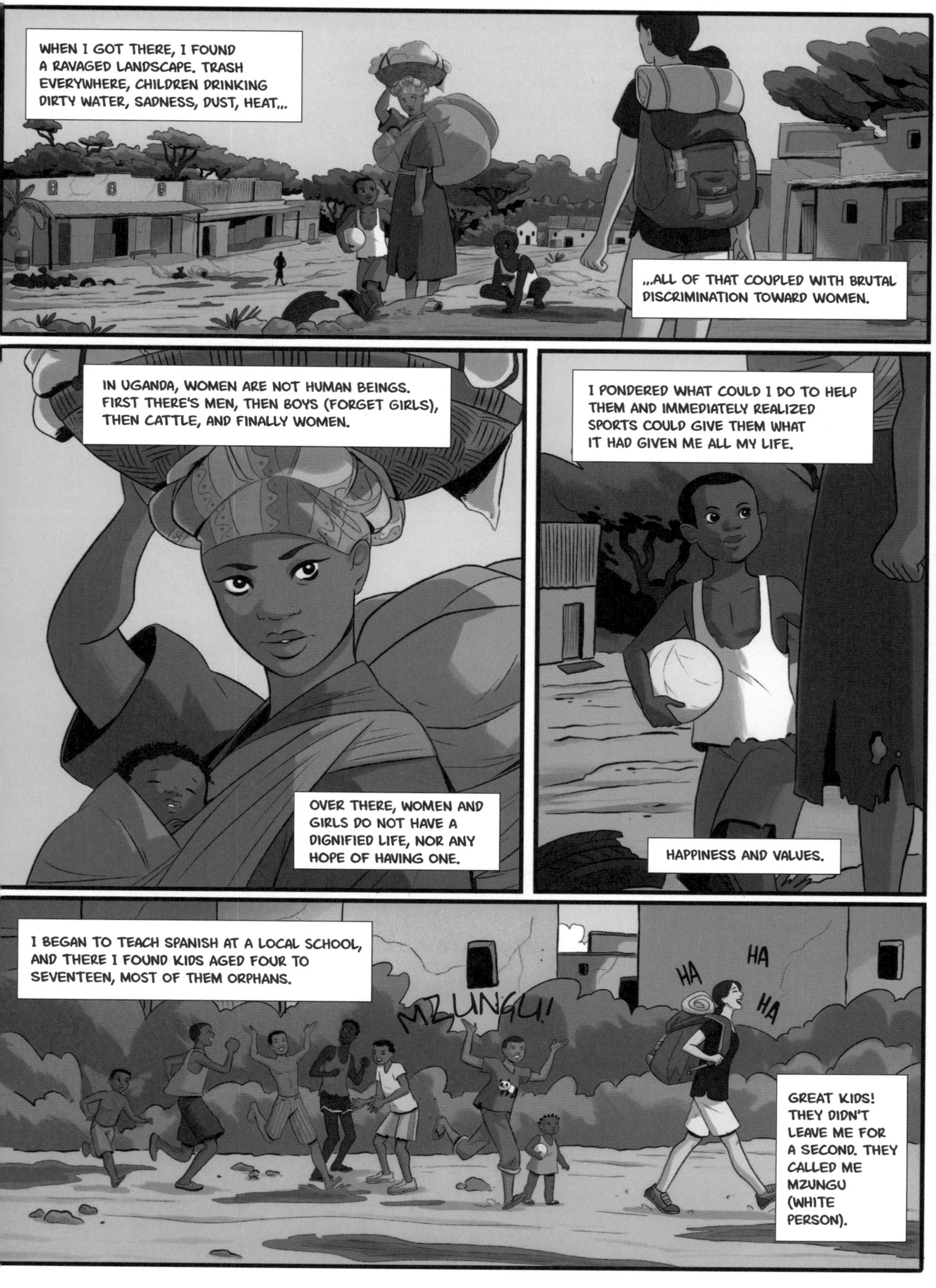
WHEN I GOT THERE, I FOUND A RAVAGED LANDSCAPE. TRASH EVERYWHERE, CHILDREN DRINKING DIRTY WATER, SADNESS, DUST, HEAT...
...ALL OF THAT COUPLED WITH BRUTAL DISCRIMINATION TOWARD WOMEN.
IN UGANDA, WOMEN ARE NOT HUMAN BEINGS. FIRST THERE'S MEN, THEN BOYS (FORGET GIRLS), THEN CATTLE, AND FINALLY WOMEN.
OVER THERE, WOMEN AND GIRLS DO NOT HAVE A DIGNIFIED LIFE, NOR ANY HOPE OF HAVING ONE.
I PONDERED WHAT COULD I DO TO HELP THEM AND IMMEDIATELY REALIZED SPORTS COULD GIVE THEM WHAT IT HAD GIVEN ME ALL MY LIFE.
HAPPINESS AND VALUES.
I BEGAN TO TEACH SPANISH AT A LOCAL SCHOOL, AND THERE I FOUND KIDS AGED FOUR TO SEVENTEEN, MOST OF THEM ORPHANS.
MZUNGU!
HA
HA
HA
GREAT KIDS! THEY DIDN'T LEAVE ME FOR A SECOND. THEY CALLED ME MZUNGU (WHITE PERSON).

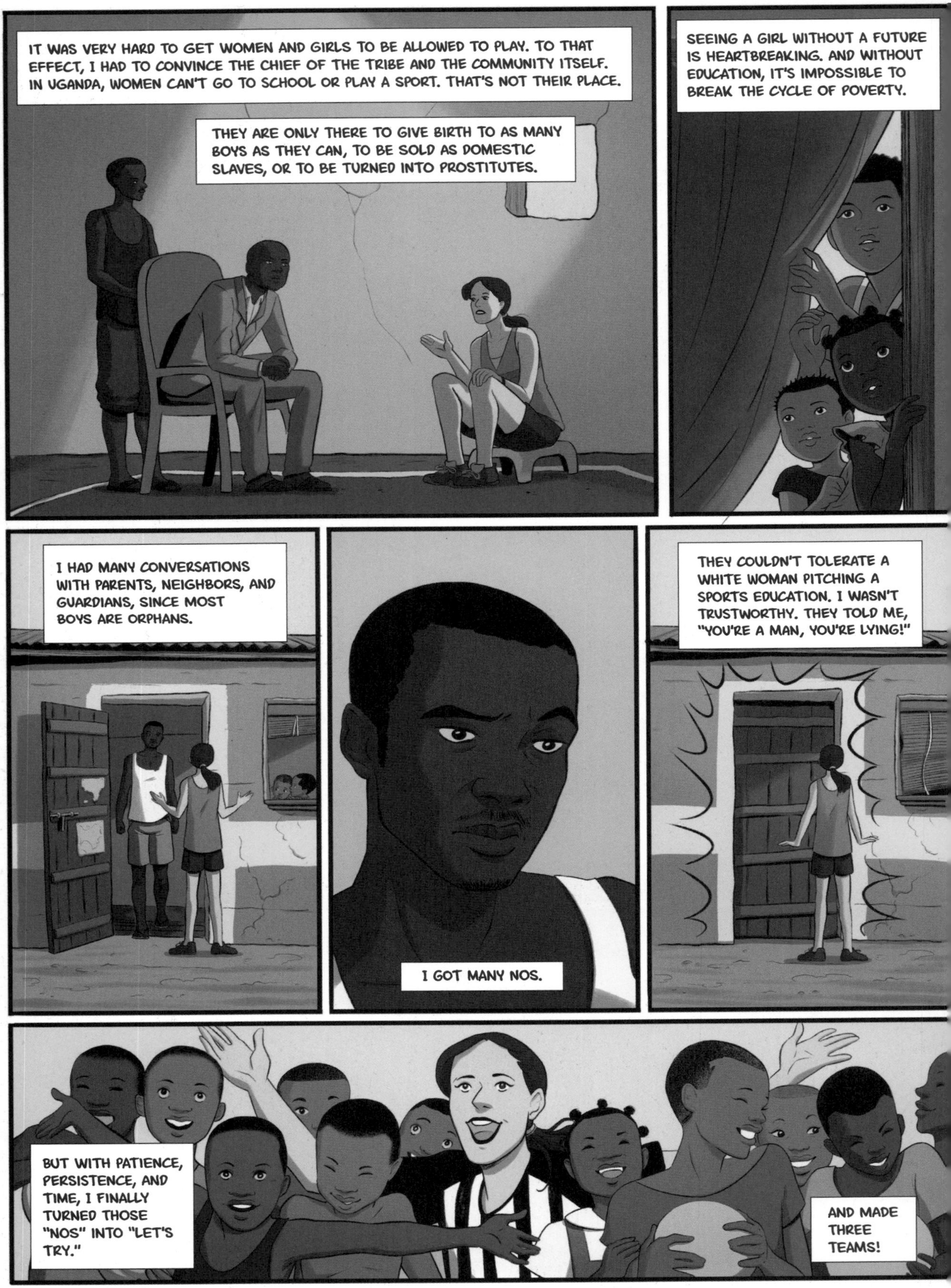
IT WAS VERY HARD TO GET WOMEN AND GIRLS TO BE ALLOWED TO PLAY. TO THAT EFFECT, I HAD TO CONVINCE THE CHIEF OF THE TRIBE AND THE COMMUNITY ITSELF. IN UGANDA, WOMEN CAN'T GO TO SCHOOL OR PLAY A SPORT. THAT'S NOT THEIR PLACE.
THEY ARE ONLY THERE TO GIVE BIRTH TO AS MANY BOYS AS THEY CAN, TO BE SOLD AS DOMESTIC SLAVES, OR TO BE TURNED INTO PROSTITUTES.
SEEING A GIRL WITHOUT A FUTURE IS HEARTBREAKING. AND WITHOUT EDUCATION, IT'S IMPOSSIBLE TO BREAK THE CYCLE OF POVERTY.
I HAD MANY CONVERSATIONS WITH PARENTS, NEIGHBORS, AND GUARDIANS, SINCE MOST BOYS ARE ORPHANS.
I GOT MANY NOS.
THEY COULDN'T TOLERATE A WHITE WOMAN PITCHING A SPORTS EDUCATION. I WASN'T TRUSTWORTHY. THEY TOLD ME, "YOU'RE A MAN, YOU'RE LYING!"
BUT WITH PATIENCE, PERSISTENCE, AND TIME, I FINALLY TURNED THOSE "NOS" INTO "LET'S TRY."
AND MADE THREE TEAMS!

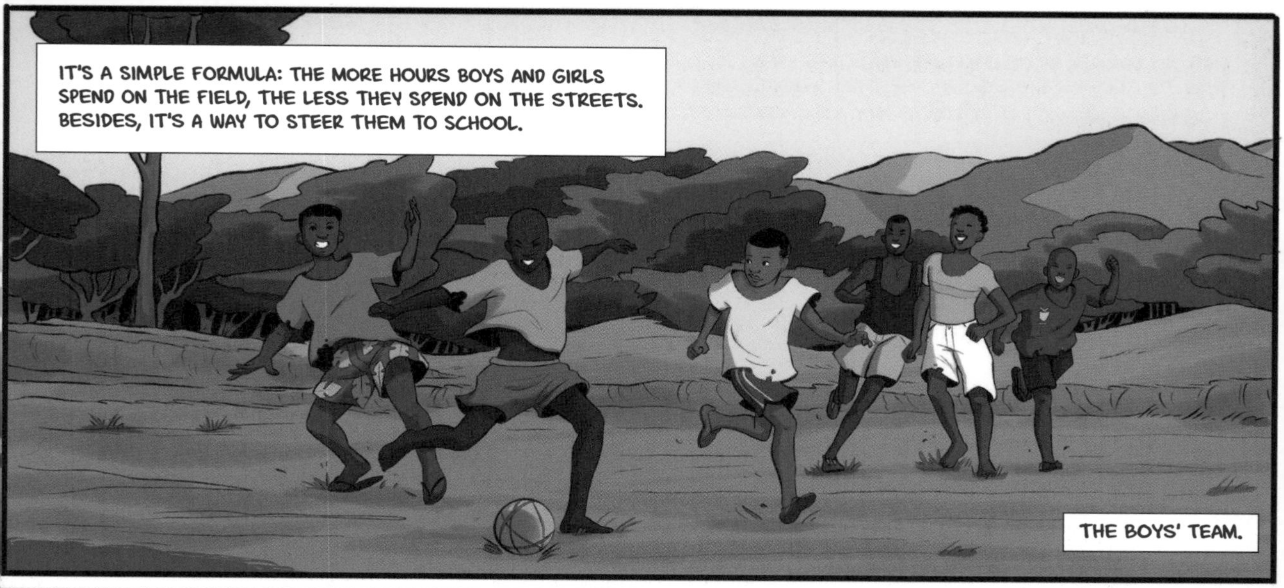
IT'S A SIMPLE FORMULA: THE MORE HOURS BOYS AND GIRLS SPEND ON THE FIELD, THE LESS THEY SPEND ON THE STREETS. BESIDES, IT'S A WAY TO STEER THEM TO SCHOOL.
THE BOYS' TEAM.

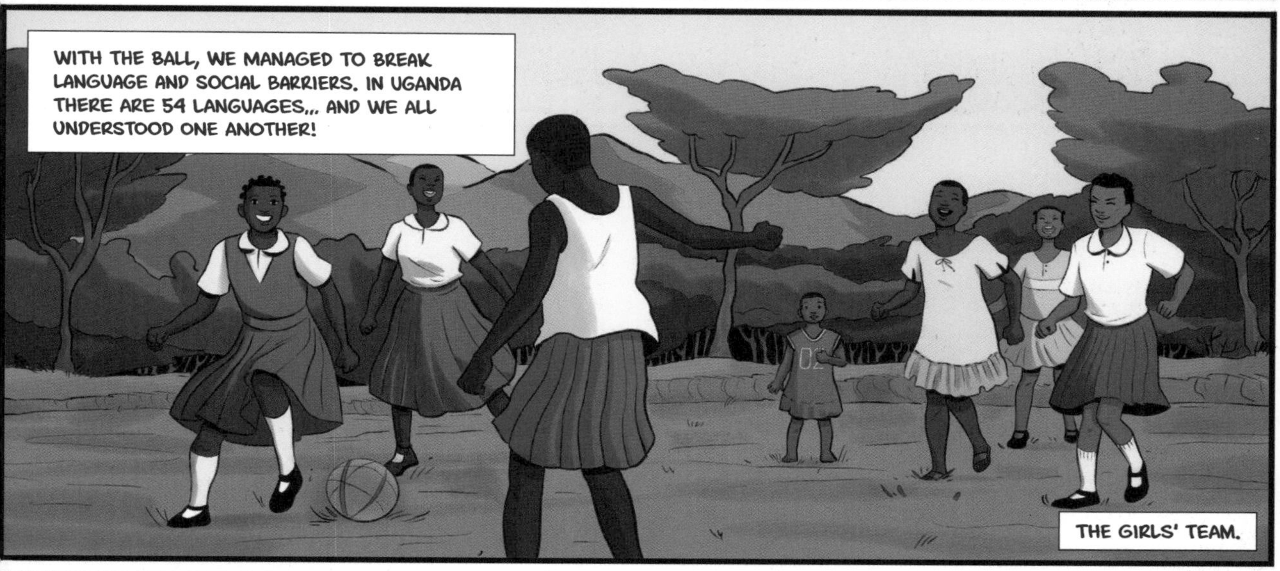
WITH THE BALL, WE MANAGED TO BREAK LANGUAGE AND SOCIAL BARRIERS. IN UGANDA THERE ARE 54 LANGUAGES... AND WE ALL UNDERSTOOD ONE ANOTHER!
THE GIRLS' TEAM.

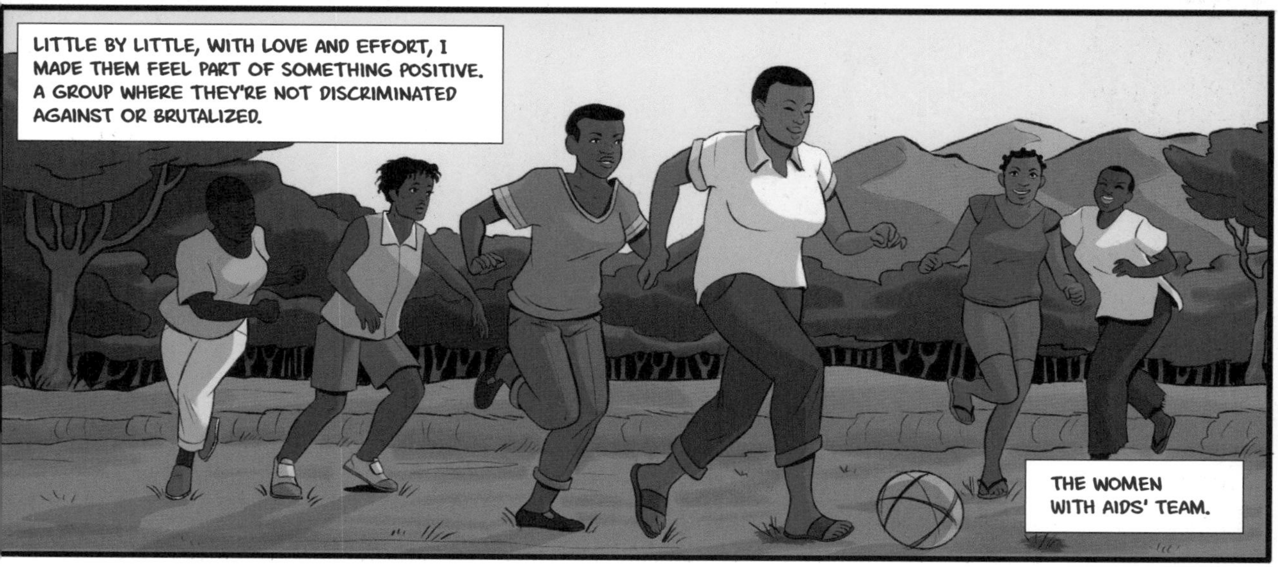
LITTLE BY LITTLE, WITH LOVE AND EFFORT, I MADE THEM FEEL PART OF SOMETHING POSITIVE. A GROUP WHERE THEY'RE NOT DISCRIMINATED AGAINST OR BRUTALIZED.
THE WOMEN WITH AIDS' TEAM.

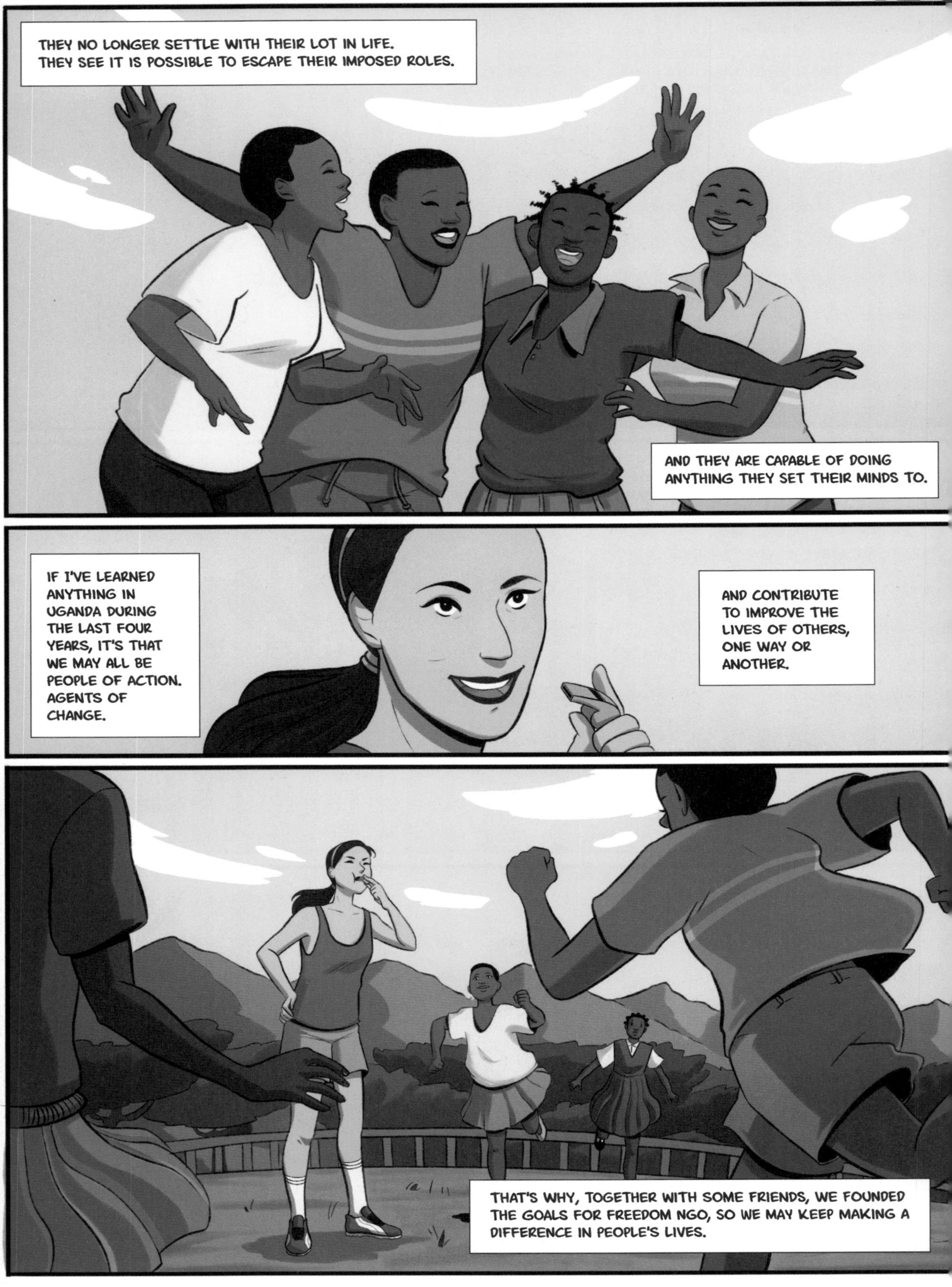
THEY NO LONGER SETTLE WITH THEIR LOT IN LIFE. THEY SEE IT IS POSSIBLE TO ESCAPE THEIR IMPOSED ROLES.
AND THEY ARE CAPABLE OF DOING ANYTHING THEY SET THEIR MINDS TO.
IF I'VE LEARNED ANYTHING IN UGANDA DURING THE LAST FOUR YEARS, IT'S THAT WE MAY ALL BE PEOPLE OF ACTION. AGENTS OF CHANGE.
AND CONTRIBUTE TO IMPROVE THE LIVES OF OTHERS, ONE WAY OR ANOTHER.
THAT'S WHY, TOGETHER WITH SOME FRIENDS, WE FOUNDED THE GOALS FOR FREEDOM NGO, SO WE MAY KEEP MAKING A DIFFERENCE IN PEOPLE'S LIVES.

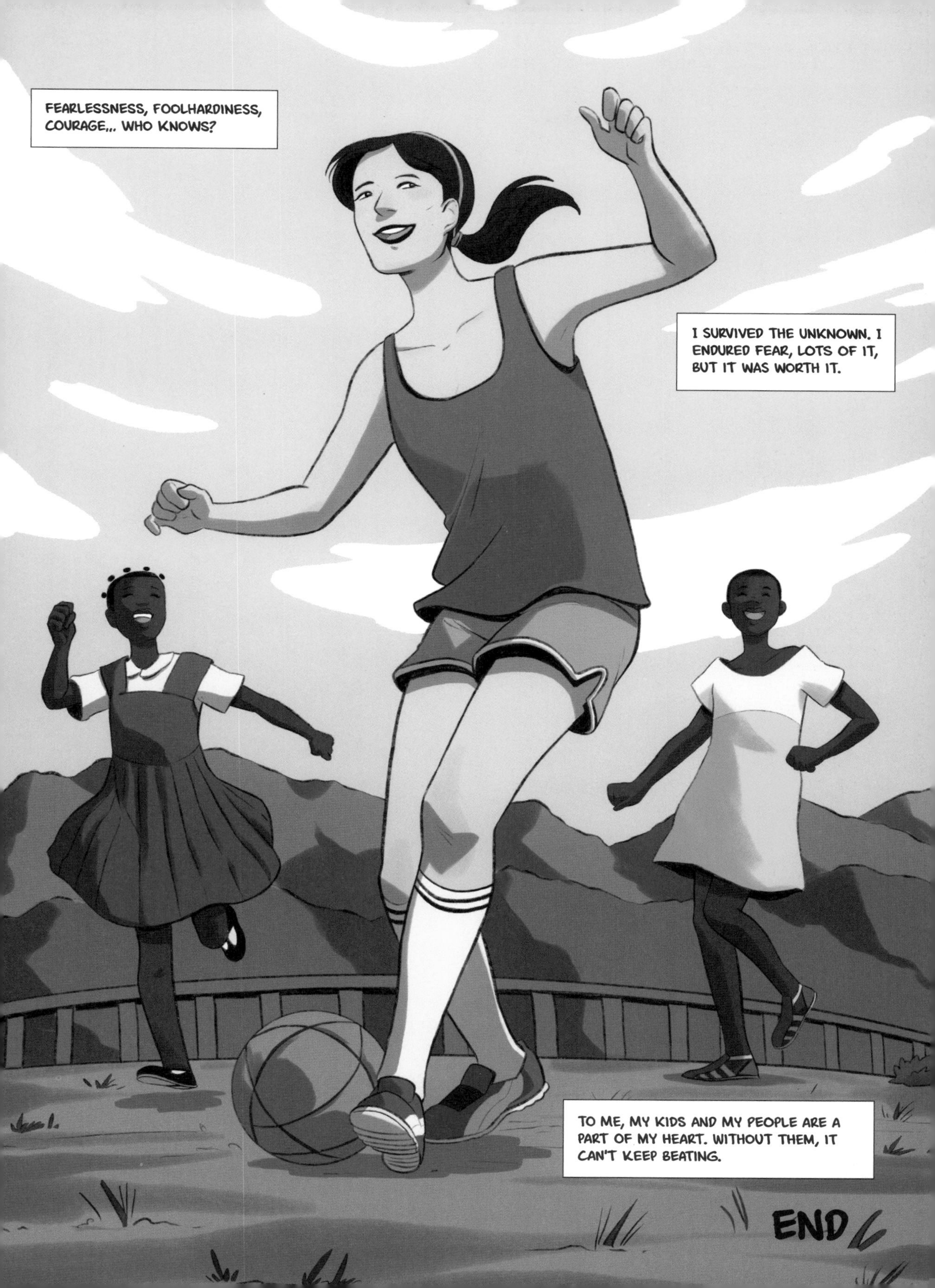
FEARLESSNESS, FOOLHARDINESS, COURAGE... WHO KNOWS?
I SURVIVED THE UNKNOWN. I ENDURED FEAR, LOTS OF IT, BUT IT WAS WORTH IT.
TO ME, MY KIDS AND MY PEOPLE ARE A PART OF MY HEART. WITHOUT THEM, IT CAN'T KEEP BEATING.
END

A FEW WORDS

Esther Gili:

"**D**avid, the anthology editor, suggested I make a few comic pages, but lack of time meant I had to turn him down. Regardless, he persisted, knowing I had to be a part of the project--and, truth be told, I looked forward to joining in with such amazing women. So when he asked me to illustrate the cover, I thought it was perfect. He already had a clear idea and handed me a sketch his girlfriend had made. They weren't keen on it, but I found a way to work with it. My job was turning this rough sketch into reality."

Esther Gili (Madrid, 1981). Studied illustration at Madrid's *Escuela de Arte No. 10*. Since then, she has worked as an illustrator for many publishers and regularly collaborates with USER T38 on film and advertising commissions. At Lunwerg, she published *39 semanas* (2016) and *El legado de Catherine Elliot* (2018) with Gemma Camblor, and for Planeta Cómic she made the *Voices That Count* (2021) cover.

Julia Otero:

"**T**o be honest, I'm not a comic book person. I quit comics years ago, along with my childhood and adolescence, so this is a great comeback. One day I saw myself before stories drawn by Spain's best, and intuition led me to Ada Diez. Meeting her and sharing personal stories over coffee was an interesting experience. Despite our age difference, we saw ourselves reflected when exchanging memories. That's the thing about being a child: we often share similar experiences, especially bad ones (those, no matter how much time passes, remain). Ada, and the good company of women I love and admire, did the rest. So here I am, happy to see them all drawn and told."

I'm **Julia Otero,** a Catalan born in Monforte of Lemos, or a Galician living in Barcelona, it's all the same.

I arrived in Cataluña with the immigration wave of the sixties. I was a good girl always, a committed student, the only child of a trumpet player and a housewife. I thank the social elevator I got into thanks to my parents' effort and a state grant. I love communications and, because of that, listening even more than speaking. I graduated as a philologist because I loved writing. However, the words I've been working with for the last thirty years vanish into thin air. I've been a feminist since I can remember and have educated my daughter to carry the torch.

Ada Diez:

"This comic shows the importance of an unconditionally supportive family environment, the necessity of the right educational groundwork as a feminist principle, and the key to fight for your dreams--understanding the importance of an individual's independence, forgetting what's been established by gender rules.

What began as the need for protection thirty years ago is still a current history of empowerment, since every little step fighting for that independence gets us closer to real equality. A continued struggle where every small step matters.

Working on this comic turned out to be interesting, with a relatable, simple story about the humble values of rural Spain and an honest portrait about how the love for our offspring changes the known perspectives of what's comfortable. The curious aspect of the journey, seen through the eyes of different generations, shows the evolution of how feminism is incorporated in due time, like a seed planted three decades ago that takes root, allowing a unique testimony in the telling of common social narratives in our world, incorporating nontraditional places into the different genres. Women join the social, professional, and educational world. Men take on the roles of educators, confidants, and fathers beyond the concept of parenting.

Plus, taking in the language of comics adds a great graphic encouragement to appeal to any age group, helping with the visualization of everyday issues."

Ada Diez, Valencian illustrator, was a Universidad Politécnica de Valencia (UPV) Fine Arts bachelor who ended up specializing as a graphic designer, expanding her versatility through a Design and Illustration master's degree, which allowed her to be a part of different projects as well as national and international exhibitions, such as collaborating with Nástio Mosquito for the Fondazione Prada (Milan).

She dedicated most of her career to the layout and design of various proposals for the Confucius Institute of the Universidad de Valencia until 2013, when she undertook advertising work, posters, and illustrated campaign graphics in addition to making several incursions into the world of comics. Co-creator of the sonographic project "Hits With Tits" and the Truenorayo Fest, she also handles art direction of both her own work and that of other illustrators.

Lola García:

"**A**t first it seemed to me that this comics thing had nothing to do with my profession in journalism. But decoding reality is my job, and that may be done in different ways, all of them good if you behave professionally. In France, for example, it is very common to use this resource to portray politics. I also have an eternal nostalgia for the comics that absorbed me for hours when I was a child, so I did away with my prejudices and took a chance with this little story. After seeing Agustina Guerrero's intuitive and delicate work, which breathes life into the main character, I no longer had any doubts regarding the storytelling power of illustrations."

Lola García (Badalona, 1967) is the deputy editor of *La Vanguardia*. She was previously deputy editor for the Politics, Living, and Sports section of the same newspaper. Previously, she worked at *El Periódico* of Catalunya, first in "*Cosas de la Vida*" and then as editor-in-chief of the Politics section. She has a degree in Journalism and Political Science, is the author of *El naufragio (Ediciones Península, 2018)*, and has contributed to the anthology *Voices That Count* (2021).

Agustina Guerrero:

"**W**hen I had Lola García's story in my hands something magical happened: I was seeing it in images, something that hardly ever happens to me since I usually draw what I write myself. But this time her story, the story of all of them, took me by the hand, and the lines came out by themselves. I strongly maintain that so many silences that us women live through should start to be heard, and this anthology is going to create some wonderful noise."

Agustina Guerrero (known as "La Volátil") was born in the small Argentinian city of Chacabuco more than thirty years ago. She has lived in Barcelona since 2003. After working for a while as a graphic designer, she decided to devote herself to illustration. In 2011, she created her autobiographical blog *Diario de una Volátil*, which reached thousands of followers in a few months and was an immediate success in social networks. She is the solo author of six books, which have been translated into several languages and have been a great success among her readers: *Nina, diario de una adolescente* (Montena, 2011), *Diario de una Volátil* (Lumen, 2014), *Mamma mia!* (Lumen, 2015), *Érase una vez la Volátil* (Lumen, 2016), *A calzón quitado* (Lumen, 2017), and *El viaje* (Lumen, 2020), besides her contribution to the anthology *Voices That Count* (2021).

When someone asks her what she does for a living, she sometimes tells it by drawing little pictures.

Diana López Varela:

"For many years, I hesitated about writing about my experience with anorexia nervosa. I have always believed that there are certain topics that, because they affect a very vulnerable part of society--teenage girls--should be treated delicately and without falling into the temptation of making dangerous apologies. My fears vanished when David Hernando came to me with me the possibility of telling a personal story in comics form. It was the first time I used this format, and, together with Akira Pantsu, we managed to focus on anorexia as an infection no one is immune to at fourteen, when sexism rules personal relationships."

Diana López Varela (Pontevedra, 1986) is a journalist and screenwriter. She has written and co-written different projects for film and television and also theater, premiering her first play, *No es país para coños*, in 2015. In 2018, she premiered her first short film as a director, *Feminazi*, a parody of chauvinism. As a columnist, she has collaborated with *Jot Down, Diario de Pontevedra*, El Nacional.cat, and Radio Galega. She currently collaborates with *Diario Público* and Onda Cero while she works as a script writer for TVG shows. She is co-responsible for the congress of opinionated women "As mulleres que opinan son perigosas." In 2016, she published her first book, *No es país para coños*, and in 2019, *Maternofobia*, a portrait of a generation facing motherhood. In 2021, she contributed to the anthology *Voices That Count* (2021).

Akira Pantsu:

"Joining this project has been a challenge for me, especially when dealing with such a delicate subject that affects so many people. In this case, with Diana's experience--who has been very brave to tell her story--I have tried to capture it with respect, and at the same time show its harsh reality. I hope it will support and help raise awareness on the issue. Thank you very much for counting on me."

Akira Pantsu (Madrid, 1998) studied at ESDIP (Madrid), earning a Conceptual Art and Graphics for Video Games master's degree. She also participated in a course on comics, taking part in a contest organized every year by the school and winning first prize in 2018. That's how she began her career as a comics author, debuting the following year in Planeta Manga with *MidoriBoshi* (2019) and its sequel *MidoriBoshi: El Diario de Kiku* (2020), in addition to collaborating with the anthology *Voices That Count* (2021). She has also participated in different fanzines with illustrations and short comics. She always tries to be creative with layouts, and likes to experiment with storytelling and the use of lots of symbolism. Her fluid combination of the surreal and the real, as well as her frequent use of LGBT characters, deserves special mention.

Estefanía Molina:

"Taking part in this anthology has symbolized a kind of personal catharsis for the possibility of giving courage to other women to fight against those pitfalls, sometimes self-imposed, that form in a society where there are still fewer female authority figures in the public-political sphere than male. All this came about through a deep reflection on the impact of life role models. How amazing that Ana Oncina, my successful illustrator, identified with these experiences, perhaps because many of us have been like this at one time or another."

Estefanía Molina Morales (Igualada, 1991) got a degree in Journalism and a degree in Political Science and Administration at Pompeu Fabra University (UPF) in Barcelona. She is a political analyst for print and mass media (La Sexta, Onda Cero, *El Confidencial*, Catalunya Ràdio, SER Catalunya). She left at a very young age to work in Madrid, where she has developed her professional career since 2015 as a parliamentary chronicler following Congress, the Senate, Government, and parties since the crisis--economic, political, territorial--rooted itself in her country. She began her career as a consultant in political-electoral communication and public affairs. Curious about international politics, she was awarded the Global Cities: Barcelona-Los Angeles summer scholarship at the University of California, Los Angeles (UCLA). She graduated cum laude at her two majors at UPF. She participated in the Beers and Politics Madrid Club for lovers of political communication. She has also collaborated with the *Voices That Count* (2021) anthology.

Ana Oncina:

"**D**espite the fact that Estefanía and I have totally different jobs, I have been able to completely identify with her experiences. The different situations are a wake-up call for us to stop punishing ourselves for being ambitious and to believe more in ourselves. Being part of this project and, in particular, getting to work with Estefanía, has made me feel even more united with my colleagues."

Ana Oncina (Elda, 1989) exploded in 2014 with her series *Croqueta y Empanadilla*, which reached thousands of readers and won the Audience Award at the International Comic Fair of Barcelona in 2015. It was also nominated for the Best Spanish Work Award at Ficomic. In 2017, Ana Oncina was listed by Forbes as one of the most influential creators under thirty in Europe. In recent years, she has published *Los f*cking 30* (Zenith, 2019), short stories "Neko Grl" and "Mangaka" in Planeta Manga (2019, 2020), and has collaborated with the *Voices That Count* (2021) anthology.

Eva Amaral:

"Our solitude, our little daily struggles, and the great battles fought by all those who once were and by successive generations of those we now are...this anthology is a witness to those who will come. It is an honor for me to take part in it, surrounded by women capable of moving mountains, and I am thrilled to see 'Loneliness' illustrated by María Hesse, an artist I follow and admire, both for her work and for the message she conveys through it."

Eva Amaral Lallana (Zaragoza, 1972) is a composer and singer, considered one of the best Spanish vocalists. Together with Juan Aguirre, she formed the band Amaral for two decades, with which she has recorded eight studio albums and won the most prestigious national and international awards, such as the National Award for Contemporary Music, the MTV Europe and Spain Awards, *Premios Ondas*, and the 40 Music Awards, in addition to earning several Latin Grammy nominations.

Because of the way they understand their work--from commitment and freedom--Amaral has become an indisputable reference in Spanish music. Eva, trained at the School of Arts and Crafts in Zaragoza, began her career in music as a drummer in a rock band. She currently plays different instruments; is a lover of photography, sculpture, illustration, fashion, and any artistic discipline; and has an enormous fascination for nature in general and birds in particular.

Due to her liberated, committed, and nonconformist character, she has been linked to causes and social entities in defense of human rights, respect for animals, the fight against climate change, equality, and the elimination of gender violence, among others.

María Hesse:

"I loved being able to illustrate Amaral's song--their music has accompanied me in many, many moments of my life. The lyrics of 'Loneliness' are full of so much strength and meaning, and it has been a pleasure to immerse myself in it. To participate in a project like this, surrounded by so many women and colleagues whom I follow and admire, is a real gift."

María Hesse (Sevillian by adoption, 1982) became an illustrator at the age of six. She didn't know it yet, but her teacher and her mother did. A few years later, after finishing her studies in Special Education, she picked up her pencils and jumped into the illustration field. She has worked as an illustrator for various publishers, magazines, and commercial brands, and her work has been displayed in several exhibitions. After the publishing phenomenon that was her first illustrated album, *Frida Kahlo. Una biografía* (Lumen, 2016), translated in fifteen countries and winner of the Brazilian National Children's and Young People's Book Foundation Award, she published *Bowie. Una biografía* (2018), which is being translated into eleven languages, in addition to *El placer* (2019) and *Marilyn* (2020), all with Lumen. She has also collaborated with the anthology *Voices That Count* (2021). María Hesse's illustrated work stands out through her gouache and ink strokes. Her illustrations exude naivety and sensitivity. They are often accompanied by coming-of-age metaphors and allegories. Her work has been described as feminist, and in it, women are represented far from any clichés.

Leticia Dolera:

"It has been very exciting to see how Lola Vendetta (Raquel Riba Rossy) shaped a chapter of *Biting the Apple*, that intimate exchange between two friends that takes place in a cafeteria in Madrid around a slice of cheesecake. Each new email from Raquel felt like opening a surprise gift, discovering how these two characters, as they passed through her eyes, were filled with new shades of color, which filled me with joy."

Leticia Dolera is an actress and film director. She has worked on TV shows such as *Al salir de clase*, *Los Serrano*, *Hospital Central*, and *El barco*, and in films such as *El otro lado de la cama*, *Spanish movie*, *REC 3*, *Kamikaze*, and *La novia*. In 2015, she wrote, directed, and starred in her first film, *Requisitos para ser una persona normal*, which won the awards for best new script, cinematography, and editing at the Málaga Festival and was nominated for three Goya Awards: Best New Director, Best Editing, and Best New Actor. Faithful to her feminist convictions, in August 2017 she starred in the Madrid City Council's *No Means No* campaign against sexual abuse.

Raquel Riba Rossy:

"It has been very interesting to get into Leticia Dolera's universe and graphically adapt her story--looking for a color palette that connected me to the story and the author, placing the characters in the streets of Madrid, and dealing subtly with the sorority shared between two friends. Once again, women unite to say, 'Enough is enough.'"

Raquel Riba Rossy (Igualada, 1990) had a clear goal since childhood: she wanted to convey messages through her characters and stories. The daughter of architect Jaume Riba and multidisciplinary artist Clara Rossy, she was nurtured by the creative environment of a family of painters, draftsmen, architects, and musicians. From an early age, she drew without counting the hours and sang as if she lived in a musical (without thinking about the volume). She studied Fine Arts at the Universitat de Barcelona and illustration at the Escola de la Dona in Barcelona. In 2017, she entered bookstores with Lola Vendetta, the main character of her *Más vale Lola que mal acompañada* books, *¿Qué pacha, mama?* (2018) and *Lola Vendetta y los hombres* (2019). She also collaborated with the anthology *Voices That Count* (2021). Through art, she has learned to know herself and network with many women around the world. In 2021, she released her first album, *El Primer Canto*, launching her music career with ten songs of her own. She also designed the album herself, thus achieving the alignment of her two favorite languages: music and illustration.

Sandra Sabatés:

// Joining this project has been the most rewarding experience. It is the most personal work I have done so far, a tribute to the struggle of the great women in my life, and this gives it added emotion. I am enormously grateful to Sandra Cardona for the love she has put into illustrating this story that appears alongside those of great women I follow and admire. Simply wonderful."

Sandra Sabatés (Granollers, Barcelona, 1979) has a degree in Audiovisual Communications. Her professional career has been linked to television since early on, first as a local news anchor in L'Hospitalet and TVE of Catalunya, and from 2007 in La Sexta, thus making the leap to national television. Since 2012 she has presented the humorous news program *El intermedio* on La Sexta with great success.

She has been awarded the CIMA TV Festival de Vitoria Award (granted by the Asociación de Mujeres Cineastas y de Medios Audiovisuales) and the Meninas Award in 2018 (granted by the Government Delegation) for her segment *Mujer tenía que ser*, in both instances. Additionally, she has also been awarded the 2018 Premio Ondas as Best Television Presenter, has written the book *Pelea como una chica* (Planeta, 2018), and has collaborated with the *Voices That Count* (2021) anthology.

Sandra Cardona:

// Illustrating a generation of women who have lived a reality so different from our reality today has been incredible to me. The most important thing about this anthology is to give visibility to those brave women, and…what better way to do it than through comic books?"

Sandra Cardona (Granollers, 1986) started in comics after finishing her studies at Escola Joso, doing some collaborations with France and Spain. After several years dedicated to graphic design, she returned to comics with French screenwriter Olivier Milhaud to make the graphic novel *Bouillon* (Marabout, 2018) that brought together their love for Wes Anderson's cinema, Ghibli movies, and Art Nouveau.

In 2019, during her author residency in Québec, she started a project with screenwriter Cédric Mayen under the name *Sac-à-Diable* (Dargaud, 2021) where her other loves are present: witches, monsters, and magical worlds. She has also contributed to the *Voices That Count* (2021) anthology.

Almudena Grandes:

"How happy am I that a young creator as talented as Sara Herranz illustrated an old story of mine. I have always found it enviable to know how to draw and to be able to condense so many things in a single image. That is why I am especially excited that it was precisely this story, *Over a Banana Skirt*--in which my own family past intermingles with my way of writing and the value historical memory has for everyone-- that forms part of this anthology."

Almudena Grandes (Madrid, 1960) became known in 1989 with *Las edades de Lulú*, winner of the XI Premio La Sonrisa Vertical. Her novels *Te llamaré Viernes, Malena es un nombre de tango, Atlas de geografía humana, Los aires difíciles, Castillos de cartón, El corazón helado*, and *Los besos en el pan*, together with her books of short stories, *Modelos de mujer* and *Estaciones de paso*, have made her an essential author. Several of her works have been made into films and plays and have been awarded, among others, the Premio de la Fundación Lara, the Premio de los Libreros de Madrid, the Rapallo Carige, and the Prix Méditerranée. With *Inés y la alegría* (Premio de la Crítica de Madrid, Premio Elena Poniatowska, and the Sor Juana Inés de la Cruz) she inaugurated the series *Episodios de una Guerra Interminable*, which includes *El lector de Julio Verne, Las tres bodas de Manolita, Los pacientes del doctor García* (Premio Nacional de Narrativa, 2018), and *La madre de Frankenstein*, a story of unpredictable love and redemption.

Sara Herranz:

"It has been a pleasure to be able to work with the prose of a writer I admire as much as Almudena Grandes and an honor to be part of this anthology. We need more stories that tell how women see the world."

Sara Herranz (Tenerife, 1986) is an illustrator. Her first book, *Todo lo que nunca te dije lo guardo aquí* (Lunwerg, 2015), has reached its sixth edition and more than 25,000 copies sold. In 2017, she published *La persona incorrecta*, also with Lunwerg. And in 2021, she collaborated with the *Voices That Count* (2021) anthology. Vogue Spain, Gucci, and Chanel are some of the brands that have relied on her work. The visual story that Sara Herranz proposes contains the strength of color simplicity, the overwhelming power of her female characters, a fragile and elegant expressionist style, and, among other traits, the place of women in our reality. Sara Herranz's work is characterized by its firm line work and the use of red. Her illustrations invite us to enter a universe where the main cast address the problems of today's world in a mixture of everyday life, intimacy, and irony.

Patricia Campos:

"**M**y experience has been very positive. On the one hand, I have immersed myself in the world of comics and loved it. Also, it has been a joy to meet Sara and discover her art, because it is impressive what she can communicate with drawings. Best of all, this comic will be a source of inspiration for many girls who see themselves reflected in each of us. I'm sure it will bring a lot to all the girls and boys who read it."

Hello! My name is **Patricia Campos**. I was born in 1977 in Castellón, although I spent all my childhood in Onda. Since I was a little girl, soccer has been my life, and my dream was to be able to dedicate myself to it professionally. Over time, flying became another of my passions, and that is why becoming an aviation pilot was on my list of goals to achieve.

I studied Audiovisual Communications at the Universidad de Valencia. When I finished my degree, I prepared for the demanding exams to enter the Armed Forces. During my career in the army, I became the first female jet pilot. Eight years after joining the military, I decided to fulfill my other dream--to play soccer--so I traveled to the United States to become a soccer coach. The truth is that it was not easy, but the motivation to overcome those obstacles and the desire to live life my way allowed me to make every dream I have set for myself come true.

While I was in the United States, I decided to go to Uganda with a soccer ball and sneakers to help children and women with AIDS, and to try to improve their living conditions and their future through soccer. Embarking on this adventure changed my life. Currently, I live in Valencia, I am a pilot, TV and radio soccer commentator, TV presenter, *LA Times* and *As* columnist, and a Goals for Freedom volunteer.

Sara Soler:

"I have never had a good relationship with soccer. Since I was a little girl, I have seen it as an elite sport they wouldn't let me join because I was a girl. I had to grow up and participate in this anthology to make peace with it. And it has been thanks to another woman, Patricia Campos. Because of her, I have realized the power the sport has when based on kindness, community, and nondiscrimination. I hope this story touches you as deeply as it did me. It has been quite the experience to take part in a story full of wonderful people!"

Sara Soler (Barbastro, 1992) is an Aragonese comic book artist and illustrator. She currently lives in Barcelona, where she settled to begin her studies of Fine Arts, as well as the Graphic Arts course at Escola Joso, where she developed her passion for comics and took her first steps into the publishing world, placing short stories in several fanzines. She has worked as a costume and set designer for the play *Morpheus* by Factory Productions, at animation studios as a storyboard artist, and also as a background designer for the film *Memorias de un hombre en pijama*.

She began her career in the world of sequential storytelling in 2017 when she won the second round of the "carnet joven connecta't al cómic" grant, which allowed her to publish her first work, *Red & Blue*, as a complete author. From then on, she worked for various national and international publishers such as Planeta and Dark Horse. You can see her name in several published titles such as *Dr. Horrible Friends Forever*, *Primavera Graphic Sound*, *En la oscuridad*, and *Planeta Manga*, as well as the *Voices That Count* (2021) anthology.

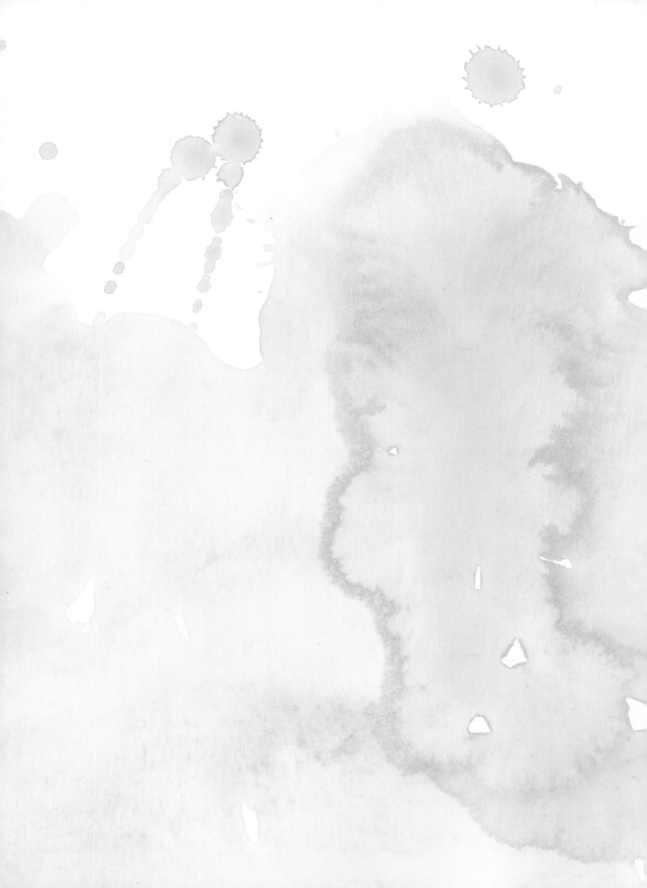